spark of madness

EMBER GLEN | BOOK ONE

BRYNN FORD

Spark of Madness (Ember Glen, Book 1)
Copyright © 2022 Brynn Ford
Published by Brynn Ford

ISBN: 978-1-955349-30-7

Cover Design Copyright © 2022 Qamber Designs and Media
Interior Formatting by Qamber Designs and Media
Editing by Silvia Curry at *Silvia's Reading Corner*

All rights reserved. No part of this book may be reproduced or transmitted in any form, including electronic or mechanical, without written permission from the publisher, except in the case of brief quotations embodied in critical articles or reviews that are cited appropriately.

This is a work of fiction. Names, characters, businesses, places, events, and incidents are either the products of the author's imagination or used in a fictitious manner. Any resemblance to actual persons, living or dead, or actual events is purely coincidental.

This book is licensed for your personal enjoyment only. This book may not be re-sold or given away to other people. Thank you for respecting the author's work.

<u>More from the Author</u>
www.brynnford.com
brynn@brynnford.com

content warning

This is a dark romance series involving many triggering elements which may be upsetting for some readers. A complete list of tropes and triggers can be found on the author's website.
www.brynnford.com/triggers

series note

Spark of Madness is book one of three in the Ember Glen trilogy. It is not a standalone; the books must be read in order. Books one and two end on cliffhangers.

reading order

EMBER GLEN
Spark of Madness
Blaze of Misery
Embers of Mercy

playlist

Stream on Spotify
bit.ly/spotify-brynnford

Arsonist's Lullaby by Hozier
Devil's At Your Door by SWARM & TINYKVT
Savages by MARINA
Devil on My Shoulder by Faith Marie
Never Alone by Krigarè
Soldiers by FJØRA & Neoni
Witch Hunt by VISTA
Almost Touch Me by Maisy Kay
Pyrokinesis by 7Chariot
Heaven by Julia Michaels
Dangerous by The Tech Thieves & Besomorph
Devil Inside Me by Halocene
Repeat After Me by KONGOS
Do You Love by machineheart
Rise by Katy Perry

For all the women who were told what to believe…
Seek truth through the madness,
and when it's necessary, dissent.

chapter one
Mercy

CHAOS LOOMS, THEN sharply descends like the quick stab of a blade through supple flesh. My anxiety over tonight's service has reached its peak, pounding through my heart and pulsing adrenaline through my veins.

Tonight, we serve the Impulse beneath the full moon.

We serve, though lately I've come to think of it as something else—something I don't have a word to describe, and I wouldn't dare speak it even if I did.

Hyatt Price circles the flickering orange flames of the bonfire, his golden eyes glowing like a predator's in the night…and they're fixed on me. I knew he would seek my service tonight. He's been whispering his intentions to me every day for the last week. The anticipation of it has given me adrenaline fatigue.

I step backward in my short black lace-up boots, a twig cracking beneath my feet as they carry me toward the surrounding forest's tree line. He sees me retreating and his pace quickens toward me.

Why me?

Debauchery falls like the black embers cast from the licking flames, sparking ash spewed out from the fire. It rains down to set our world on fire with the release of the Impulse in a monthly ritual where our men purge.

Servants have already been claimed. One woman is being ravaged in front of the fire, while another is beaten senselessly in the shadows. All around, the air is ripe with the scent of smoke, sex, and sin.

And Hyatt approaches to use me.

He marches right past three unclaimed servants dressed in their black corsets and lace. One of them is Ivy Jane, who I know for a fact takes great pleasure in serving the urge for violence. Yet after a quick appreciative glance at her curves on display, Hyatt continues, heading straight for me.

I take another step back, though I know there will be hell to pay if anyone sees me retreating. I should be marching toward him. I should be waiting on my knees for him, knowing he's coming to use me. But no matter how hard I try, I can't plant my feet. I can't bend. I can't sink to my knees and welcome his purge.

I'm a sinner…a rebel.

I'm weak.

I watch as Hyatt's expression hardens, his pace quickening toward me, violent rage gleaming in his deceptive glowing gaze.

And then a hand closes around my wrist.

Jerking me toward him, Theo Hughes pulls me into his hard chest and bends to kiss me, claiming me before Hyatt can even reach me. I allow a sigh of relief against his bruising lips. Theo's urges are nothing to balk at, but they're manageable. I can survive Theo—I have time and again—but I don't know if I'd survive Hyatt.

As Theo drags his soft lips from mine, he turns his head, looking over at Hyatt, who's standing at our side. "Better luck next time," he says, clapping him on the shoulder. "Mercy's mine."

"You'll be done with her eventually," Hyatt says, his lips twisted devilishly at the corner of his mouth. "And then I'll take my turn with her."

"I wouldn't wait around," Theo replies, reaching around me and curving his palm around my ass cheek.

I swallow hard as Hyatt narrows his eyes, holding my stare.

Heat burns through his gaze, scorching me with the promise of untold violence and pain. He holds me there, forcing me to take the fire before he blinks and turns his eyes to Theo. "Fine. Plenty of other servants." He reaches out to pluck a strand of my long blonde hair, twisting it sharply around his finger. "Just know I have my eye on you, Mercy Madness."

He turns on his heel, returning to the bonfire where Ivy Jane stands with a proud smile upon her cheeks as he approaches her. Hyatt glances over his shoulder at me before fully giving his attention to her.

"You're lucky I'm looking out for you," Theo murmurs.

I look up at him as a moment's relief tugs away the incessant throb of adrenaline, allowing me a brief reprieve. "Thank you."

He lowers his voice. "I saw you retreating from him. Someone else could've seen. You need to get yourself together, Mercy. You're a *servant*, and you need to accept it."

"I accept it," I tell him, though it may be a lie.

My lack of acceptance is rebellious, but I don't aim to rebel. I want to survive here, though sometimes I find it difficult to justify that desire.

Theo's hand latches around my throat and he squeezes, restricting my air flow as he pushes me back against the tree trunk. His other hand slips beneath the torn black lace of my skirt, shoving it aside and quickly seeking my sex, finding me bare without the barrier of undergarments—which we aren't allowed to wear during service. He unceremoniously shoves two fingers inside me, his rough skin scraping along my dry inner walls.

"Why aren't you ready for me?" he growls as he leans against me, his lips beside my ear. "What do you think Hyatt would've done to you if he'd found you dry and unprepared like this?"

I turn my head to the side, looking out at the campfire and the licking orange flames as depravity claims our village. Theo pumps his fingers harshly, grunting as he grinds his body against mine. He's trying to draw slickness and desire out of me, though it's for his benefit, not mine.

I sigh, watching as Hyatt playfully threatens to push Ivy into the flames. She screams and he laughs, a pulse of collective pleasure at the sound of her horror ripping through the crowd.

Men thrive on our horror, our pain, our misery. It's their burden to carry as they live their lives suppressing their natural and overwhelming urges—that instinctual, primal need for violence and sex, and the mixture of them together.

It's why we serve the Impulse tonight. It's why we allow them a regular outlet to purge. It's why we live to serve.

Purging is the only way they can control it.

Except I don't believe that.

Theo's hand leaves my throat, but only to allow him space to sink his teeth into the side of my neck, eliciting a yelp from me.

"I want to hear you scream like that," he whispers.

I gulp, assured that he will make me scream like that if it's what he wants.

"For fuck's sake," his voice is tinged with agitation, "get wet for me already."

"I'm sorry," I whisper. "I'm trying."

"It doesn't matter," he snarls, pulling his fingers out. He grips my shoulders and turns me before throwing me down on the dirt. I land sideways on my hip, a puff of soil caking my skirt. "Hands and knees."

I obey, though everything within me begs to resist.

Theo will hurt me and use me, but it won't be as bad as it would've been with Hyatt. I should be grateful to serve Theo's needs.

I'm not grateful to serve any man.

The boning of my black corset digs into my pelvis as I maneuver into position for him. I arch my back as he flips up my skirt, exposing my bare bottom to the world—but I'm still more covered than most of the women around us.

Grunting, groaning, screaming sex fills the air.

I'm supposed to let it take hold of me, to let it fill my heart with passion for service so it can sink me in pleasure—pleasure derived from serving any violent or sexual desire that's demanded by the men of Ember Glen.

But it never works for me, and as far as I can tell, I'm the only one. I'm the only woman who seems to think this way, or maybe the others just don't let on. I'm having a harder time hiding my truth as time goes on. I'm a bad seed, and I deserve to feel the pain of service.

Except…I don't deserve it at all.

Theo slams inside me, thrusting into my dry pussy with painful force as he grips my hips.

"It only hurts because you weren't ready for me." Always trying to shift the blame. "What's wrong with you?" he asks as he fucks me from behind.

Nothing's wrong with me.

Everything around me is wrong, but it makes *me* wrong to think it. To speak it would get me killed, so I pinch my eyes shut against the burning pain between my legs as Theo thrusts, and I let the single teardrop stray from the corner of my eye in aching silence.

I keep my mouth shut and let Theo sink into his cravings. Eventually my body succumbs to his movement, slickening with fake arousal to ease the sharpness of his intrusion.

We live to serve; we serve to live.

I repeat our mantra in my mind, pretending that I actually believe it until some part of my mind that aches to please demands control. I let that part of me take control, happy to let it, knowing that it will give all the other parts of me some sense of peace. Maybe not peace, exactly, but a reprieve, nevertheless.

With his brute strength, Theo flips me over, my back landing harshly on dirt and stones and twigs. He hooks his fingers into the top of my corset and yanks, forcing my breasts to peek out of the top.

I blink up at him, reminding myself that sometimes he's kind, that he stepped in to spare me from Hyatt's raging, that he's someone I might consider a friend if we ever interacted outside of service. But as he bends over me, planting his fists in the dirt on either side of my head, all I can see is a faceless foe.

Maybe something *is* wrong with me.

I wish I could be like the others. I wish I could let myself enjoy this. I wish I could feel my purpose in this as I'm meant to.

He lifts his hand and tucks my hair behind my ear, almost sweetly, deceptively so. Then he sinks inside me again, thrusting with slow, deep strokes, coaxing something out of me, too kindly tricking me into pleasure. I feel it for a moment, a tug deep in my core, and a single shockwave of pleasure I know I should let myself sink into.

But it's lost when he slaps me across the cheek so harshly that my head snaps to the side. His palm presses to my cheek and the pressure of it soothes the ache for a moment—until the pressure becomes too great. He presses down against my face with bruising force as he picks up his pace, fucking me harder, faster.

Gradually his hand slips down, fingers wrapping around my throat, squeezing. I reach for his wrist, grabbing hold of it with both hands after a minute of painful pressure takes my breath away.

He's unrelenting.

He's supposed to be.

"That's fucking beautiful," he groans as my eyes widen, silently begging for air. He loosens his grip just long enough for me to suck in a greedy breath before his hand tightens again.

I panic as he skirts the edge of release, as his thrusting turns to manic fucking. His eyes darken as he pants, teasing me with his breaths that I'm not afforded the same privilege of having. My body bucks beneath him as he comes, as he shouts his pleasure into the night, and it mingles with the sound of so many others.

Moaning, panting, shouts of pleasure…screams of pain.

After Theo spills inside me, he hoists me up by his grip around my throat, pulling me into a sitting position with my legs still spread for him, my knees bent at his hips while he kneels between them.

His hand slips up to pinch my chin, forcing it up as he bends down over my face. "It's no wonder Hyatt wants you to serve him; once you're warmed up, your cunt is divine."

He spits in my face, and I flinch, turning away as his hand slips back into my hair. He holds my head steady as the other hand strikes my cheek again.

"Happy to serve," I mutter half-heartedly, speaking my script as he rubs his saliva across my cheek.

His fingertips drag to my mouth, wiggling against my sealed lips until I let them part. He shoves two fingers inside, stroking them along my tongue, toward the back of my throat until I gag. Only then does he drag them back out.

"Damnit, Mercy," frustration touches his tone, "give me something. Fucking *anything*."

I have a nasty habit of disengagement during service.

I've been told by others that using me is like fucking a corpse— but I have to disappear to avoid speaking my mind, to keep myself quiet, to stop myself from fighting.

I should be more enthusiastic to serve my purpose, but I'm simply not. I wish I could be like all the others.

I close my eyes, trying to find the actress within, though she's buried so deep. "How can I serve you better?"

He bends, my back arching as he looms over me, pressing an almost sweet kiss to my cheek. "Give me something. Literally any emotion would serve me. Passion, lust, anger, hatred…fight me if that's what you feel. Just wake the fuck up and *engage*." His lips slip back along my face, coming to stop at my ear where he whispers, "Everyone's watching you, Mercy."

My eyes snap open to take in the scene where sex and violence surround me. I glance around at the clusters of people, taking in the sight of women offering themselves with passion and purpose—because it *is* our purpose in Ember Glen. They fall to their knees, part their lips, spread their legs…They take a hit and rise for another; have their head slammed to the ground, only to lift it again for more.

But no one is watching me that I can see.

I turn my head to look at Theo. "What?"

"People talk about you," he says, catching my gaze with his dark eyes. I see honesty there—there's no room for anything but raw, painful truth when giving in to the Impulse. "They call you a sinner."

"I'm not a—"

He clamps his hand over my mouth. "It's what you look like when you give me nothing. You're supposed to serve happily, so do your God-given duty."

"Just tell me what you—"

He drops me, and I land hard on my back as his eyebrows knit together. "Get on your knees and offer your service with enthusiasm." His eyebrows lift expectantly. "Now."

I steel myself as I scramble to get on my knees, blinking up at him. "I offer myself to honor the Impulse." I speak the scripted words like a prayer at the altar of his feet. "How can I serve you?"

His hard chest rises and falls, his palm landing on the side of my head, stroking down my white-blonde waves. "That's better," he murmurs. "You know I'm only looking out for you."

I know he is…I do.

I know he cares about me.

Yet the more I serve, the more everything around me feels so wrong. I'm not doing a good enough job of hiding that, and I really need to. I need to bury my internal dissension so deep that no one can dig it up.

But how?

I nod, forcing a small smile. "I know. How can I serve?"

"No!" a sharp cry pierces the night, collectively jerking our attention toward the sound.

I twist to keep my eyes on her as a girl with wild eyes shoves a man near the campfire and runs toward us, racing for the forest just beyond. The entire village hesitates from their collective madness at the brilliant sound of a word no servant should ever speak, especially not while serving the Impulse.

I recognize the girl with the wild mane of long ashen hair—Delle Carter. She just turned sixteen last week, and this is the first time she's serving. My heart races as I see the fear on her face—I recognize it as the same fear I had when I had turned sixteen over four years ago.

Her eyes catch hold of mine as she approaches, her skirt floating behind her and shadowing the firelight at her back as she runs. The world around me slows, as if I'm trapped in a nightmare with her, trying to outrun a threat that's moving faster. But reality snaps back into focus as she blurs past us, chased by three men in quick stride.

"Who is that?" Theo asks, and when I turn my eyes to look up at him, I find his are fixed on the girl beyond my back being chased into the forest.

I clear my throat. "Delle. Tonight is her first—"

He holds up a hand to silence me, his gaze fixed far beyond me—and I already know he's going after her.

It's fine.

He can have whoever he wants.

But it's not fine—I need him to claim me to keep me safe from the others.

"I'm going after her," he confirms, but I hardly hear the words because he's already running.

I look over my shoulder to see him dart off into the darkness of the forest, his strides quickly carrying him to match the speed of the other men chasing the poor girl before they all disappear into the night.

I hold my breath as they vanish in silence, waiting for the inevitable sound of it…and it comes, her scream piercing through the night once she's caught.

I turn forward and bow my head as I release my breath with an unsteady huff, my fingers curling into the lace covering my thighs. I should stand. I should go and find one to serve. But I can hear my pulse thrumming, pumping behind my ears, adrenaline running like rivers through my veins.

Run.

I want to run, too.

I want to disappear into the darkness.

I push to my feet and straighten my skirt, then press my modest breasts back into the corset and adjust it.

I raise my foot to take a step forward, intending to walk back to the campfire and present myself for another's use. And that's when another piercing scream, more horror-striking than Delle's, rips across the night.

My wide eyes snap to the burning fire, and I see it shift.

Feral flames streak away from the containment of the bonfire, rushing across the camp, but it's not a blaze set along the forest floor or burning through the trees. It's a servant, her skirt bathed in fire that threatens to consume her whole. She runs, flames chasing her, burning up the fabric, racing to greet her skin and burn her flesh.

Hyatt Price stands behind her, holding a torch of his own making, his twisted smile bright with delight for what he's done to her. It's not until her beautiful, raven-black tresses catch flame that I realize it's Ivy Jane screaming and running, begging for help.

But she'll get none.

She'll go down in literal flames to serve the Impulse.

And she'll be honored for her sacrifice.

I lurch as bile rises in my throat, bending sharply with a dry heave and catching myself with my hands on my thighs. I swallow it down, panting heavily through my sudden nausea. When I lift my head, I see Hyatt move in my direction. He sees that I'm unclaimed, that Theo has left me, and now I'm on my own.

I rise and take a step back as he picks up his pace.

Another step, then another, committing the sin of retreat with each pad of my foot against earth.

A sin with my right foot, a sin with my left...

And when I realize I no longer care if anyone sees me retreating, knowing my fate is sealed no matter what I choose, I turn on my heels, and run into the forest.

I stood as a servant, and now, I run as a sinner.

chapter two

ARLO

THE IMPULSE DRIVES my hunger, the same as it does for everyone else. But it's the anticipation of our nights of purging that's the most thrilling for me—sometimes even more thrilling than the nights themselves.

The Impulse is painful for some—the suppression of a man's natural, God-given urges for sex and violence. I suppose I've always been a little twisted finding pleasure in that pain. The denial is intoxicating for me. Skirting the edge of release for as long as I can amplifies the relief once I finally let go. And there is no better way to skirt the edge than with a little voyeurism.

I take a sip of ale from my mug, then tilt my head back to rest against the tree trunk at my back. I feel one with my primitive nature, sunk down low against the earth, sitting on soil with one knee lifted to rest my arm against. If I were to press my palm to the ground, I imagine I might feel the vibration of pleasure from Mother Earth as we submit to our primordial needs—as our women fulfill their purpose by serving our masculine urges.

I have every intention to participate in tonight's festivities, but not until I'm ready. As a member of the Control, I'm used to standing back and watching. It's actually a rather fitting role for me to be one of the authority of Ember Glen. I have a level of patience unrivaled in our village. That patience is what allows me the ultimate release after extensive time spent in persistent, delicious anticipation.

There's always a mad rush at the beginning of a night of purging, such as now. The hounds have been released, so to speak, and the men of Ember Glen chase their prey like rabid dogs, quickly seeking and selecting a servant to unleash upon.

Watching this is my favorite part.

Taking another long sip from my mug, I cast my glance around the glowing firelight at the center of the camp…watching, waiting. I reach down with one hand to undo the two buttons of my waistcoat which I wear over a gray button-up. The leather gloves I often wear are placed on top of the coiled rope resting on the ground beside me. My sleeves are rolled up to my elbows, and the gradually cooling air breezes across my forearms.

I watch the flames dance against the dark shadows of the campsite and the black trunks of trees looming beyond. It's rustic, a good setting for primal release, though I enjoy my clean, elegant living at the Homestead with the other members of the Control. Yet being out here in this part of our village, with the servants and men of our community, it makes the impulse to purge that much stronger.

This night is feral.

A scream near the campfire draws my attention, and when I glance over, I see Hyatt Price playfully threaten to push Ivy Jane into the fire before pulling her away. Her fright sends out a pulse through the village, an electric shock which triggers desire to use and abuse.

I slowly inhale, dragging in an aching breath of anticipation as I let my desire simmer deep inside. Several servants are unclaimed; I could take any one of them now and satisfy the throbbing ache of my thickening cock, but still, I bide my time.

I scan the circle from where I'm seated, my gaze settling to watch one pair and then the next, observing the men of Ember Glen as they use their creativity to purge with servants. I spot Ellary Hill stark naked, on her hands and knees in the dirt, getting fucked from behind. My gaze travels her naked form appreciatively—I think I'd enjoy sinking inside her, but I don't think she'll be the one I take to satisfy me first tonight.

Nearby, I see Cambria Miller, still fully clothed, hugging a tree. Her wrists are bound with a rope on the opposite side of the trunk. She screams with pure delight as Killian Cole—a fellow member of the Control—spreads her legs and drags the tip of a blade down the back of her thigh, a thin stream of blood slowly tracking down her bare leg.

My pulse quickens as I watch the blood flow, the subtle violence of the act and the slow drip of blood along her medium brown skin builds anticipation that rushes through my veins with an insistent *whoosh*. I adjust my cock with one hand as I shift against the ground, then take a long drink of ale as I continue to watch.

"No!" The shout of protest immediately catches my attention, my head snapping toward the sound.

Servants don't say no—on this night or any other—and it won't be tolerated. I see Delle Carter dart from the campfire, running toward the forest, her hair whipping wildly behind her as she sprints away. I scramble to my feet, prepared to run after her, but another villager and two members of the Control are already chasing her—two more than necessary to bring a servant under control.

And then I see one more, Theo Hughes, take off at a sprint to chase the group into the dark forest.

That's interesting.

He's a member of the Control, too, and surely, he sees enough men are after her already. In his wake, he leaves a girl on her knees… the same girl he chooses nearly every time we purge.

Mercy Madness.

I'm perplexed by her.

She's attractive, though her appeal has declined over the last year or so—at least that's what I hear from my brothers. By all rights, she should be in high demand. Supple flesh, round curves, skin like porcelain begging to be reddened with a smack of a hand or the flow of blood. Pink lips that dip to a perfect, permanent pout, sinful, sultry bedroom eyes, and soft waves of long, white-blonde hair.

She is service in the flesh, a feast for the eyes, though her passion is severely lacking. It's the reason my brothers find her less appealing than she should be. It's also the reason the Control has been watching her. Her history is riddled with small rebellions which, kept unchecked, could lead her to revolt.

I gaze upon her curiously as she tucks her breasts back inside her corset. She hesitates, gathering herself, as if she isn't enthusiastic to find another to serve.

What is she doing?

A shriek breaks through the night like a lightning strike, so thunderous and bright it can't be ignored. The chaos is drawn to the fire, and soon I see why—Hyatt Price holding a torch and Ivy Jane awash in flames.

I'm mesmerized by the walking fire for a moment, the movement of the orange and yellow glow as it burns her skirt to ashes, licking at the ends of her long, black hair. There's a stagnant pause as silence surrounds us, allowing the sounds of her horrified screams to echo through the trees as she chokes on her own voice.

I say a brief prayer in honor of this sacrificial servant, "*Malo mori quam foedari.*"

Death before dishonor.

It's quite a glorious end for a servant so willing as Ivy Jane. I can't imagine she'll survive this.

I could put her out.

It's an odd voice inside me that thinks such a thing, and I don't understand it. Though I suppose I didn't always understand my natural impulses, either. I had to be taught to sink inside every dark thought in my mind and push myself to indulge each of them without prejudice in these nights of purging.

I was taught to indulge any impulse that begged from deep within me…so perhaps I should indulge this strange impulse to put her out all the same.

I set my mug on the ground and retrieve my black overcoat. Then my feet carry me in Ivy's direction, intent on covering her to smother the flames. As I walk toward her, I see Hyatt move around her, staring at the spot where I saw Mercy standing. I turn to look and see if she's there, though I'm not sure why I bother.

She *is* there…but she takes a step back.

Oh, don't you dare.

Don't you fucking dare, Mercy Madness.

Don't retreat.

She turns, and she *runs*.

Hyatt sprints, zipping with his torch alight, the heat of the flames brushing over my skin as he streaks past me.

Two servants have now retreated—Delle and Mercy. They've run from their purpose and have fled into the forest.

This won't be tolerated.

They'll face punishment for this.

I drop my coat and chase after them.

chapter three

Mercy

MY CONSCIENCE NAGS as my lungs burn, fear running blazing heat through my veins. I glance back as I run—*I'm not supposed to run*—and the only thing that's visible is the orange glow from Hyatt's torchlight. He'll burn down the whole damn forest just to light me on fire.

I don't know exactly where I am in the darkness, but I'm comfortable among the trees. I'm familiar with the feel of twigs cracking beneath my boots, and the meager piling of leaves just beginning to fall, crunching with each step. I often travel through the forest to get to the open fields of wildflowers beneath the mountains that surround Ember Glen. So while I can't see my hand in front of my face, I don't fear the dark; I don't fear colliding with the trees blocking my path.

"I'm going to bathe you in flames, Mercy Madness!" Hyatt shouts, his voice is faraway, but echoes through the trees.

My heart slams against my ribcage, pulse thrumming with the insistent need to get away.

Get away, get away, get away.

Tears burn behind my eyes as I pump my legs harder, faster. There's going to be hell to pay for doing this, for running away, but I think—I *hope*—the punishment can be no worse than being set on fire.

I'm fast, but I'm not fast enough to outrun the pace of his determination. His voice is too near when he calls my name again.

Climb.

I skid to a stop, reaching out into the darkness and grappling to find the nearest tree. My knuckles scratch across the bark when I find one, and I press my palms against the trunk, reaching in front of me and high above my head in hopes of finding a low hanging branch I can climb. I circle the tree with quick side-steps, feeling all around.

Good fortune finds me. The side of my hand bumps up against the stubbed remains of a branch that must have fallen away. Feeling around, I find another branch above it, just within reach. I think I can pull myself up onto the remains of the broken branch and climb higher.

It's that or continue trying to outrun Hyatt, and my lungs are already screaming.

Climb.

Grabbing hold of the higher branch, I plant my foot on the tree trunk and hoist myself up. I grunt with the effort as I climb, managing to place my foot on the stub. I use it as leverage to climb onto the higher branch. I steady myself, ensuring it will hold my weight as I find my balance before reaching, searching for another branch to climb.

The orange glow of Hyatt's torch approaches, burning enough light around me that I can see the shadow of a limb at chest-height in front of me. Without hesitation, I scramble, jumping from the branch I'm standing on to wrap my body around the one in front of me.

The lace of my skirt catches and tugs behind me, as if it wants to pull me back. But I pull against it, lifting my leg over the limb, pulling enough that the lace snags and rips, a piece of it tearing off as I wrap my body sideways around the branch, hugging it, and holding on tight.

I settle just in time to see firelight move into the space beneath me and the dark shadow of Hyatt's form attached to it.

He's not running.

He's slowed to a walk.

He must know I'm nearby.

Turning my head, I place my cheek against the rough bark, and I can see the torn strip of dark lace caught on the stub I climbed from. I squeeze my eyes shut, ridiculously wishing that *he* can't see it if *I* can't see it.

"Mercy," he sings my name tauntingly as he creeps between the trees twenty feet below me.

All he has to do is look up, and he'll see me.

Quick footsteps from behind him pad across the dirt, plodding to an abrupt stop. "Where is she?" I hear a second male voice, along with the sonorous pounding of my heart.

I open my eyes to look down, wondering who it is, uselessly hoping it could be Theo, that he might be willing to rescue me. I know it isn't him, though. I saw the look in his eyes when he ran after poor Delle—he was lost to the Impulse.

"She's near," Hyatt replies as I see the top of another head approach. "I'm claiming her. She's mine."

"I'll help you find her."

No!

"Help me find her if you wish, but I'm telling you now, she's *mine*. I've been waiting for my turn with her," Hyatt says.

"And you should've had your turn by now. She retreated, and that won't go unpunished."

"She won't need punishment from the Control by the time I'm through with her. My impulse to defile her is strong."

"Then find her and purge." I see the other man snatch the torch from Hyatt. "But don't burn the forest like a damn fool just to spite her running from you."

"I need the light." Hyatt lurches forward, reaching for the torch, but the other man draws his arm back, holding it away from him.

"You're lost to the Impulse. I won't allow you to set fire to the trees just to serve it."

Hmm.

A rational thought from a man during a purge?

Hyatt postures, stepping closer to him, moving unnervingly close into his space. But this other man doesn't step back; in fact, not a single muscle twitches as he stands his ground.

"I have an impulse to fight," Hyatt hisses in a way that would be intimidating to me…

But it isn't intimidating to the man in front of him. He takes a step forward, forcing Hyatt to move back. "Then go find your servant and fight."

Hyatt places his hands on the man's chest and shoves. "Maybe I'll fight you."

He takes a step back to catch himself but pushes forward again, shoving into Hyatt's space, coming in chest to chest. "Back off, Price. I'm warning you."

Hyatt throws his fist, but the other man catches it in his palm as it *smacks*. I stifle a gasp as he twists Hyatt's arm, spinning him to face away before kicking the back of his knee, causing him to buckle. When Hyatt drops to kneel, he wraps his arm around Hyatt's neck, squeezing him into a chokehold.

The man is strong, holding him with one arm, the torch still held out in the other while Hyatt claws at his forearm, trying to pull his grip away. Hyatt struggles against his hold, but the man's hold remains tight, keeps him still, squeezing and squeezing until suddenly, Hyatt collapses. His arms drop away and his body slumps, and when the other man lets him go, Hyatt falls sideways to the ground, unconscious.

He choked Hyatt until he passed out.

I watch with wide eyes, afraid yet curious for what will happen next. The man holds the torch over Hyatt's still form, watching him for a few beats, as though he's making sure he's really down.

Then, with a snap, he turns his head in my direction, chin tilted, eyes landing on mine as if he's always known how to find them in the dark.

He takes a step closer, gaze locked on mine as the fire crackles, and a curious expression spreads across his cheeks. "I believe it's now your move, Mercy Madness."

Arlo Rainn.

My heart drops to my stomach as I realize who stands before me. He's one of the Control. He's witnessed the extent of my failures as a servant.

Retreating.

Running.

Hiding.

I'm a sinner…and he's going to send me straight to hell.

chapter four

ARLO

THERE ARE SEVERAL words that could describe how I'm feeling about this situation—interested, fascinated, and curious all come to mind. Yet none of them quite capture the pleasure that comes from the anticipation of her next move.

I didn't have a plan when I ran after Hyatt chasing Mercy into the forest, and I don't have one now. I could walk away if I wanted, let her do what she will, knowing that she'll face punishment for her insolence once the sun rises. I could pull her down from the tree and use her to serve my needs—finally satiate the sexual desire rushing through my veins from the thrill of the chase.

Instead, I take a step closer, then I stop and wait.

I watch as she slowly pushes herself up to a sitting position on the branch, the shadow of her form gradually moving where she straddles the limb. Her hands remain in front of her, pressed to the branch between her legs, gripping it with fear.

She should be frightened.

"It appears you have two choices." I casually take another step toward the tree. Her bright blonde hair gleams behind the firelight as I move the torch in front of me to cast her in the light. "You can stay where you are, and hope that I have no interest in you. You can pray that I'll walk away so you can remain here in hiding for the rest of the night—regardless of the fact that you've already crossed the line so severely that you'll never recover from the punishment you'll receive. That is a choice you could make…though, you should also consider that perhaps I'm just as lust-blind as Hyatt." I creep closer, inch by inch. "Perhaps I'll set the tree on fire. Perhaps I'll rip you from it and burn your flesh just to hear you scream."

Her shoulders straighten and her face hardens. "You won't."

My eyebrows lift in surprise. I'm surprised she spoke, because for some reason, I expected her to be meek and fearful. After all, she ran from her duty when she should've been kneeling, grateful to serve, regardless of the pain inflicted.

"Your other choice is to run," I finish. "Come down from your perch, little sparrow. I'll even let you have a head start." I take a step back, sweeping my arm out to the side as if welcoming her down to the forest floor.

I let silence settle between us, though I can sense it's unsettling for her. A grin twists at one corner of my lips as I wait, savoring the festering quiet which precedes her response.

I'm not sure what I expect her to do.

I'm not sure what I hope she'll do.

With a sharp movement, she lifts one leg, bringing it over the branch before turning sideways to sit. She hesitates, her hands pressed to the bark on either side of her hips. She looks down at the ground, then her eyes flicker sideways to glance at me surreptitiously. She kicks out her foot and lets it swing, as if she were going to jump, but thought better of it.

"What will it be?" I prod.

She looks over at me. "What will my punishment be? How will I be punished for running from my duty?"

"I don't know," I tell her honestly. "Your cowardice will be brought before the authority of the Control for a vote."

"So it's cowardice, then?" she scoffs. "Not wanting to be set on fire?"

She asks as though she doesn't know, and my eyes narrow at

her, wondering why she's so combative about who she is meant to be, how she is meant to serve her community. "Coward, weak, spineless… *selfish*. Choose whichever word draws the most meaning for you."

Her lovely lips part in surprise as her eyes narrow, taking personal insult from the words. They aren't untrue; she knows her role, her purpose, her duty—not only did she fail to fulfill it, but she *ran* from it, and hid from it.

Remarkably, it's this sentiment that gives her a nudge, and she makes the leap, pushing her bottom off the branch and falling to the ground. She lands hard, her knees buckling from the momentum of leaping from such height, but she manages to keep herself upright as she bends.

She rises slowly, and my breath catches in my lungs as I watch her shadowed form lift from the ground. Perhaps it's the sweep of her long, platinum waves over her shoulder which brush over the swell of her breast. Maybe it's the gradual manner with which she lifts her chin, her eyes rising to meet mine. It could be the intoxicating manner in which she fills the black corset…or maybe it's the glow of her pearly smooth skin stretched taut around her fleshy thigh where it peaks through the split in her skirt, begging to be marked.

Sweet sin.

"I'm not selfish," she says defiantly.

I smile at her, amused by her boldness. I suppose she knows just how much trouble she's already in and assumes she can't make it any worse—though, I'm certain she can make it much, much worse.

With one arm, I shrug off my waist coat, then move to a brush-free clearing a few steps away where nothing but soil covers the ground. With a suddenness that makes her audibly gasp behind me, I drop the torch, the flame flaring as it catches air on the way down. As soon as it hits the dirt, I open my waistcoat, position it above the flame, and drop it. The light goes out with a puff of smoke as I effectively smother the fire.

I hear her step back, her boots crunching over twigs and leaves—one small step, then another.

I whip around to face her, but remain in place. "Are you going to run?" I'm met with silence…sense-heightening silence. "Think twice, Mercy. Because a chase sounds like fun for me."

I hear the breath she forces out with a frustrated *oomph*, and her annoyance calls to me. I've never interacted with a woman in quite this way before—where she's combative, hostile, resistant. I think I'm enjoying the resistance, though I know I shouldn't. It's should put me off entirely because her actions are disgusting. She's defiant of the ritual sacrifice she was born to give each month beneath the full moon; the sacrifice of self to satiate the hunger of men.

I listen for the crinkle and crunch of leaves and twigs beneath her boots, though she tries to muffle the sound with each slow step.

Why hasn't she run yet?

Hyatt groans, stirring from his unconsciousness nearby, and that seems to be the trigger she needs to act. I hear her turn, hear her padding with quick steps along the forest floor, and I give chase.

I run, following the sound of her footsteps until I can see her outline in front of me. I open my arms and wrap them around her waist as I barrel into her, grabbing hold as I plant my feet to stop. I lean back, lifting her from the ground as I step backward to steady myself.

"Hyatt…" she whispers with urgency, her quiet plea in protest of my capture.

My back hits a tree behind me. I set her down and spin her in my arms to face me, turning and shoving her spine against the tree.

"Please don't—"

I slap my palm over her mouth when I hear Hyatt move, creeping to his feet in the darkness.

"Quiet, or he'll hear you," I warn.

She stills, though her anxiety rises. I feel the warm puffs of breath from her nostrils as they rush down the back of my bare hand. I feel her soft lips against my palm, and I want to feel her softness against every inch of me. I move closer, molding my body to hers, pinning her to the tree.

Sweet sin.

The way she feels is divine. Her soft curves are a perfect contradiction to her sharpened tongue. The lust she inspires is maddening—something that wraps around me and takes hold with a swiftness I couldn't have predicted.

My cock thickens, straining behind my slacks, and my hips jut forward to seek relief. I shift my hand across her lips, along her cheek as I move in close, whispering against her ear, "Quiet. Don't make a sound. Remain silent and I'll do the same." I comb my fingers through her hair, threading through the silky strands. I feel the wisp of her breath against my cheek. "Stay quiet and I'll keep you safe, right here, until he loses interest and goes away."

She doesn't stir.

She doesn't speak.

Her chest is the only part of her that moves, the gentle rise and fall as she breathes rocks me into a state of blissful longing.

I wonder how soft she is between her legs...Are those lips the same precious pink as the pout on her face?

I let my free hand move as footsteps crunch in the distance, and I hiss, "shh," against her ear as I sweep aside her skirt. I brush my knuckles along the inside of her thigh, nearly groaning at the silky smoothness of her skin and how her muscles tense against my touch.

Slowly, I drag a finger up her leg until I reach the apex of her thighs. She flinches, stifling a gasp as I pull my finger along her slit, dipping in to the knuckle. She rises on her toes, her body slipping upward as though she's trying to lift away; yet, when I push a little deeper and press against her inner wall, she drops in my hold.

Her hands, which she'd pinned to her sides before, snap up to clutch my biceps, the burrow of her fingertips pressing buttons inside me I didn't know existed. My lips press to the side of her neck as I stroke inside her, adding another finger.

"I—"

"Not a word."

Sinking deeper, I curl my fingers, stroking and gently pumping, savoring the wetness that so easily coats my fingers. I wonder if it's all from her or whether Theo's release is still dripping from within her.

Her grip on my arms tightens while I stroke her, tightens further when I grind my cock against her body. I'm finding it difficult to contain myself, and a groan beckons from deep in my chest, threatening to roll up my body and escape with a roar. I smile against her neck as I swallow the sound, feeling the muscles in her throat contract as she swallows, too.

I bring down my thumb to circle her clit, and with a jolt, her back arches from the tree. Her face falls forward to land on my shoulder. Somehow I find my free hand swooping around her, stroking down her soft hair, caressing with a gentleness that doesn't make sense.

It's when her hips roll forward to seek more pressure from my hand that I feel overwhelmed with the need to make her come. I bring my hand from her hair to her hip, fingers curling around her ass and dragging her into me. With the squeeze of my hand, I encourage her to move—I need to feel her fuck my fingers with gratitude for the unearned concealment I've offered her from Hyatt.

She feels incredible, inconceivably warm. Her cunt is unlike anything I've ever felt before, though I can't place exactly why. It isn't just her cunt, though—it's every inch of her.

Our breaths mingle with heat as she rocks on my hand. "Come for me," I demand, "but don't you dare make a sound."

chapter five

Mercy

I'M WARM AND wet, pleasure circling my center in a way I've never felt before.

I feel weak.

I feel strong.

I feel shame for the release that threatens to unravel me…yet I crave it all the same.

I dig my fingers into his arms as my core tightens, clenching around his pulsing digits. My breaths quicken as I rock against his hand, intoxicated by the way he holds me, the warmth of his body aligned with mine…the way his hardness presses to my stomach.

I feel held by him, and somehow, it's centering yet disorienting all at once.

I bury my face in the crook of his neck as my climax awakens, pulsing through my swollen clit while his fingers work with mastery.

Come, but don't make a sound.

A command I can follow.

I'm not unfamiliar with my body or the feeling of self-pleasure. All of us—the servants of Ember Glen—would spend a week at Sanctuary following a night of service. We'd gather to rest and reflect in reverence of fulfilling our duty; we'd heal and mend those injured in violence.

For many nights, we would share our experiences with one another in a safe space. No one is allowed in Sanctuary except for servants and the Control who watch over us. And even they can only enter with the permission of us all. It's the only time we have any power in this place.

Some weeks in Sanctuary were living hell—if someone had served an excess of violence, we lived their pain with them as they healed. But occasionally, there were nights of service more manageable than others, when no one was injured, and we'd spend our nights recounting our experiences in sexual service.

Inevitably, there would be some girls who would become lustful in their remembrance. Self-pleasure isn't allowed unless a man demands it of a servant during a night of service beneath the full moon—which they rarely did because men don't care about a woman's pleasure. I suppose that tiny rebellion was part of the appeal. It was an unspoken secret we kept for each other, the silent seeking of release by one's own hand beneath the sheets when the lights went out.

I was never left particularly wanting after serving; though, like so many of the others, I was left unsatisfied all the same. Service is about the men, but those nights are for us. And I would sometimes indulge while in our safe space. Though I did it out of spite and contempt—not as a lust-fueled rebellion that I'd seek forgiveness for by dutifully serving.

And that was how I had always come before, silently, secretly, because I never once came from service.

Arlo turns his head, running his nose along the sensitive skin behind my ear, letting out a soft hum as he exhales, and that tips me over the edge. My body spasms, my grip tightens, and I arch against him as every muscle in my body tenses. Then comes the release as a strangled moan fights its way up my throat.

His hand moves to cradle the back of my head, pushing my face down into the curve of his neck. "Bite down and keep quiet," he whispers, and *oh*, how that makes me clench around his hand, spurring my release to its peak.

I clamp down on the soft fabric covering his shoulder and let it muffle the moans that wish to escape. I've never climaxed from the touch of another, and it makes my head spin.

How did he do that?

How did he make me come like that?

He strokes my hair as I twitch, as my body suddenly goes limp against him. His lips press to my cheek as he holds me through this oddly comforting let down.

"See?" he whispers. "You can be obedient when you want to be. I think Hyatt's gone away now. I don't suspect he heard a single moan," he thrusts forward against my middle, "or whimper."

I feel breathless and shaky. "H-how can I serve you?"

He lets out a groan that vibrates across my cheek. "That's what I wanted to hear."

With a suddenness I don't expect, he releases me and steps back. My knees are so weak that I slump as they buckle beneath me, the fingers of one hand grazing the dirt as I brace myself with the other palm against the trunk of the tree. I steady myself, then push back up to standing, watching him retreat into the darkness.

He's silent, taking a step back, then another.

I can't stand the silence.

"Do you want me to—"

"I want nothing from a sinner like you, Mercy Madness. Enjoy the remainder of your night in the forest. The Control will decide your punishment soon enough."

I hear leaves crunch as he turns and runs away. He runs away, leaving me there, panting, overwhelmed, stunned…and alone.

I SAT WITH my back to the tree for a while, basking in my confusion over what had happened and my fear of what will happen to me next. Somewhere in the midst of deciding whether I should return to camp and try to fulfill my duty as a servant, or give in to the fact that I'm already in deep trouble, I fell asleep.

Awakening now, the sun is rising, fog overcasting the streaks of orange glow that draw lines between the trees. The purging is over now that the sun is rising, and I know I'm safe. No man will touch me—not until next month's service under the full moon.

I push myself up from where I'd slumped over sideways across the ground, yawning as I draw up my knees to brush dirt from my bare legs, which are covered in goosebumps from the chill of night.

I inhale the fresh morning air as I let my head fall back against the tree, looking up at the branches overhead. Flashes of last night rush through my mind's eye—running, climbing, leaping from the limb, and trying to get away...Flashing to Arlo grabbing me and shoving me against the tree at my back.

A trembling breath shakes through my lungs as I recall the way he touched me. How his touch felt good, welcomed. And then he'd left me alone, and I couldn't understand it. I couldn't understand how he was so hard, how he had me at his mercy, but had somehow dragged himself away during a night of purging. He hadn't asked me to serve his needs, and I'm entirely baffled by it.

Why didn't he use me?

I should return and check in with my friends. They may worry about me now that the purge is over and I'm nowhere to be found at camp. I shouldn't be out here in the forest.

I drop my head forward, glancing around to gauge my location so I can find my way back to camp. The hazy orange sunshine tries to tear its way through the fog, peeking between the ash-colored tree trunks and casting a glow over the teardrop-shaped marigold leaves which are scattered across the forest floor. They're starting to fall rather early this year.

I stand, brushing dry dirt from my hips and smoothing down the torn remnants of my lacy black skirt. My shoulders sag as I walk, the brightly colored leaves beneath my feet sparking images of walking fire and the memory of Ivy Jane awash in flames. I wonder if she survived the night. If she's dead, we'll know it soon enough. Either we'll see her at Sanctuary or we won't.

Maybe I won't be seen at Sanctuary.

Maybe I'll be dead by then.

A shiver creeps up my spine as I recall just how badly I've behaved and how much I've sinned in failing to fulfill my purpose. Arlo Rainn had promised that punishment would be coming, but what that punishment will be or when it will fall is anyone's guess.

Perhaps I'm in so much trouble that it will be days before retribution finds me. I imagine my transgressions will be brought to the full attention of the Control, and a collective decision will be made. Slow-burning fear already crawls through my veins at the thought of what penance I'll be made to pay.

I come upon a fallen tree laying sideways across the ground in front of me. I lift my leg to step over it, and as my boot comes down to land on dirt on the opposite side, I gasp because my eyes land on the other servant who ran last night.

Delle Carter.

Her small frame is curled around her center and tucked against the fallen tree. Her corset is gone—I spot it discarded a few feet away. Her skirt remains, but it's torn and tattered around her bruised legs. Her bare back is covered with a bloody crisscross pattern of welts, made by a whip.

Is she dead?

I shake myself from my hesitation and run to her, crouching beside her, and placing my hand on her arm. "Delle…"

She jolts, swinging her arm back with the force of her entire body turning toward me, hands coming up defensively, prepared to fight me off. I fall back, landing hard on my ass, but quickly shift onto my knees and scramble toward her again.

"It's okay," I soothe, gently grabbing hold of her swinging arm. "It's okay...it's over. You're okay."

Her pretty hazel eyes widen, her expression awash with fear. But as she blinks, her gaze moves across my face, flickering down my form and taking me in for what I am—a fellow servant and not a threat.

She takes in a stuttering breath. "I-I'm..."

Nothing follows.

I push matted hair from where it sticks to her forehead, where I imagine sweat slicked her skin as she was used last night. "It's okay. The night is over. You don't have to be afraid anymore."

You always have to be afraid.

I let a small smile touch my lips to offer her comfort, but the comfort only allows her space to grieve. I watch as she swallows so hard that her throat bobs, as tears gloss over her eyes, as her breaths quicken into a hiccup which turns into a sob. She clutches me as she begins to cry, and I grab hold of her, easing her closer as she turns onto my lap. She lets her tears spill onto my bare thigh at the spot where my skirt splits.

I stroke her hair as I sniff back my own tears.

I feel relief that this girl I hardly know has survived.

I feel pain for what she must have gone through.

I feel hopeless that serving will never become easier.

"Let it all out now," I tell her softly. "Release everything you're feeling right now because you can't take it back with you, love. We're meant to be strong through this; we're meant to be proud to serve."

She sits up with a sharp snap and looks at me pointedly. "I'm not proud!"

Her arms cross over her chest as she realizes her top is bare. She blinks and her face contorts, twisting from anger to embarrassment as her eyes meet the ground.

What do I say to that?

I'm not proud either, but I'm meant to be. We all are. And before this very moment, I've never heard another servant say as much aloud. I'm frightened of our shared sentiment because it means she'll suffer the way I have suffered for years—lacking the ability to take pride in our God-granted duty like the others.

I swallow the unease climbing up my throat. "It's a lot to take in. The first night isn't easy for anyone—"

"The *first* night? Is *any* night easy? How could it be? How could this ever become easier?"

"Delle, I—"

"I can't do this! I won't do this again!" she shouts.

I grip her cheeks, squeezing enough that she can't shake from my hold as I turn her face to meet mine. "Don't ever let me hear you say that again." I narrow my eyes on her. "If they hear you say that, the consequences will be dire."

She opens her mouth to argue, but I silence her with the force of my words.

"*No.* Listen to me." I lean in close, our noses nearly touching as I hold her stare with significance. "I understand you. I do. But no one else in Ember Glen ever will, and if you speak the thoughts in your mind, you will pay dearly for them. You may already be in trouble for running from service. I can only hope the Control will offer leniency as it was your first night." I loosen my hold, allowing one of my hands to stroke the side of her head with a sisterly kind of comfort. "You don't share these thoughts inside your mind. You hold your head high. You show your pride for service. You do what you must to survive. And when the emotional burden of your sinner's thoughts becomes too great, you speak of it to me and *only* to me. Do you understand?"

She blinks slowly, a lonely tear slipping from the corner of her eye, trickling down her rosy cheek. "I'm not a sinner."

I close my eyes and let my forehead fall to hers. "I know." Her hands wrap around my wrists where I hold her steady, though she isn't trying to pull them away—she's holding on. "I know you're not." I let go and pull her close, wrapping my arms around her, trying to give her the comfort I wish someone had given me after my first night of service.

I let her hold on to me for as long as she needs. Eventually, she loosens and pulls away. I stand, retrieve her discarded corset, and bring it back to her.

"Just hold it in front of you," I tell her as she positions the garment to cover her breasts. "We can tend to your back at Sanctuary."

Delle gives me a small nod, and a softly uttered, "Thank you," before we begin our walk back to the campsite, which is on the way to the village and Sanctuary.

I see the smoke of the extinguished bonfire rising in the distance, the gray tufts of ash slowly lifting between the trees. It brings me a contradictory sensation of panic and relief all at once.

The service is over.

The purge has ended.

The Impulse of men has been satiated...for now.

Yet, I still hold the fear from witnessing what had happened to Ivy Jane—from Hyatt chasing me with a torch and what he meant to have done to me.

Arlo Rainn saved me from that...and brought me pleasure in its wake. I place my hand over my pounding heart as we emerge from the trees.

"Mercy!" I hear Ellary call and turn my head to see her rushing toward me.

A smile touches my cheeks when I see her. Her straight brown hair flows behind her as she runs to me. She collides with me, pulling me into a hug that I welcome. Then, with my hands on her shoulders, I nudge her back to arm's length, quickly looking her over from head to toe—a habitual check for injuries. There's a bruise on her collarbone, but otherwise, she looks well.

"Where have you been? Were you dragged into the forest?"

"You could say that..." I hope she doesn't ask for more. "Are you okay? Are you injured?"

"No, I'm fine," she tells me, and by the look on her face, I can see she's being truthful. "The Higgins brothers claimed me and took turns with me the entire night."

I exhale with some relief. The Higgins have strong sexual urges, but they've never been particularly violent.

"Where's Cambria?" I ask, concerned that she hasn't approached yet.

Ellary's expression twists. "I need your help to take her back to Sanctuary...she's injured."

Urgency tenses my shoulders. "Where?"

She leads and I follow. We rush around the smoky remnants of the bonfire, to the opposite side of the circular clearing surrounded by trees. I hear Cambria's hissing and labored breathing before she comes into view. Her onyx hair forms a tangled frame around her beautiful face, though it's contorted in agony where she lays. She's on the ground, curled on her side, rope still twisted around her wrists where she must have been bound, though I can see the other end has already been cut free.

"Cambria." I slam to my knees at her side, and Ellary mirrors me. "Where are you hurt?" I ask, scanning her form.

"Everywhere," she hisses.

Her legs are streaked with dark, dried blood. Her skirt—which covered down to her ankles last night, despite the slit that cut all the way up her thigh—had been torn to shreds. It hangs in tattered pieces where a knife must have slipped through the fabric to cut her skin beneath.

"Oh..." Delle breathes out on a whisper of horror from where she stands somewhere behind me.

As I carefully inspect her skin, I see the knife has touched Cambria nearly everywhere except for her face. Bloody streaks have dried down her arms and across her chest—her skin must be burning from the sear of it.

"We'll help you back to Sanctuary," I tell her. "Can you stand?"

"My toes…" she whimpers.

"What?"

I look to Ellary as she explains, "I think they might be broken."

"Her *toes*?" Delle gasps.

Ellary nods. "Her right foot. The other seems to be okay."

I feel too much.

I feel her pain as if it were my own, and I feel my face grimace with her agony.

"Oh, Cambria…" Ellary's voice is laced with empathy and pride as she brushes her knuckles comfortingly along Cambria's cheek. "*Malo mori quam foedari.* You served so bravely last night."

My eyes snap to Ellary, my jaw tensing against her words.

Malo mori quam foedari—an ending to our prayers so often spoken in Ember Glen. It's said to mean that we should seek death before dishonoring our roles of service. Everyone in Ember Glen says it, but the prayer is really only meant as a reminder to servants.

I know Ellary means well. She only says what she's meant to say; she only thinks what she's meant to think. She's a victim of our indoctrination as much as anyone else. And just like everyone else, she's entirely unaware of it. She means to honor Cambria and her strength— of which, they both have mountains worth—but my sins have overcome me in such a way that my mind sees it all differently now.

They still serve with pride in the name of our god.

Why can't I believe the way they do?

A glance down at Cambria shows the small smile that touches the corners of her lips while tears glass over her dark eyes. I see the gratitude she has for her agony.

Regardless of what I believe and what I don't, this is our reality. This pain is real, and I wish I could bear it for her so she didn't have to. But this pain can't be held by any one of us alone—it must be held by all of us.

It's our burden.

Our duty.

Our curse.

With great care and taking our time, we help Cambria from the ground, working together to carry her through the trees and back to the village of Ember Glen, seeking out our Sanctuary from the madness.

We come out through the trees like warriors returning from the battlefield—injured and tormented from the horrors of war.

Only this isn't a war.

It's our life.

chapter six

ARLO

THE CONTROL STAND watch over the foggy morning as those who serve begin to emerge from the forest. The seven of us stand side by side, forming a line across the large open space of the village square. It's a matter of showing honor for our women who have served the Impulse as they cross to return to Sanctuary—a space where they can rest, heal their injuries, and reflect in reverence of the good work they've done.

I bend to brush away dirt that hides the shine of my black derby shoe beneath the tapered leg of my fine-cut black slacks. I huff as the dirt only attaches itself to my black leather gloves and rise while I brush my palms together. I adjust my waistcoat over my gray button-up before shoving my hands into my pockets.

"Be still, brother." Theo's head is turned toward the trees, away from me, and he watches carefully. "You've been fidgeting all morning."

I blow out a heavy breath. "I'm unsettled."

Theo briefly glances at me with furrowed brows before turning his attention back to the forest. "Perhaps if you'd purged as you were meant to, you wouldn't feel that way."

"I had my release."

I hadn't.

I was desperate to come when I'd left Mercy.

I'd meant to grab another woman to serve me, but the mere idea of it felt…unsatisfactory. I should've fucked Mercy. I'd even gone back into the forest to find her once I realized she hadn't returned to the campsite to serve her duty. And I had found her, at that very same tree where she came on my fingers.

The clouds were clearing from the sky and the full moon shone brightly above her, as if it were placed there just to bathe her in moonlight for my eyes' pleasure. Her bright blonde hair glowed like starlight shining down from above.

Yet, when I saw her there, pacing, fighting an internal battle I couldn't see with my eyes, I'd been too fascinated with watching her to approach. Fascination had quickly turned to obsession, and I couldn't tear my eyes away from her. Not as she paced, not as she sat, not as she reached between her legs and rested her fingers there with confusion in her expression—she was confused about me and what I'd done to her.

I'd wondered if it was the first time she felt pleasure.

I'd wondered a lot of things about her…so many things that minutes creeped into hours. I watched until she fell asleep, and before I knew it, the night was coming to a close. I had to leave her to return to the Homestead before daylight—and without a single release of my own.

I'd squandered my only opportunity to satisfy my impulses for the next month. I missed out on the physical pleasure I was meant to take, all because I'd lost myself to the curiosity in watching *her*.

"Here she comes," Theo mutters, running a hand through his mess of sandy blond hair, and I don't know exactly who he means.

I look across the vast, gravel-covered square toward the trees, and I see her.

Mercy.

Her platinum hair shines in stark contrast against her black clothing. And she's not alone. She's helping Ellary carry Cambria—and I'm not surprised. From what I've gathered, the three girls are close.

However, I am surprised to see young Delle close behind,

clutching the remains of her corset to cover herself. Frankly, I'm surprised to see her walking on her own. Last I'd seen, she was taking a harsh whipping.

We watch as the group of girls make their way across the open square, small pebbles crunching and kicking up around their feet. It's thirty paces or so from the trees to the end of our line, and we stand in waiting as they pass the first of us.

"Thank you for your service," Owen says from the end as they pass.

Another two paces ahead, they cross Ryker. "Thank you for your service, ladies."

Each of us thank them in turn, standing still as they huff and struggle to carry Cambria across the vast square. They pass Theo, who offers his thanks with a cursory glance at Delle. And as they approach where I stand—second to the last in our line—Mercy's eyes meet mine, though she quickly looks away.

A grin curls my lips. "Thank you for your service, *sinner*."

I'm not entirely sure why I feel compelled to remind her that she's sinned, but I do. And the way her gray-blue eyes narrow on me as she sets her jaw makes something inside me stir—whatever it is slithers up my spine, coiling around my nerves and squeezing.

She doesn't say a word as they pass. She arcs an eyebrow as she gives me an appraising look, and then her eyes leave me, stealing my breath as they do.

The way she turns from me feels as though I'm a flame being snuffed out by the breeze of her disapproval.

My fingers twitch in my pockets with the desire to put pen to paper—she's walking poetry and my hand aches to write her. I don't know how she's managed to evade my senses for so long or how she's suddenly triggered such an awareness within me.

It's no matter. Her demeanor is insolent. She's sinned and punishment awaits her.

BY MID-MORNING, THE girls are all accounted for and safely tucked away at Sanctuary, save for one. Ivy Jane's remains are being prepared for grievance and honor at a servants' ceremony that will take place later in the week. It's probably good she didn't survive being lit on fire; I imagine the recovery from such an event would have been excruciating.

The seven of us cross the village square. The town is at our backs, and the Homestead manor is in front of us. Gravel crunches beneath our feet as we walk the empty space to the sprawling mansion estate where we reside. The people of Ember Glen live in their humble homes in the village, but we—the seven men of the Control—live here at the Homestead. Our space is superior and separate from the residents.

Our manor is made for kings, which we are in our own right. Perhaps not kings exactly, but keepers of our realm.

Decision makers.

Overseers.

High priests ensuring the godliness of our domain.

Our stone manor spans the square, from the forest line on the eastside, to the Sanctuary on the west. Rising high behind the Homestead are the peaks of the Ember Glen mountains. Beautiful and shielding, the mountain range surrounding our valley village serves the purpose of keeping us separate from the outside world, protected from its evils.

I glance over my shoulder at the Sanctuary—the old cathedral on the westside of the square—before looking over at Theo. "You left Mercy Madness alone last night."

"I did."

"Hmm."

"Did you have a thought about that, or are you just verifying facts?"

"I'm curious about it…You frequently claim her on nights of service."

Theo sighs. "For a long time, I found her fascinating. She thinks differently, and it was fun to entertain it for a while. However, as of late, her thinking has turned in the direction of defiance and apathy."

"Are you aware that she ran last night?"

I feel the collective attention of the Control turn their eyes to me, Theo's head swiveling to look at me squarely as we move toward the wide stone steps leading up to the manor.

"No, I wasn't aware," Theo says, a twinge of concern detected in his voice.

"Who ran?" Killian asks from down the line.

"Mercy Madness," I say. "She ran and hid from service in the forest."

My foot comes down on the first step, and I stop on the second step when I realize everyone else has halted. I half turn to face the group.

"Unprovoked?" Owen asks with his pensive blue-eyed stare.

"Not exactly." I turn completely to face them, moving down to the first step. "It was after Hyatt Price set Ivy Jane on fire. I saw him run after Mercy with his torch."

I see unease strain Theo's features—dark eyebrows drawing a line over his brown eyes as his shoulders tense. His reaction—that he has any reaction at all, really—to my story about Mercy causes something like jealousy to bubble up in my chest, and I'm not fond of the feeling.

"I left her unclaimed when I chased after Delle Carter," he says.

"And Hyatt noticed. He came after her, and instead of welcoming her fate to serve his violent urge, she fled in cowardice." I swallow around the word. I'd said it to her last night, too; and while it's the appropriate word, it just somehow doesn't taste quite right.

"Delle ran, too," Ryker points out.

"She's sixteen," Theo counters. "It was her first service."

"This needs to be addressed immediately. We should take it to the Elders," Killian suggests.

I nod. "I agree. It's a transgression worthy of severe punishment."

"It may be worthy of death considering how rebellious Mercy's been as of late. She's developed a history of bad behavior. How long do we allow it before losing all control over our community?" Killian's stare narrows in consideration. "That girl thinks too much for her own good."

He's right, though I admit to myself that Mercy's unpredictable thinking is what drew my attention to her last night. There was a strong anticipatory thrill in not knowing exactly what she would say or do, whether I could find a way to break her, shape her, to discover her buttons and exactly how to push them to get her to do what I wanted her to do.

She's a challenge…not easily controlled.

And though the mere idea of overcoming her is exciting, I understand why it can't be tolerated. Allow one woman to think for herself, and all control is lost. She becomes a danger to herself with her foolish ideas and poses a risk to the very values our community was founded on one hundred and fifty-two years ago.

Intrigue on my part isn't enough for me to argue for her life.

Was I thinking about arguing in favor of her life?

Theo sighs before making his way up the steps. "I've warned her about that."

We follow behind, all of us climbing the thirteen stone steps to the concrete landing.

Killian scoffs, showing me his profile and his tuft of brown hair tied back in a knot. "And yet she still had the audacity to run and hide during service? She makes a fool of you in extending that kindness to her. At her age, she should be a model servant."

Theo reaches the main entrance first, two large wooden doors, intricately carved with images of wildflowers that seem to leap out from the wood itself—dozens of three-dimensional flowers that resemble the grassy fields leading out to the mountains. He pushes his sleeve back to reveal the black band permanently fixed around his wrist—just as all the men of the Control have. He waves the device adorning his wrist over the concealed scanner above the door handle, and the locking mechanism beeps once before we hear it release.

"I've been more than kind to her," Theo agrees as he pushes the door open, and we all filter inside. "I claimed her last night, as I did the first time Hyatt went after her. I'm aware of how brutal his impulses are, and some part of me wanted to spare her. I know I shouldn't have…I should have let him have her. She offers me nothing in service—no passion, no pride, no gratitude."

We cross the ornate floor where the burgundy and gold tiles are laid to form a sunburst pattern—a massive design that expands all the way across the large, circular foyer. The sun's center lies directly beneath a golden chandelier that's more decorative than it is functional. The space is dimly lit, save for the natural light filtering through the large windows on the west side—our home can seem a little grim, I suppose.

"She's been given too much leniency," Killian says.

Naturally, we gather in a circle surrounding the sunburst—not intentionally nor ritualistically. This is simply how we've always come to stand together and discuss important matters.

Wesley rubs his dark palms together. "It's not like we can manage every ill-formed thought that flits through the servants' minds."

At that, I find myself wondering what ill-formed thought is flitting through Mercy's mind right now. I wonder whether she'll think of the way I made her come on my fingers when she lays her head to rest at Sanctuary tonight. The idea of it makes my cock twitch.

Sweet sin.

I should've fucked her last night while I had the chance.

"Something has to be done about Mercy Madness. The new servants are impressionable," Killian says, "and this sets a poor example for them."

"Then something should also be done about Delle Carter because she ran, too," Ryker adds.

"I think Delle could be afforded some leniency," Theo says, crossing his arms. "It was her first night."

"It's no excuse, whether it's the first or the fiftieth. How many first-timers have behaved that way?" Killian asks.

"None come to my mind in recent memory," I reply.

"Exactly." Killian points to me. "They know their place before their first service."

"I don't think Delle presents a concern," Park offers, tossing his head as a strand of black hair falls across his tawny skin. "I'm sure she's learned her place after last night." He looks to Theo. "You went after her. What happened once she was caught?"

"She was effectively put in her place," Theo confirms. "I don't think she'll be an issue again."

"It's Mercy who poses the threat," Killian says. "The pattern of defiance she's developed; the fact that she ran and hid last night… How long has she been in service? How old is she now, twenty? Four years of monthly service. Her actions last night were blasphemous. She's a sinner, and we have to make an example of her."

The men nod in agreement, as do I.

She *is* a sinner.

And yet…there's an odd prickling at the back of my mind that makes me feel uneasy. I can't place the feeling or why it's there. Perhaps it's my weakened state since I didn't effectively purge last night.

Yes, that must be it.

My impulses are clouding my mind, and I need to be careful about my thoughts and decisions until I can satisfy my impulses at the next service. My brothers in God are right; Mercy is a sinner, a bad example for the younger servants, and she must be made an example of.

She must be punished.

I let out a heavy sigh, forcing my breath to blow away that useless feeling of unease. "Then it's decided. Mercy Madness must be punished. I'll alert the Elders that we need to meet."

53

chapter seven

I ROLL MY pen along the dark wood table as we discuss the fate of a sinner whose name stirs lyrical thoughts inside my mind—thoughts which beg to be put to paper.

This is a manner of torture for me, having jumbled words inside my mind without the time or space to scratch them out with my pen. It has me struggling through this collective discussion between the three ruling Elders and the seven members of the Control.

I clear my throat and push back to straighten in my seat, intent on engaging with reason and sound judgment, as it is my duty.

The Control are seated at the black semi-circular table in the courtroom here at the Homestead. The room is a large, barren square, starkly different from the rest of the manor, where everything is elegant and opulent.

This room has black walls and furniture, and a cold, slate-tiled floor. The two light sources are strategically placed—one above the center of our semi-circular black table, and the other directly above a spot on the opposite side where it can serve as a spotlight over the accused who would stand before us.

This room is where we cast judgment over the sinners and lawbreakers in Ember Glen. Fortunately for us, this room is hardly used, thanks to the grace of our God. Because God commands that we indulge during each full moon, the Impulse of men is satisfied, such that the rest of our days are free from violence, debauchery, and sin.

The three Elders appear on the projected screen on the black wall opposite where we sit. Due to their advancing age, they remain physically excluded from the general population. It's crucial their health be maintained so they can provide guidance to Ember Glen, to ensure we follow the guiding principles set forth by their forefathers, who founded our community set away from the world after a new civil war split the nation.

We were all lucky to have been born here.

No one knows what horror still exists in the world around us, what vile demons and sinners lurk on the other side of the mountains that surround us.

"I have a suggestion," Clyde says, snapping me from my thoughts. The flickering triangle of light points from the projector across to the far wall, showing his face in its own square on the screen aside the other two Elders.

"Please," Killian says, "we'd be grateful for your guidance."

"It hasn't been done for a while," Clyde continues, "but I think it's necessary to reassert your authority. You must send a message to the other servants that their sins won't be tolerated. I think Mercy should be made to participate in the Trials of Dissension."

I lean away from the table, my head tilting in curiosity as my arms fall to the armrests of my chair. "The Trials haven't been executed in what, forty years? Fifty? Certainly not in my lifetime."

"Yes, forty, maybe forty-five," Clyde confirms with a nod. "It certainly has been a long time. I was a child then, maybe seven or eight years old."

"If I heard correctly," Theo says, "they tried to do away with the Trials altogether after that last round. Why is that?"

Ryker leans back in his chair, lacing his fingers together over his wavy, dark blond hair, and stretches back. "They stopped because they lost five servants."

"Five? That many chose to participate?" Owen asks.

"There was an unusually high number of participants that year," Edgar—another of the Elders—confirms. "The sinner was required to participate, of course, but then four other servants volunteered."

"And none of them passed? None survived?" I ask.

"They all survived the first round, much to be expected," Clyde says. "I think three survived the second round, and the final round took the rest."

"I think it's fair," Killian says. "Mercy Madness should be made an example of."

"I don't think anyone here disagrees with that," Owen says, "but perhaps we should take some time to discuss the past trials. I'd like to be fully aware of the punishment we're proposing."

Park leans forward, placing his forearms on the table and clasping his hands. "I'd like to do that review, as well. I suppose I don't have a good understanding of the trials, as I can't imagine why a servant would *volunteer* to participate."

"For a chance at freedom," Lawrence—the third Elder—explains. "A sinner is forced because they've already dissented from our ways. But if a servant thought that they somehow deserved a different life than the one God chose for them, then they could volunteer to participate with the promise of a new role in our society should they pass the trials—the promise of a domestic life."

"But no one ever passes," Park says.

"Right," Lawrence confirms with a sharp nod. "Because the trials weren't meant to be passed."

"And yet there were volunteers?"

"Who could possibly understand the mind of a woman?" Clyde chuckles. "Their judgment is poor, and the decisions they make are untenable. Some are as boldly brave as they are stupid, thinking that somehow they will be *the one* to pass."

I realize I'm tapping my pen on the table and abruptly still my hand. "Then the trials are torture. A means of punishment for a sinner, and a device by which to draw out any other servant with divisive thinking."

"Precisely," Edgar says. "Use the trials to draw the approval of the villagers—it will be seen as a fair ruling and prove to be healthy entertainment for them. You give the promise of absolution for the sinner's soul through their participation in the trials. And any servants who might find your sinner to be…*inspirational* will be put in their place. Either they'll volunteer to participate, or they'll see what the sinner faces in the trials and remember why it's best for them to keep their mouths shut, their silly ideas to themselves, and serve with pride and dignity."

"So, what about Delle Carter?" Theo asks, and I'm starting to see the pattern of his concern for her fate. "Admittedly, I feel a pang for how far Mercy's fallen. I've tried to be a friend to her, to keep her in the light, but clearly, I've failed. I understand that an example needs to be made of her," his leg twitches beneath the table as he speaks, "but Delle…she's young. She has years of service ahead of her. She can be managed, reformed in the eyes of God."

"But fleeing from her purpose? It's shameful, regardless of her age and experience," Killian counters.

"Transgressions can be forgiven with atonement," Theo reminds him.

"The three trials *are* atonement—reparations for the sake of the soul before death. The sinner will prove herself through the ultimate acts of service: Service of the Flesh, Service by Sacrifice, and Service from Bloodshed," Clyde recites the three trials.

"But I think Delle's soul can still be saved in *this* life," Theo asserts. "She'll witness Mercy's trials, and she'll learn. If she's a true sinner, we'll know, won't we? If we allow other servants to volunteer, she'll come forward, we'll know, and then the trials will take care of her."

"Fair point." Killian nods.

"I think we're all neglecting to ask a question with a very

important answer here," I say. "What happens if a servant survives the trials?"

The Elders laugh, then Lawrence says, "That won't happen. If they survive the second trial, it's the third that will seal their fate… and you make sure of it."

We make sure of it.

So, that's it, then. The Trials of Dissension are a certified death sentence.

"Let's put it to a vote. All in favor of Mercy's participation in the trials…" Killian says.

Hands rise in favor from Killian, Wesley, and Ryker. Theo seems reluctant, but then slowly lifts his arm.

Breathing you in is sweet sin,
transgression worthy of fire and brimstone.

Words suddenly spring free in my mind, words that need to be chased and explored.

Mercy needs to be chased and explored.

With the thought, I immediately raise my hand in agreement. She draws too much interest and is clouding my every thought. She needs to go, or else I may lose myself in the overwhelming intrigue of her strange personality.

Park and Owen raise their hands as well—a unanimous agreement, of course.

"It's settled then," Killian declares. "Mercy Madness will participate in the Trials of Dissension."

"You'll need to elect a warden," Lawrence says. "Someone who will be responsible for looking after the trial participants. They'll be moved to reside in the Homestead manor during the time between trials."

"Why?"

"For several reasons," Clyde says. "First, to ensure they are immediately separated from the other servants. The last thing we need is a sinner sullying the minds of our most precious commodity. They'll also need to be protected from the villagers. There's record from one of the earliest runs of the trials where the villagers took it upon themselves to round up the participants, tie them to stakes in the center of the village square, and burn them alive."

Ryker chuckles. "Well, that certainly seems more expedient."

"It offers no absolution for the soul," Theo explains. "Isn't that the ultimate goal at the end of the trials?"

"Yes," Lawrence confirms. "And allowing them to seek that absolution absolves us of any responsibility in judgment. The trials decide their fate."

Absolves us of responsibility?

My mind must truly be muddled, as that sounds like hypocrisy to me. How can we say that the trials decide their fate if the trials are fixed? If we're meant to ensure their fate by the third trial, then how do *we* find absolution?

I shake my head and run my leather-gloved hand across my short beard. I didn't purge last night. I must be out of my mind.

"How do we select a warden, then?" Owen asks.

My hand lifts and I speak beyond conscious thought. "I'll do it. I'll volunteer to be the warden."

What the hell am I doing?

I need to stay away from this girl, this sinner who makes a mess of my thoughts.

"That was easy enough. Anyone opposed to Arlo serving as warden?" Ryker asks the group.

To my detriment, no one disagrees. I've just volunteered to keep myself close to Mercy Madness as we bide time until her death. Though that worries me for my clarity of thought, it excites me for the anticipatory denial that being in her presence will bring. I won't be able to have her, and that will only heighten my anticipation for the next full moon when I can purge my impulses with another servant.

Yes. This will be good practice in self-control.

"Congratulations, Warden Rainn. You get to babysit the sinner," Killian says, drawing a low chuckle from the Control.

"It will be my pleasure," I say…and I think it actually will be.

I CLIMB THE marble steps to the second floor and turn right at the landing. My steps are quick as I pad over the runner covering the hardwood floors in the hallway—a traditional rug design of crimson and gold. My room is at the far end of the hall, and when I reach the door on my left, I use the band around my wrist to unlock it.

I slam it shut behind me and ensure its locked before crossing the ivory carpet to my desk. I pull out the chair and sit, huffing out a heavy breath as I stare at the beige wall. My desk is pushed up against it, sitting between two windows that look out to the rolling mountains.

I open the drawer on my right-hand side and pull out my leather-bound journal and fountain pen, placing them on the neatly organized desktop before me. I peel off my leather gloves and drop them onto the desktop.

I stretch and flex my fingers, observing the uneven texture and pinkened color of the scars from my old burns. The roughly textured surface of scarring on my left hand extends from my wrist, twisting along the back of my hand, and stretching to the bends of my pointer and middle finger. A circular patch covers the back of my right hand, thankfully stopping before reaching my fingers, allowing me full movement without pain—if I couldn't write, I don't know what I'd do.

I keep my hands covered most of the time, but not because I'm hiding them. I keep them hidden because these scars are for *me*. My scars are a reminder of how little self-control I had in my youth.

I unwrap the leather cord from around my journal and flip to the next empty page, smoothing my hand down the center to press it open. I uncap my pen and quickly scribble the two lines that had come to me earlier:

Breathing you in is sweet sin,
transgression worthy of fire and brimstone.

I move my pen to the next line, letting a dot of ink bleed out from the tip—hoping the words will bleed out from me, too. And soon, they do.

You are heat.
You are flame.
You are smoking ash which floods my lungs with each delicious breath I take.

My breaths quicken as I draw my pen across the page. Memories of Mercy in my hold as I brought her to pleasure dance across my mind. I remember each drag of my fingers inside her—each twist, each stroke, each thrust—and the sound of her secret, warm breaths puffing delicately against my skin.

I'd never felt anything like her before.

Burn, sweet sinner, and I'll bathe in flames with you.

Heat washes over me as the image of her sets fire in my mind's eye. She is the same as the flames where I burned my hands in my youth—a flickering light that calls to me, heats me, begs me to be burned.

I will disintegrate to ash at your feet.
And my remnants will beg for your grace, your sin…your mercy.

"Mercy," I breathe her name aloud. "Sweet, *sweet* Mercy." I scribble on the page.

Send me to hell, you demon of delight.
Burn with me.

I drop my pen, suddenly heavy with the weight of words I didn't know I was holding inside my mind. I lace my fingers behind my head as I stretch, leaning back in my chair. My cock is hard, and it's all because of this girl—this *servant*—I had hardly noticed before.

What is it that changed?

What removed her cloak of invisibility?

It was her running that made me stand and take notice, but I don't know if that's where she drew my sudden obsession.

No.

It was the grip of her fingers on my biceps and the rocking of her hips as I made her come. It was the way she bit my neck to muffle the sound of her orgasm.

It was her pleasure…the way she fought against it but took it all the same.

"Fuck." My palms drag down over my face.

I slap the journal shut, coil the leather cord around it, drop it in the drawer, and slam it closed. I hadn't felt a need to lock that drawer before, but I feel the need now. The poem must be kept secret, a shameful thing I need to hide.

I use the band on my wrist to engage the magnetic lock on the drawer before shoving to my feet so forcefully that my chair topples over backward. I ignore it and march toward the bathroom, stripping my clothes off as I go.

I walk straight across the white-tiled floor to the far corner of the bathroom. The shower has no doors, just a rainfall showerhead from the ceiling and a drain at my feet that I can walk straight beneath.

Naked, I step beneath the showerhead before turning it on, letting the cold water spill down my body. I don't turn the tap to warm—I need the shock of cold to wake me from this shameful longing.

There's nothing to be gained from wanting Mercy Madness. She's been sentenced to death, and I've volunteered in a way to be her reaper.

I rub cold water over my face as I wonder what the fuck I was thinking volunteering to be the warden of the trial participants. I find myself hoping other servants will volunteer, because then there will be others to focus my time and attention on.

Yet, I also find myself hoping Mercy will be the only one, hoping I might have moments with her alone.

What sins would I commit with her alone?

A shudder rips through my spine.

I'm going to need a bathtub full of ice cubes to shake this blasphemous desire.

Breathing you in is sweet sin,
transgression worthy of fire and brimstone.

You are heat.
You are flame.
You are smoking ash which floods my lungs with each delicious breath I take.

Burn, sweet sinner, and I'll bathe in flames with you.

I will disintegrate to ash at your feet.
And my remnants will beg for your grace, your sin…your mercy.

Mercy.
Sweet, sweet Mercy.

Send me to hell, you demon of delight.
Burn with me.

chapter eight

Mercy

I SLEPT ABOUT as much as Cambria did last night, which is to say not much at all. She was in pain, and though she was stubbornly, bravely calm about it all, her silent screaming called to me.

I stayed by her side, waking every time she did. We splinted her toes as best we could, but I'm afraid they won't heal well. I worry she'll be in pain, that she'll walk with a limp. The cuts all over her body were mostly superficial, though painful nonetheless, I'm sure. Only a few of them were deep enough to need stitches, and Ellary took care of those with her nimble fingers.

I'd laid in the bed beside Cambria's in the chapel where we all sleep, our beds forming a large circle in the open square room. Pews once filled this space instead of beds—I once saw an old, faded photograph showing when they were still in place, but it must have been long before Ember Glen was founded. This space has been for servants to gather and rest as far back as I can remember.

Though I'd laid down to rest last night, I didn't really sleep. Between Cambria's pain and my concern for Delle, I couldn't find peace. The wounds on Delle's back were tended to, but her soul was broken. My ears strained all night, listening for the sound of her crying as I knew the tears would come eventually. And when they did, I was there to comfort her in an instant, staying by her side until she fell back to sleep.

Then, when I went back to rest again, Cambria's whimpers of

pain called me to her, though she'd urged me to go back to bed. There wasn't much I could do except be there for her.

I hate it.

I hate watching someone I care about be in pain. I wish I could take the pain for myself, so she didn't have to.

The sun shines through the stained-glass windows, signaling the girls to awaken, though I've been awake for hours.

"Mercy," Cambria calls in a tired voice.

I move from my position on the floor at her side, rising onto my knees and taking her hand. "How are you feeling?"

"I'll be all right," she says quietly. "Did you sleep at all, or have you been up worrying all night?"

She knows me well.

I give her a small smile. "You know the answer to that question. Are you in pain?"

Her features wince as she shifts, and she presses her eyes shut. "You know the answer to that question," she parrots.

I sigh. "I can get you something for the pain."

"No. It's not that bad. And you know I want to feel it."

She always wants to feel the pain. She revels in it, as do many of the others. They take pride in their injuries and feeling them deeply, knowing it means they've served well.

It saddens me in a way I can't explain, in a way I *wouldn't* explain to anyone in Ember Glen. No one would understand me.

I take hold of her hand and squeeze gently. "I know you do, but I wish you didn't. I hate seeing you ache."

She rolls her head on her pillow, turning her face to look at me. Her black hair is matted around her sweaty cheeks, and she gives me a smile. "Be happy for me, Mercy. I served well."

My chest tightens. "You always do."

"Did you rest at all last night?" Ellary's cheerful voice comes from behind me.

I glance over my shoulder and smile at her approach, glad she's not injured as well. "Not at all."

"Well, I'm up now," Ellary says, her striking green eyes showing a calmness I've never felt. "I'll watch over Cambria. You should get some rest."

"I'm too alert to sleep. My mind is already flooded with thoughts."

"Your mind is *always* flooded with thoughts." She grins, shaking her head as she lowers to sit on the bed at Cambria's feet. "What have you been up thinking about all night?"

Pain.

Torment.

Fear for the future.

"Nothing interesting."

"Are you going to tell us how your night of service went?" Ellary asks. "What happened to you in the forest?"

She leans forward with interest, and I feel Cambria's eyes on me as well. Both wait with something akin to excitement to hear what happened to me.

What do I tell them?

That I'm a sinner awaiting punishment?

Do I tell them that I ran? That I hid?

That Arlo Rainn made me come against a tree?

A wave of pleasure from the memory ripples out from my center, rushing an odd feeling through my core that instantly makes me feel shame. I blink and shake my head to rid me of the memory. "I was…taken into the forest. There's nothing else to tell."

"Something interesting happened to you, *finally*," Cambria says softly, "and you won't tell us. I'm insulted." She giggles and Ellary chuckles with her.

I force a smile to touch my cheeks, but humor and happiness evade me. The memory of Arlo Rainn floods my veins with contradictions—heat and pleasure through my belly at the recollection of the way he touched me, fear and fury for the threatening promise he made for punishment.

"I want nothing from a sinner like you, Mercy Madness."

I swallow a lump in my throat at the recollection of his words and the unearned shame I somehow feel about them.

I know I'm a sinner in his eyes—in everyone's eyes, soon enough.

But I don't feel like I am.

I only feel like a woman trying to survive madness.

My heartbeat quickens, and I suddenly feel overwhelmed. I quickly climb to my feet. "Don't feel insulted." I pat Cambria's hand. "I promise, there's nothing interesting to tell you." I look at Ellary. "I think I'll go get some fresh air. Promise you'll look after her?"

"I always do," Ellary promises.

I grin, blowing them both a kiss before I turn away. When I do, the smile quickly drops as I let my face fall to accurately reflect my melancholy. I don't expect anyone to see, but I glance sideways and catch Delle's gaze fixed on me from where she sits on the side of her bed. She sees my expression, the emotional ache of my soul radiating through my frown. Instinct tells me to cover it with a smile, but before my lips twist, I see it—the same soul ache within her.

She's a mirror, reflecting me exactly as I was at her age four years ago, when disdain dripped from my pores.

But I know better now.

I know I have to hide it.

I let it slip and she saw it, and I don't want her learning bad habits from me that might get her into trouble.

I have to get away from here.

I smile at her before marching toward the two wooden doors that lead out to the village square. Grabbing hold of the long metal handle, I pull the heavy door open, letting the morning sun shine in and cast its rays across the dark wood floors.

I grip the layers of my black mid-length skirt. Though servants must always wear black, we're allowed to make more modest clothing choices outside of nights of service. I've put on a long-sleeve, form-fitting black top that covers my shoulders and has a sweetheart neckline. My high-waisted skirt is made of layers of lace that float around me in asymmetric tiers, and I always wear the same lace-up ankle boots. Lifting my skirt up to my knees, I prepare to run.

I plod down the stone steps and sprint over the gravel, sprinting across the open village square. My eyes are set on the tree line of the forest ahead, the small stones crunching beneath my feet.

I spare a single glance at the Homestead as I run parallel to the massive structure, sneering at its pretension before turning my focus ahead to the trees.

Are they in there right now deciding my punishment?

Has it already been decided?

I push harder, running faster, sprinting to the trees as my lungs burn.

But I don't stop.

I don't stop as gravel turns to dirt. I don't stop as open space becomes cluttered with tall trees that surround me as I cross into the forest. I don't stop for fallen branches, leaping over them as my feet crunch over twigs and leaves on the forest floor. I don't stop until I reach it—the tree where I keep it hidden.

I slow to a walk as I approach the tree and circle around to the other side. Stopping, I step in close, raising onto the balls of my feet and reaching my arm high. Slipping my hand into the open knot of the trunk, I feel around as I stretch, my cheek pressed against the bark. My fingers touch leather and I grapple for a grip on it. When I have a firm hold, I pull out the leather-bound journal and lower to my flat feet.

Looking down at it, I brush the dirt away—my mother Mira's journal. I'd found it three months ago while cleaning out my father's home in the village after he died. It was in the table beside his bed, which was odd because I'd never seen it there before. It was almost as if I were meant to find it—almost as if it were meant to find *me*.

I tuck it beneath my arm, and head deeper into the forest, heading for the one place where peace always finds me.

chapter nine

Mercy

AS I COME through the trees, my mother's journal held in my grip, I'm overcome by the radiant sunshine that dares to exist after such a dark night of service. Tufts of white clouds dot the brilliant blue sky, and the sun is warm where it touches my skin. I can't help but let it bring a smile to my face.

Ahead of me is the open meadow. It's laid out beneath the rolling hills, which lead out toward the mountains—my own personal sanctuary.

Wildflowers in shades of amethyst and ruby dance in the breeze with the tall grass—gems of color that shine brightly through a bleak world. It's a sea of bright life that calls to my soul. I breathe deeply, savoring the floral scent that mingles with the fresh mountain air as I walk among the wildflowers, my skirt dusting the grass as I move through it.

I hear a child giggling and look off into the distance to see a domestic woman and her little girl playfully chasing one another through the field. The grins and laughter between them bring a joyful expression to my face, yet it also brings a twinge of heartache.

Moving to my perfect spot in the center of the field, I tuck my skirt beneath me before lowering to sit, my head still turned to watch them play a few moments longer. The longer I watch the little girl—who's maybe seven or eight—the more my sadness grows.

That child is destined to serve—she's already been marked for it. I can see the lines of black ink on her forearm from here; and though the image isn't clear from so far away, I know exactly what it looks like all the same. All who've been selected to serve bear the emblem.

I set my mother's journal beside me and push back my sleeve, revealing the same design tattooed on my arm. Two black lines wrap all the way around my forearm, splitting apart an image of the same wildflowers I sit amongst, only the design on my arm is colorless.

I think the founders of Ember Glen must have imagined us as wild—colors too bright and bold invading their grassy meadow that they needed to subdue. In a way, it's quite a sad image. Black lines draw the floral landscape on my arm, but the image is devoid of color, lacking the joy that the real flowers bring.

I sigh, knowing the little girl would've been marked for service when she was five—that's when all the girls in Ember Glen have their fates chosen for them. The Control decides who will be marked to serve and who will be left for "domestic bliss"—their words, not mine. Though if you ask the Control, they'll say God speaks through them to select the future servants, and that they don't make the decisions all their own.

It's a lie if you ask me.

In truth, we all serve, but domestics will never have to serve the Impulse. Domestics are given the grace of a home, a husband, and children. Sometimes the children are their own, born of artificial implantation, and sometimes they're born of servants and assigned a family unit. In any case, the child playing happily in the meadow bears the mark of a servant, and it gives me the urge to charge after her, pick her up, and run with her up the mountains.

It's just a fleeting thought, though. It's not as though I could ever leave Ember Glen. Even if I could survive the trek to see what's on the other side of the mountains surrounding us, I don't know what horrors await.

There was a civil war born of politics and greed before Ember

Glen was settled, and it destroyed a country they once called the greatest in the world—at least, that's what we're told. It's always said that we're lucky to have been born here.

I turn away and lay back, letting myself disappear among the green, purple, and red. I lift my mother's journal to rest against my belly, feeling the stitch of a small ache that never really goes away. It's not an ache of the physical nature…it's spiritual.

When I was younger, I naïvely hoped for children of my own one day, but that was before I understood my role as a servant. Once I began to serve, God saw fit to bring life to my womb on five separate occasions, yet he took it away every single time.

Each loss brought me such pain, tearing holes in the fabric of my soul that will never be repaired. But with the pain of lost life came gratitude for a tormented future that was spared. I couldn't bear the thought of bringing a daughter into this world, and so I knew the miscarriages were for the best, even though they pain me still.

Lifting the journal, I open it to the leather strap down the center of the page I had left off on. I find the next entry, dated July 8, 2171, when I was just a few weeks shy of my sixth birthday.

> Sometimes I look at Mercy and wonder if I made a mistake allowing her to be born. I wonder if I should have found a way to end the pregnancy as soon as the successful implantation was confirmed. But that thought never lingers long because the thought of how beautiful and perfect she is quickly replaces it.
>
> Her smile is sunshine, bright and wide and warming everything she shines upon. She's full of lightness and life, naturally caring and concerned for the well-being of others. She notices when I'm sad—when melancholy over her future in service breaks through and shows on my face.
>
> She comes to me in those moments and climbs onto my lap. She touches my cheek with her soft, tiny hand and smiles with those naturally pink lips and her unique silvery-blue eyes glowing up at me.

"It's okay, Mama," she'll say. "I'm here with you." Then she snuggles in close, hugging her arms around me tight.

And when she does, the whole world feels perfect...until she lets me go.

Then, all I can think about is her future of service. All I can think about is how she'll be hurt, how she'll be used by men.

They want me to take pride in that. They want me to be proud that I have such a beautiful daughter—a daughter who will serve so many in nights of purging.

But I'm beginning to think everything is wrong. I'm beginning to think God doesn't exist. Because if He does exist, how could He possibly allow this to be done to our daughters? How could He allow them to live through such horror?

Am I the only woman who sees this?

Am I the only one?

Am I wrong?

Am I a sinner with a demon's thoughts in my mind?

Should I take pride in knowing how Mercy will serve?

I don't know how I ever could.

My pulse pounds as I read my mother's words. She was afraid for me. She questioned the beliefs of our community, just as I do. She wondered if everything we're told to believe is wrong. Her mind was that of a sinner's, her thinking so similar to mine.

Did she condition me for divisive thinking?

Are my thoughts rebellious because hers were?

Did she indoctrinate me against having pride in service?

Was she a sinner who made me question my beliefs?

No...No!

I refuse to believe any of that.

I'm not a sinner, and neither was my mother.

But if we aren't sinners, then that means everyone else is wrong. Air rushes from my lungs on a sigh. Nausea rolls through my gut with the dissonance of it all. Either she and I are right and everyone else is wrong, or she and I are wrong…and we both deserve to burn in hell for our sins.

Where is the truth in this madness?

I flip the page to read the next entry, dated a week later, on July 15, 2171.

I'm a sinner.

I have sinned.

I don't think there will be absolution for me.

Elijah found me with her.

I don't dare write her name, though it wouldn't matter if I did. They already know; they all know. The Elders, the Control, Elijah…

Oh, how I've hurt Elijah.

He found me tangled with her in our bed. I honestly hadn't expected him to return home so soon, and I was stupid. We were stupid.

We're sinners.

It's the only explanation.

I must have been wrong, so wrong to think against our beliefs, to question the existence of our God, to wonder whether the ways of our community are right or wrong. They're right…of course they're right, and I have sinned beyond forgiveness.

There must be a demon inside my mind, giving me the same sexual impulses as those of men. It tricks me, deceives me, convinces me to carry out sexual acts with a woman, and I'm weak. Women are weak…too weak to handle the Impulse. It's why God only burdens our men with it. They have the willpower to wait for the full moon to purge, while I had none.

I wanted her.

I needed her.

I thought perhaps I loved her.

But it's only the demon in my soul.

I'm a woman possessed.

I'm a sinner.

Elijah had to report my transgression to the Control, and my fate awaits their decision of punishment. I know I deserve whatever punishment they bring. I just hope that when I'm gone, another domestic can help Elijah raise Mercy to be stronger than me, holier than me.

All hope for me is lost.

But perhaps Mercy will grow to become the proud, willing servant I know she can be.

I flip to the next entry, dated July 21, 2171—my sixth birthday.

I've said goodbye to Mercy, and nothing in my life has been harder than that. My daughter, my love, the light of my life... She turns six years old today, but it's the last birthday I'll ever see.

My life will end tonight.

I know my fate is death; I've accepted it. But I don't accept the condemnation of my soul for all eternity. I asked to find absolution for my soul, but no grace was given by the Control. They find me too abhorrent. Perhaps God will grant me grace at the stake when I'm doused in flames.

Unless...there is no God.

Unless there is nothing after death.

If that's the truth, then dare I say, I'm glad I loved that incredible woman while I could. My hand shakes as I write this— the words are blasphemous, I know. But what does it matter now that I'm sentenced to death and my soul is already damned?

There's a simple spark of hope in my chest that maybe this is it. Maybe death is the end. Maybe eternal suffering won't find me, and life will simply be over when I die. That hope is all I have to cling to in these final hours of my life.

But oh, how I fear for my Mercy. How I hate myself for doing this to her, for sinning so catastrophically and leaving her behind. The tears running down her pink cheeks as I told her I was leaving forever were enough to shred what was left of my tattered soul.

She was fearful and sad and looked at me as though I'd broken her world. I have broken her world because I sinned.

But tonight I'll stand humbly at the stake, and I won't scream when they set me on fire; I won't protest. I'll receive my punishment, and though I know it's too late for my soul to be saved, I'll pray for God's mercy all the same. Likewise, I'll hope that God doesn't exist at all, and that this will be the end of my suffering forever.

All I ever wanted was to love and to be loved. It was never there with Elijah, though he never treated me poorly. It was only with her that I felt it, and I regret nothing.

No.

I regret everything.

I regret our stolen fates.

I regret our carelessness.

I regret that we didn't spend more of our numbered days together, sinning in secret.

I regret that I won't be here to protect Mercy.

Tears well, and one breaks away from the corner of my eye, slipping down the side of my face. My heart is broken. My mother had loved and been loved in return, and because it wasn't with the man she'd been assigned to be with, she was persecuted. She'd found love with another woman, and they murdered her because of it.

Love is a rare and precious thing in Ember Glen—something scarcely seen and only found by sheer luck. Domestic women are assigned their male counterpart, and the likelihood of them loving one another is improbable. Though I can't deny the hurt I feel for my late father over her adultery, the anger I feel for my mother's demise overshadows it.

How can murder be justified for one person loving another?

A shadow quickly obscures the sunlight from overhead, startling me. My heart sinks heavily into my stomach, but it splashes in the acid, scattering droplets that burn my insides as I look up and see why the sunlight disappeared.

A man stands above me, feet straddling either side of my hips.

"Good morning, Mercy."

I blink against the tears clouding my vision.

The sunlight glows like a halo around Arlo Rainn's head.

"Good morning," I return politely, curious about his appearance.

I swallow anxiously that he's caught me with my mother's journal—and on the page with an admission of her sins, no less.

I don't want anyone to see what's within these pages—it's my mother's personal thoughts. But more than that, it tells of her indiscretions. It tells of all her secrets, and my thoughts are scribbled in the margins. So, as he watches me, I move slowly, careful not to draw attention to it, careful not to move so quickly as to make it seem like I want to hide it.

I fold the journal closed and gently slip it down to rest on the ground beside me, releasing it, though I have the urge to hang on for safe-keeping. I know if he sees me willing to let go of it, then perhaps he'll assume there's nothing of great importance in there.

I press up onto my elbows, wishing I could sit up at least, unnerved by laying beneath him. The way he stands above me, feet straddling my hips, prevents me from moving.

"Is there something I can do for you?" I squint against the sunshine halo around his face, tilting my head and bringing one hand up sideways against my forehead as a shield.

"I could think of several," he returns, "but the night of your service has passed."

I swallow the lump rising in my throat. "There's always the next one," I say, my voice dripping with sarcasm.

I shouldn't have said those words, at least not in that sardonic manner. It's as though I can't help but try to get myself into trouble.

Careful, Mercy.

A soft smile tugs at one corner of his thick lips, twisting into his tawny beard and highlighting the long line of his dimple. He's handsome, there's no denying it. The glow of sunlight all around him really amplifies the hint of orange in his brown hair and beard—it reminds me of fire.

Orange and yellow flames flicker through my mind, rushing me back to the other night. Images of Hyatt and his torch flash to pictures of Ivy Jane moving as flames engulf her, which distorts into the flash fire I felt rushing through my veins when Arlo had me against the tree and made me come—

"There likely won't be a next one for you, I'm afraid."

I sinned.

I ran, and I hid.

I rebelled from my soul's purpose, and I was promised punishment.

He's come to punish me.

As soon as the realization hits me, I scramble, kicking against the earth to push myself backward and crawl out from beneath him. He ignores me as I awkwardly rush to my feet and back away; instead, he bends to pick up my mother's journal.

No!

I lunge for it, but he jerks his hand away, holding the journal beside his head.

"Give that back."

"No," he says plainly.

He slowly lowers it in front of him, thumbing open the pages.

I lunge again to snatch it, but he only steps back, narrowing his eyes at me with his head tilted toward the pages. "Stop. Your property is my property now."

"What?"

What is he saying?

I'm entitled to have my own things.

Except, the Control has license to take authority over the personal property of sinners.

And I'm a sinner now.

I feel frozen as I watch him flip through the pages, reading a sentence here and there. A shiver runs up my spine despite the warmth of the sun, and I hug myself, running my hands up and down my arms. Movement in the distance catches my eye; standing at the tree line, at the edge of the meadow, are the other six members of the Control.

Watching.

Waiting.

The notion of my death claws through my mind, scratching away all other thoughts.

Have they come to kill me?

Will I die today?

How will they do it? Burned at the stake like my mother?

"What is this?" Arlo asks, closing the journal and holding it up. "Is this your mother's?"

I hear him, but I struggle to respond. The very essence of my being is trapped behind a thick wall of ice inside my mind, frozen and paralyzed to thoughts of punishment and death.

"Forget it," he says with exasperation. "Come with me."

He holds out his palm, covered with a black leather glove, and I stare at it as if it's the strangest thing I've ever seen, as if it's the most terrifying thing I've ever seen…because it is.

If I take his hand, he'll lead me away, only I don't know where to and I don't know what will happen then. I don't know if I'll be hurt or tortured, or if I'll be killed immediately.

I lift my gaze from his hand to meet his stare. "Are you going to kill me?"

His eyes are blue—bright blue, like the clear sky above. They sparkle as he watches me, waiting for me to take his outstretched hand.

I think it's the first time I've ever really looked at him. I've only known him by name and in passing before the other night in the forest. I knew *of* him; I'd seen him and could identify him easily. But looking at him now, I know I've never truly *seen* him before.

"Not personally, and certainly not today," he offers. "Come along now. We have things to discuss."

"What things?"

He takes a step closer, and instinctively, I step back.

"Mercy."

"What's going to happen to me? Please. Can't you just tell me now?"

"I'm not going to ask you again." His offered palm twitches with threat. "We will drag you away if you insist on resisting."

Part of me wants to resist. If my fate has already been decided—and I suspect it has—then resistance won't change the outcome. Resisting might make me feel like I did something, that I at least tried. That part of me makes my knees bend with the urge to run.

Likewise, though, there's no point in that fight if it changes nothing. Something tells me I should save my strength for a battle yet to come, though I don't know what it is.

I take a step closer to Arlo, and slowly, I reach out to him, watching our hands come together in contrast beneath the bright shine of sunlight. The black leather looks menacing, held out above the colorful wildflowers and grass that sways in the gentle breeze. As I lay my pale hand atop his palm, his hand closes tightly around mine, caging it in his suffocating grasp.

My lips part with an abrupt inhale as he pulls me sharply, easily tugging me into his hold as his other arm—still grasping the journal—whips around my waist. I raise my head to look up at him, and he catches me again in his stare. The intensity of his blue gaze grabs hold of me and flashes through my memories, making my stomach flutter.

I remember the warmth of his bare hand as his fingers pressed inside me. Part of me wants to feel that warmth against my palm now held in his grip—but the leather grips me instead. His thick eyebrows furrow, drawing a line above his blue eyes. His expression is forever changing—it shifts and twists so quickly that my darting eyes can't keep up as they flicker about his face. I see the curve of his throat bob as he swallows, his arm shifting along my back.

Why is his arm still around me?

Why does he still hold me this way?

He blinks and his eyes shadow, like a shade slipping down and hiding the brightness. Still holding my palm in his, he releases his arm from my waist and turns before shifting into a fast walk, dragging me along beside him. "I'm taking you to the Homestead. You'll be under my charge for an undefined period of time."

"What does that mean?"

"Do you know how to be quiet?"

"I just want to know what's going to happen to me."

"You'll learn soon enough. Patience is a virtue, Mercy. You should practice it."

I huff out in stressful frustration as he pulls me toward the trees. The Control turns their attention to me as we charge toward the center of their gathering at the edge of the woods.

"Mercy Madness," Killian Cole says. "About time you were brought to justice."

"It's your reckoning day," someone else calls, but I don't see who as Arlo drags me past them, marching me through the forest.

"Bring the sinner to her judgment," another says, their voices following close, taunting me as they take me away for God knows what.

The taunting continues through the forest, twigs breaking beneath my feet, the crunching echoes bouncing off the trees all around me. The men's voices seem to drift into a swirling chorus that loops around tree trunks, swirls through the empty spaces between them, and bathes me in taunting noise.

As we break through the trees, the noise crescendos with the sound of voices ahead in the village square.

Adrenaline pulses through my veins as I stumble behind Arlo's quickening pace. My eyes take notice of who the rising voices belong to. The entire population of Ember Glen is standing in wait in the village square, just in front of the steps leading up to the Homestead.

Waiting.

Waiting for me.

chapter ten
Mercy

FEAR GRIPS ME, bringing my feet to an abrupt stop. Arlo jerks, but I plant my boots on the gravel, anger contorting my expression. His grip slips from my hand to my wrist. I try to pull my arm away, bringing my free hand to push down against his grip.

"Let go of me!" I shout, and my cry is met with the sudden deafening silence of the world around me.

Arlo stares at me, his anger bringing a sneer that pulls his lips across his cheeks. In a surprise move, he releases me and takes a step back. I turn to run, but I crash straight into Theo's broad chest.

I look up at him. "Theo…"

His expression is somber, sad, regretful—and that scares me more than anything. "I'm sorry, Mercy."

I take a step back as the Control circles me, making it clear there is no escaping my fate.

"You sinned when you were meant to serve," Theo says, as if the logic is sound and should be enough to make me accept this. "But it was the culmination of your dissenting thoughts, and it can no longer be ignored." He lowers his voice. "I warned you…"

He did warn me.

He told me I was being watched before he ran after Delle that night.

Heat envelops me, like a fire burning at my back as Arlo steps in close behind me. My pounding heart skips a beat. His fingers are too light, too gentle as they capture strands of my white-blonde hair and lift them back over my shoulder. His breath breezes across my ear as he leans in.

"Come with me, sinner. Walk with dignity to your reckoning, and I'll stand beside you."

I turn my head sharply, meeting his eyes as he slowly circles to stand at my side.

"I'll stand beside you."

I don't know what to make of such a contradictory statement.

I'll cast judgment upon you while standing at your side?

Righteous indignation catches fire in my chest as he once again holds out his gloved palm for me to take. I feel the snarl tug a sour grin from my lips.

Everything in Ember Glen is a contradiction—our faith, our beliefs, our values…Everything is just one sickening contradiction after the next.

So let them call me the sinner.

Bring forth my judgment and reckoning.

I won't pretend I believe their lies any longer. I won't go with willing acceptance to my death like my mother did.

I swing my arm to smack Arlo's hand away. "I don't need anyone to stand beside me, least of all men like you." For good measure, I spit on the ground beside his feet, out of my mind with fury.

My action stirs chaos, and the men descend. My eyes are caught on Arlo's, but he can't even get to me before another has their arms around my waist, lifting and dragging me away. I stare as Arlo remains fixed to the spot, as my body is carried away with the Control surrounding me, all except for him.

In his own rage, the sight of him draws me in, keeps my furious attention locked on him while I'm dragged away. His chest rises and falls as anger flares his nostrils; but strangely, there's a fluttering inside my stomach at the way his piercing eyes narrow on me.

He looks at me with passion.

He looks at me with fierce determination, with intent, with a plan. That shouldn't trigger my curiosity, yet it does.

It keeps me drawn in, zeroed in on him as he stomps after me. Arlo's rapt attention fuels me with anger, and I thrash against the arms that hold me, letting rage build as I'm spun away and dropped heavily to the ground again.

I land on my boots, but the forward thrust pitches my weight, causing me to stumble ahead. I'm determined not to fall. I find my balance and start walking before they can push me, moving toward the villagers gathered in the square.

The day is too bright for these dark events.

The villagers watch, confusion and anticipation mixed in their expressions. They probably don't know *why* they're gathered; they're probably just excited *to be* gathered. They must know by now that I've done something wrong. My sin is their entertainment—whatever my punishment will be is a spectacle for them.

Murmurs and whispers carry to my ears as I'm marched up the concrete steps toward the Homestead. Three of the Control climb to the landing ahead of me. They stop and turn to face me so abruptly that I nearly lose my balance trying to stop myself from falling.

A hand latches around my wrist, another pressing to the small of my back. The touch of fingertips grazing my spine with delicate control is shocking, causing a shudder to ripple through every nerve ending.

My head turns, and I'm not surprised when I lock eyes with Arlo. It's his leather-clad hand on my wrist, his palm on my back. With a quick jerk, he spins me around, and I suck in a gasping breath.

Clustered together in the center of the large gravel-covered square is everyone I've ever known. They're staring at me, judging me, waiting on bated breath to know why I've been brought to stand before them.

This is perhaps the first moment I've ever been glad that both my parents are dead—at least I don't have to see them gathered, staring with fear and embarrassment in their eyes.

A mass of servants, all dressed in black, emerge from the Sanctuary, realizing that there's a gathering that they hadn't been called to. It's only because it's the week after service—they're meant to be left alone in reverence, and this is a disturbance.

I'm a disturbance—a ripple in the perfectly flowing current of life in Ember Glen.

My heart pounds as the girls from Sanctuary quicken their pace, my stomach clenching in shame as Ellary recognizes me standing on the steps and rushes, pushing through the cluster of servants to meet the gathering of villagers.

I can't look at her.

I turn my head, gazing off toward the line of trees, quietly wishing I were back in the meadow among the wildflowers.

Too soon, Killian's bellowing voice drags my attention back to the unfolding nightmare. "Mercy Madness has sinned."

The dramatic hisses and sighs of disapproval that roll through the throng is nearly laughable—as if they hadn't already figured it out.

"On the night of our purge, Mercy turned and fled from a man as he approached her. She ran into the forest and hid in a tree. She knowingly, and willfully, refused to serve the Impulse, and her transgression cannot go unrecognized by our authority. Mercy has actively engaged in rebellion, not only by fleeing during service, but in her withdrawal from her duties to serve this community. She chose her own well-being over the well-being of every other man, woman, and child in this village. She has chosen not to fulfill her purpose as a servant of the Impulse, and in doing so, has put you all in danger."

I scoff, too angry to hide it any longer.

They aren't in danger because I chose to flee rather than be lit on fire, but it's what we've been made to believe our entire lives. As I learned today, even my mother was made to believe it—though she'd questioned it just like me. They've made us believe that our community is safe because men are allowed to purge on nights of service, and servants are honored for their sacrifices.

But we were never given the choice to sacrifice, so it's not sacrifice at all…it's slaughter.

In my obvious disdain, Arlo jerks my wrist, tilting my body harshly to the side. I grimace as he twists, bending my arm at the elbow and pinning it behind me. Pressing forward, my back arches away from the pressure, and I groan.

"Quiet, sinner," he whispers.

I lift my foot and slam it back down again, stomping on his toe. His leather shoe is hard, and I'm sure he doesn't feel a thing. Still, he presses harder, making my back arch deeper. His other hand wraps around my hair and tugs, forcing my chin skyward.

His mouth is against my ear, and he speaks so quietly that I don't think the Control surrounding us can even hear. "I will bind you so tightly that your veins bulge and your limbs go numb. Don't test me." The rasp of truth in his tone is jarring, and I still myself in his hold.

Gradually, he loosens his grip, his fingers slipping down through the length of my hair until it falls away entirely. He doesn't let go of my arm, keeping it pinned against my back, but he lets up enough that it no longer aches.

"Our eyes have been on Mercy Madness for several months," Killian continues. "She has become disengaged from our community; she's indignant and self-righteous. And this last purge was the culmination of her dissension. We've known peace in Ember Glen for many years, and we owe that peace to our nights of release. Praise God for the insight he's granted us over how to be a worthy community—a community of godly men and women who know their roles and fulfill them with grace. We cannot allow one ungodly servant to threaten the peace we've worked so hard to maintain.

"Yet, we must humble ourselves in God's good graces. We must seek absolution for the sake of this sinner's soul." Killian paces dramatically along the step beneath me as he speaks. "Though her dishonorable choices must be punished, we must offer her a chance."

A chance?

A chance at what?

I'm motionless, waiting on bated breath.

"The Elders have offered us their guidance and we are all in agreement of what must be done." Killian stops, turns his head over his shoulder to glance at me with a smug grin before turning to face the villagers again. "Mercy Madness is set to participate in the Trials of Dissension."

My ears roar, not with the murmurs and cheers that swell from the villagers, but with the quickening thrum of my pulse.

The Trials of Dissension?

I shake my head. "No," I whisper, but no one hears me. "No! This is a death sentence!"

"Pass the trials, and it's not," Arlo says.

I turn toward him as rage takes hold of me, his grip loosening and letting me go. "No one has ever survived the trials. No one."

He leans forward, coming into my space, making me crane my neck to look up at him as he bends over me. I can smell his minty breath. "Then perhaps you'll be the first." An arrogant grin spreads through his cheeks.

We both know that won't be the case. No one ever survived because the trials were designed to push one past their boundaries in the ultimate acts of service. Every last participant has met their death at the end of these torturous trials.

I'm disgusted by Arlo, sickened by all the men surrounding me—smug, righteous, arrogant, power-hungry men.

Does no one see it but me?

My mother did, but she was so misled that she still mistrusted her instincts.

"Get out of my face," I hiss.

Arlo's grin remains, though his blue eyes roam my expression.

What is he thinking when he looks at me that way?

And why do I care?

"You'll hold your tongue with me and show respect, Mercy, or I will make your numbered days a living hell."

I swallow the weight of his threat, feeling my eyes widen as the smug expression melts with the honesty of his words.

Abruptly, he turns to face the villagers. "I've been appointed warden of our trial participant," Arlo says. "Mercy Madness will be my charge and my responsibility from now until the trials have concluded." He turns toward the servants, all grouped together beside the other villagers. "Servants, as is tradition with the Trials of Dissension, you are all granted the choice of participating. Those of you who are proud servants—graceful in your acceptance of your role within our community, honorable in the eyes of God—you should find it an easy choice not to participate.

"But should any of you feel a blasphemous urge to participate in these trials along with Mercy, we are granting you the right to make the choice. If you pass the trials and prove yourself through the ultimate acts of service, then you will be granted reprieve from your role as a servant and assigned a domestic life.

"But make no mistake, the trials are brutal, and none have survived before. I suggest you think again should the unholy urge to participate arise. God does not show favor in this life to those who wish to deflect their duties." He looks over at me and catches my gaze with an unexplainable heat in his eyes. "Mercy has lost her way. She travels a trail of sin." He looks back to the servants and I blink away the invisible hold he has on me. "If you're a woman of God, you'll ensure you do not follow the path she has made with demons."

Arlo Rainn—my warden, my jailor, my *captor.*

I'll be his until the day I die.

chapter eleven

Mercy

I JERK MY arm from Arlo's grip and plant my feet in the center of the foyer as the men come to a stop in front of me. The door slams shut behind me as the Control circles around, making me feel caged in.

Because I *am* caged in.

I've never been inside the Homestead before…none of the villagers or servants have. It belongs to the members of the Control and to no one else.

I spin to see all of them surrounding me. Seven towering men in their fine clothes and pretentious expressions bringing me to judgment of my so-called sins. As I turn, the tiled floor beneath my feet catches my gaze. I'm standing on the center of a golden sun with seven swooping arms reaching out to form its halo—seven arms, and one man standing at the point where each ends. A lump rises in my throat and I swallow, feeling tension pull through my shoulders.

I open my mouth to speak, but to say what, I don't know. But their madness descends without warning, and any words I might've spoken are shoved aside by the forceful protest of my scream. All at once, they close in, my cage collapsing. Hands fall on me, grabbing my wrists, sweeping my legs out from under me, bringing me down to the ground. I thrash and fight at their team effort to push me down, but there are seven of them and the fight is no use. Quickly, they have me on my back, and it's a flurry of men above me, beside me, all around me.

"Turn her over," Killian commands, and there isn't an inch of my body that isn't being touched by someone.

I scream, thrashing and twisting violently as they work to flip me. I don't know what they intend to do to me, but it isn't hard to imagine what horrible things they might do while I'm pinned face-down on the floor with seven men controlling me.

"Mercy, stop," I hear Theo say, and the sound of his voice startles me.

I glance over at him as his hand slips behind my head and grabs hold of the back of my neck. I don't know why it hurts me that he's part of this, because he's always been part of this. He's always been one of the Control. I just sometimes thought that he was my friend, too. Maybe that stopped when he chose to leave me and chase after Delle into the forest.

The overwhelming fear and heartache over what's happening to me brings tears to my eyes, and the trail down my cheeks triggers a resigned sob. My body relents in its fight and allows them to turn me, pressing me down into the hard floor, my black skirt spread across the sunburst tile like a dark spot on the sun.

I feel someone climb over my back, their knees straddling my waist. Then I feel the touch of leather kiss my skin, and I instantly know it's Arlo brushing his gloved fingers across the side of my neck. I go still, my breath held at his touch.

"Hold still," Arlo says as he pulls my hair back, brushing it aside and exposing the back of my neck. "We need to mark you for the trials. If you just hold still, it will only hurt briefly."

I'm a strong woman, but I have no strength in this moment. I'm subdued entirely, overpowered and overwhelmed. I don't even flinch at the news of pain and being marked. I just want them to get this over with—whatever this is.

I hold still, breathing heavily through several beats, doing my best to quell the waves of tears that threaten behind a sob. I feel

Arlo's leather-covered fingertip trace a spot at the base of my neck.

"Here?" he questions.

"Yes, right there at the back of her neck," I hear Killian respond.

The leather leaves and it's replaced by a metal tip, and then a sharp slice sears pain across my skin. I yelp at the unexpected burn of it—a knife slicing a quick straight line at the base of my neck.

"Don't move," Arlo commands, and I'm obliged to listen as sadness overwhelms me.

He stands, the weight of him leaving my body, but it's quickly replaced by someone else. I feel the knife tip dig into my skin a second time, then slice sharply, drawing a short line of fire beside the first cut.

I cry as I feel the warmth of my blood pooling and dripping from the cuts. I let the tears fall freely as the second body leaves me, and another replaces him, as another slice sears my skin…then another, and another. The seven take their turn drawing bloody lines at the base of my neck, and once the seventh is etched on my skin, it's over.

They let go of me, and nearly all at once move back to their points around the starburst, leaving me in the center of the burning sun. Gasping and breathless, my body curls protectively around its center, though my palms stay pressed flat to the tile.

"There's no need to fear us, Mercy," I hear Killian say. "You won't be harmed in this house now that you're marked. As a trial participant, you're granted the privilege of living as one of us until your time is…over."

Until I'm dead.

I hear Ryker chuckle. "Last rites for a sinner."

"Your warden will make sure you have what you need during your time here, however long that may be."

I push through my palms and slowly lift myself. "How long?" I ask, my voice coming out unexpectedly hoarse, low, shaken.

"The first trial will take place in a little less than a month."

One month.

Goosebumps prickle along my forearms as I bring myself to a sitting position, my gaze fixed on the floor.

"Come with me, sinner." Arlo's smooth voice touches my ears and I feel the sound vibrate through my spine. "I'll show you to your room so you can dress in something more appropriate for your new status."

I scoff at his words as I bravely, but slowly push to my feet. I turn to face Arlo and see his outstretched hand once again—still covered by the black gloves I'm coming to despise.

Arlo's pointed gaze holds my attention, his straight expression steady and severe. "Take my hand," he implores, "and come with me."

I feel my hand lift and reach toward his. I'm aware of the movement, but I feel powerless over it. As my palm lands on his, something sparks and crackles between us—a strange emotion that feels inevitable, yet entirely unexplainable.

Arlo's hand closes around mine and he tugs, just as he did in the meadow. Air escapes my lungs as he pulls me against him, and our bodies collide.

I bring up my hands to push off his chest, but they're pinned between us as he dips his head to my ear. "I expect nothing less than your best behavior," he whispers, then draws his head back to look down at me, speaking loud enough for the others to hear. "It's understood that I'm your warden, and your needs will be met through me. If there's something you need, you come to me first. No one else needs to be bothered by your requests. Do you understand, sinner?"

"You can continue to call me that but saying it doesn't make it true."

I draw a chuckle from the men behind me, but my eyes are fixed on Arlo's serious features, my gaze drawn to the frustratingly plump lips that twist into a devilishly smug grin.

I hate his lips.

I hate his grin.

I hate the long dimples that cut down his cheeks.

I hate that, despite all the ugliness inside, he's objectively handsome. But when I raise my eyes to meet his, I feel an unwanted recognition.

I can't breathe when he looks at me.

"Up the steps, sinner," Arlo says, tilting his head toward the grand staircase in front of us.

He shifts to move beside me with our hands meeting in the space between us, my palm resting face down on his as he leads me elegantly up the steps. He behaves as if this were a delicate and regal moment, helping a fragile woman make her way up such a grand staircase.

He acts as though he's honorable for leading me so gently.

It enrages me.

We step onto the landing, and we turn right before he leads me down a long hallway.

"You'll stay in the room next to mine," he says. "That way I can keep a close eye on you and ensure your needs are met."

Part of me wants to remain silent in protest, but there's a much stronger urge to speak up, to lash out, to show anger. "What needs do you expect me to have that you're capable of meeting? I don't recall a single time in my life that all of my needs have been met."

He stops abruptly, turning to face me, my hand still in his. "Then consider yourself lucky to live what's left of your life here. In the Homestead, everyone's needs are met, save for—"

"Sex and violence?" I finish the statement for him. "Don't all the men of Ember Glen have that need?" I scoff.

He arches an eyebrow. "We do, of course."

"So, not all your needs are met here."

He tenses his jaw to fight the curling of his lips at one corner. "Obviously, you already knew that. Are we playing a game of semantics?" He drops his hand and mine falls, as well. He cocks his head to the side as he considers me. "It's funny that you mention it, seeing that the very reason you're here right now is due to your choice not to fulfill man's need for sex and violence under the last full moon. Here you are now, having your own needs fulfilled until the day you take your last breath." He takes a step toward me, and instinctively, I step back. "And aren't you ashamed of yourself? It was your duty to service the impulsive needs of men, and you refused."

"I served those needs," I argue, stepping forward and closing the distance between us. "I served dutifully for four years!"

"Do you have short-term memory loss, or are you just stupid? You *ran*, Mercy. You fled and hid from service."

I flinch at his insulting choice of words but allow it to fuel my frustration. "My memory serves me well, and I'm much smarter than any man gives me credit for. I'm smart enough to know better than to let myself be lit on fire just for the sake of calling myself righteous. A god worth serving wouldn't—"

He presses closer and our bodies touch as he looks down at me with fury and passion. "Don't you dare speak another word, Mercy Madness."

I huff out a heavy breath as my eyebrows draw together in anger, my chest sinking rapidly. I want to speak, to retaliate, to agitate him. I want to rile him up further and invoke a verbal sparring match, but I don't know exactly why I want that. He's stubborn and self-righteous; a man who has the authority to uphold the doctrine I question and quarrel over in my mind on a minute-to-minute basis.

Then I realize why I want to speak against him so badly. It's because he's let me speak longer than any other man ever has. Truthfully, I've spoken more freely with him than I ever have, even with another servant. The realization is striking, and somehow, it fills me with a sense of gratitude—a sentiment he certainly hasn't earned. Yet it pulls through me, drags my shoulders back, forces me to soften my features, and concede to showing him that the sentiment is there all the same.

Sensing the change in me, he pulls back, rolling his shoulders and letting go of some tension he held there.

He lowers his voice to a heated whisper. "You'll watch your words here, lest one of my brothers with less patience than I have should overhear you and decide it would be best to drag you out and burn you at the stake…to spare the spectacle of the trials and the time granted to you in between." He turns and starts walking again. "This way."

"What do you mean?" I ask before following him down the hallway.

We approach a door—second to the last at the end of the hall—and he turns to face it. He pushes back his sleeve and uses the black band, which is forever fixed around his wrist, to release the lock. My gaze falls to the patch of skin visible between his sleeve and glove, and I notice a portion of his skin is bumpy, uneven—it looks scarred or something.

Is he hiding scars beneath the leather gloves?

He turns the handle and pushes the door open, waving his hand to encourage me inside. Reluctantly, I cross the threshold and enter the room. I take a couple of slow steps inside before I hear the door click shut behind me, and it makes me jump. I whirl around to find him in the room with me, door closed at his back.

"You're here as both a prisoner and for your protection," he tells me. "We've granted you a courtesy by making you a trial participant; we've given you a chance—"

"It's hardly a chance."

He closes the distance between us with a single, long stride. "It's a *chance*, nonetheless. A chance at absolution for your soul, if not for life itself. But make no mistake that if you fall out of line, a swift execution can be arranged. Everyone in Ember Glen is aware that you're a sinner, and though I'm sure they'll all be thrilled to watch you face the trials, some would be so inclined as to take matters into their own hands and end your life more expediently."

His finger captures a strand of my hair and I narrow my gaze on him. "You should really consider our kindness in bringing you into our home. You should be grateful that you get to live this life of luxury while you can. Because you certainly haven't proven that you deserve it. I can only protect you if you tame your maniacal thinking and keep your pretty pink lips shut." His eyes drop to my mouth and my heart skips a beat.

I swallow. "Why bother to protect me at all?"

"Because I'm your warden, and you're my ward. Because it's the duty I've been given, and unlike you, sinner, I uphold the word of God."

He moves closer as I move back, and I realize only now that we've been doing this dance the entire time. My back hits one of the four posts of a bed behind me that I haven't set my gaze on yet. I gasp, twisting my head around to see the dark stained wood post as my body crushes into it.

He bends over me, and as I draw in a shaking breath, I can smell him—mint, pine, and open mountain air.

He smells like the meadow.

He smells like my happy place, and the realization of that twists in my gut, almost pleasantly so, but it quickly turns sour, spinning into nausea.

"You'll have no privacy from me, do you understand?"

I don't understand it.

I don't accept it.

But somehow, I find my head nodding as I stare up into his disarmingly bright blue eyes.

"Good." He tilts his head, his stare lifting to look beyond me, past my shoulder. "Go run a bath."

"A bath?"

His leather-covered finger plucks a strand of my hair again, running it slowly down to the end. "Are you asking me what a bath is?"

"Do you really think I'm stupid?"

"I think you're a servant and a sinner. I don't expect you to know much of anything."

My nostrils flare as I take in a furious breath, my voice deepening to match his condescending timbre. "I know how to care for myself. I know so much more than you'll ever give me credit for."

"That remains to be seen…though I don't expect to see much before the end."

The end.

My death.

I swallow hard. "How long do I have?"

"For what?" His body sways toward mine, and I let my back press against the wood post, hard and aching as my spine aligns to it.

"Until the final trial."

"Hmm," he hums. "I don't know. But as soon as I'm aware of your final day, I'll be sure to let you know."

His flippancy about my demise sets a fire in my chest. Without thought or care, I put my hands to his chest and shove. My sudden action takes him off guard and he stumbles back, slowly lifting his head and looking up at me from beneath dark lashes.

I've incited violence, and now he'll have a fair reason to retaliate. The Control are anointed by God to meet violence with violence in the name of keeping the peace—one of so many contradictions of our religious law.

His soft, full lips stretch wide across his cheeks to form a straight, hard line, indignant at my action against him.

Two swift steps bring him against me, his hand locking around my throat, then slipping around to the side of my neck, and spinning me to face away from him. Gripping the back of my neck, his touch sends a searing burn through my spine, reminding me of the knife marks still dripping blood down my back.

He marches me along the side of the bed, moving us past it and shoving me toward an open door at the back of the room. My shoulders tense and tighten, lifting against his grip as he shoves me forward. My boot steps from plush carpet to land on cold, hard tile—the transition mimics the contrast of Arlo, and it makes my head spin.

Just as fear weaves between my ribs and ropes around my heart, he stops…and lets me go. I feel the weight of his force drift away, and I whirl around to face him. My hands come up, ready to defend myself, but he takes a step back.

"Take a bath, sinner." He stands in the doorway, leaning his shoulder against the frame, standing so casually that I don't know what to make of it because I thought he was going to hurt me. "I want you clean before your skin touches the fine clothes we have for you."

I blink at him, confused. "Are you…are you going to stay there?"

He crosses his arms as he leans. "Does my presence bother you?"

"Yes."

"That's too bad." There's no violence in his expression. Instead, he smiles, his wide, thick lips turning upward and showing the long lines of his dimples.

He's disarmingly beautiful, and I know that's dangerous.

"Go on now," he says, tilting his head forward to indicate behind me.

I look over my shoulder and glance at the white clawfoot tub in the center of the bathroom. The space is starkly white. The walls are painted a soft, gray-tinted shade of white, and square, white tiles cover the floor. The vanity even has a white marbled countertop.

White, white, white.

No hint of color.

A space for cleansing.

"You seem nervous," he says, drawing my attention back to him.

Of course, I'm nervous.

Everything in my life has just changed for the worst.

I cross my arms over my chest, caging in my pounding heart. "I can't undress with you watching me like that."

"Like what?" he taunts.

He's baiting me into this little back and forth, and it leaves a sour taste in my mouth. I choose not to respond. Instead, I turn away from him and move to the center of the room, reaching over the edge of the tub to turn on the faucet. Water pours—clear, clean, and heavy—into the oversized tub. If my circumstances were different, I would find joy in the prospect of climbing into the warmth and resting.

But that's not my circumstance.

My shoulders jump and I startle as Arlo's fingers suddenly run across my shoulder blades. I feel his hand wrap around my hair, strands catching on the leather of his glove.

"Your hair…it's the color of the stars in the night sky," he says softly.

I wonder if I imagined him saying that at first. It's said in such a gentle way, in a way of wonder. It's jarring in comparison to the way he calls me a sinner.

It makes my heart beat faster.

I feel his hand turn, fingers combing through, leather catching on a tangle as he drags his hand down the length. I wonder why he doesn't remove his gloves to touch my hair, which he seems to be so enamored with. I wonder if it's stained and matted with drying blood from the knife wounds inflicted on my neck.

His fingers reach the end, and I feel the weight of my long hair drop against the center of my back, nearly reaching my waistline. I take a breath, and I think it's the first I've taken since he reached out to touch me.

Without preamble, he touches the zipper at the back of my high-waisted skirt and tugs with a sharp jerk. He pushes the fabric down over my hips and it quickly falls to my feet. I shudder at the sudden exposure of my bare legs.

Leather brushes my skin as his fingers wiggle beneath the hem of my top and tug it up. My arms lift naturally, too easily allowing him to pull it off over my head and toss it aside. I cross my arms at the sudden chill in the room…the sudden bareness and vulnerability in the way he's exposed me.

I'm left standing in my boots, bra, and underwear. I feel rooted to the spot as I watch the tub fill with water. The sound of it splashing against the porcelain tub echoes through the bathroom, and he's just standing there behind me, too close for comfort, quiet and still. I have to arm myself against him because I feel the strength of his gravitational pull, the way it tugs at my soul in a way I've never felt before.

I feel him so strongly.

It's terrifying, and even though the pull is warming, it makes me shiver from head to toe.

"Take off the rest," he whispers.

I steel myself and harden my voice. "Where is the line for you?"

"What are you asking?"

"The line, Warden Rainn." I call him that to dehumanize him—maybe if I can remind myself that he's my captor, my keeper, then maybe I'll forget about the way his presence melts my insides. "Where is the line between asserting your authority and being inappropriate with a woman?"

"That's a bold question."

"The question is bold, but you know the line is thin."

He chuckles, the sound low and rumbling. "Do I?"

"Don't you?"

He moves around me, circling to the other side of the tub, and my eyes never leave him. "The line may be thin, sinner, but I know where it's drawn." He bends, wrapping his gloved hands around the rounded edge of the tub and leaning forward on it.

I turn my gaze away from him, unable to look directly into his blue eyes, and I watch the water pour from the faucet instead. "I don't think you do."

"Are you going to enlighten me, then?"

I shake my head.

"No? Then perhaps you should admit that you don't know as much as you think you do."

I dare to lift my eyes and look directly into his bright blue stare. "I know far more than you give me credit for."

"You know *nothing*."

"Is this how the end of my life is going to be?" My head tilts as I appraise him with narrowed eyes, my palms rubbing over my arms. "Constantly being reminded of how stupid I am?"

"If you make it necessary."

"I suppose I should just keep my mouth shut, then? Keep my stupid thoughts to myself?"

A half smile tugs at the side of his mouth. "If you wish."

Indignation burns in my chest. With a snap, I bend, untying my shoelaces and kicking my boots off in a fury. I harshly pull off my underwear, stepping out and kicking it aside. I reach behind my back and unhook my bra, ripping it from my body and tossing it to the floor. I huff as I stare at him, refusing to speak, watching him watch me.

We stand and stare, eyes locked on each other as the sound of a waterfall rushes around us, echoing through the stark space. We stare until the tub fills, and as soon as it's full enough, I lift my leg over the edge and step in. The water is too warm, but I ignore the burn as I turn and lower. Arlo's hands lift from the edge, and he backs away as I sink.

Frustrated, frightened, and completely overwhelmed by Arlo's mere presence, I slip completely beneath the waterline. The hot water sears my skin, shocking me as it touches my cheeks, but I let it burn. It takes me from the moment and makes me feel free from this nightmare.

I'd happily stay beneath the water, holding my breath and basking in the all-encompassing warmth. But too soon, I'm torn from the heat.

Arlo's hand latches around the back of my neck, and I feel his fingers and thumb dig in painfully before he lifts me from the water. I gasp in a breath of surprise as he jerks my head above the waterline with jarring speed. My arms jerk out as an instinctive reaction, and my palms grip the edges of the tub as I rise.

Sitting upright, I whip my head to see him on his knees beside the tub. Our eyes catch and lock; his are narrowed, staring with such intensity that I don't think I could look away if I tried.

"What are you doing? Trying to drown yourself?" he huffs, anger tinging his features. "Suicide is a sin."

From the corner of my eye, I catch the red swirl of blood from my neck mingled in the water as it swirls lightly in the ripples and flow.

"What difference would it make since I'm already a sinner? And I wasn't trying to drown myself; I just wanted a moment of peace." I jerk my shoulders, forcing him to loosen his grip until he releases the back of my neck. My skin burns where he held me too tightly over the fresh cuts.

He tilts his head. "Do you think you deserve peace?"

"I deserve nothing," I sneer.

"Finally, we agree on something." The crease in his forehead ripples as his eyes flicker in bewilderment.

My lips snarl as I lean my face toward his. "We agree on *nothing*. I meant that I deserve nothing that's happened to me in this life. I didn't deserve to be chosen for service. I didn't deserve to be used and abused. I didn't deserve to be called a sinner, and I most certainly don't deserve *this*."

His expression surprises me, softening instead of hardening.

"You don't believe you've sinned, do you?"

"I haven't. Not in the way I view sin."

"Sin isn't open for interpretation," his hand strokes down the back of my head, and that's when I realize he's still wearing the damned gloves.

Why didn't he take them off before reaching into the water?

Why does he wear them at all?

"It is when it requires me to put my life on the line," I tell him.

"God's requirements are clearly defined, and your role in this life is clearly defined. You defied your duties, Mercy. Argue it all you want, but you're wrong." He pushes to his feet and moves away, circling the tub. I follow him with my gaze. "You crossed a thick, dark, well-defined line in your role as a servant. The sooner you accept that, the more likely it will be that forgiveness will find you."

"What makes you think I care about forgiveness?"

"It doesn't matter if *you* care about the fate of your soul."

I pause. "Who does it matter to?"

He sighs, several beats passing before he speaks again. His eyes skim the length of my body, and I watch his Adam's apple bob as he swallows harshly. "You were right about that thin line; perhaps it's fainter than I thought. I'll wait in your room until you're done."

I watch as he leaves through the bathroom door, and I'm frozen, my fingers curled around the edge of the tub, my head permanently turned toward the door.

Why is he talking about the fate of my soul?

Why did he bring up the thin line?

Why did he lift me from the tub if he truly thought I would try to drown myself?

I know why. I won't pretend it's because he cares about my life, because I know he doesn't. It's because it would deny him the opportunity to punish me, to drag me through the pomp and circumstance of the Trials of Dissension.

I can't let him disarm me the way he threatens to. I can't let my guard down, because I can already sense all the ways in which he could ruin me. He could ruin my mind, my heart, my soul. He could find his way through my armor. He could find his way into the depths of my being.

And I can't live my last days with that kind of hope.

chapter twelve

ARLO

I SHOULD NEVER have offered to be the warden.

I shouldn't have put myself in this position with a fiery woman who inspires poetry…an attractive woman who inspires an inappropriate stirring within me.

Inappropriate.

That was the word she used to describe the thin line between authority and an abuse of my power. And indeed, that line was thin—thin, faded, and broken in places. The sight of her bare is what snapped the line for me, and it's my own damn fault because I neglected to purge. If I had, I wouldn't be seduced by her strong will, her starlight hair, or her sultry curves.

I need to pray.

I needed to purge at the last full moon.

That's the true issue at hand. It has nothing to do with her and everything to do with my failure to purge. Yet, it was her who held me so rapt with attention that night that I neglected my impulses.

I cross her room and sit in the ivory armchair facing the foot of her four-post bed. Her accommodations are fit for saints, and far too good for a sinner like her. She should consider herself lucky to spend what's left of her life here.

My eyes are fixed to her bed, to the cream-colored comforter threaded with gold stitches that create a floral pattern throughout. I hear water rolling and lapping as she moves in the tub, and I press my eyes shut, trying to focus on something else, anything else. My fingers curl around the armrests, my leather gloves soaked and uncomfortable against my skin as I dig them into the fabric of the chair.

I should just take them off, but I'm feeling vulnerable in the moment, and they serve as a shield. It's not as though I have an issue with her seeing my scars, but I'm not in the mood for her curiosity about them right now. I'm not inclined to share personal details from my life with her. I refuse to let her in, especially now when I'm reeling with urges I should've satisfied with her when I was allowed to under the full moon. If I had, I'd be thinking clearly now.

Eventually, I hear the whoosh of water as she exits the tub. I open my eyes and watch the open doorway, my pulse thrumming with the anticipation of her arrival.

My eyes want to take her in, to see her standing there, bare.

God help me.

I let out a breath when she finally appears, relieved to see her wrapped in a white towel. Her hair is dripping, and I watch droplets fall to her feet, landing on the tile and echoing in their splashing sadness for no longer mingling with her starlight tresses.

She looks at me expectantly, and I cast a glance toward the bed. "You can get dressed."

She looks at the dress I've laid out for her on the bed. Before, she only wore black—as all the servants wear—but as a trial participant, she'll now wear red, the color of blood and sacrifice. She'll have to sacrifice pieces of herself in the ultimate acts of service.

She takes a few slow steps toward the bed and reaches down, running her finger beneath the fabric. "It's beautiful."

Sweet sin.

The way the word flows from between her rosy lips makes something twist inside my chest.

Beautiful.

She looks up at me. "I'm supposed to wear this?"

I press my elbow into the armrest as I lift my hand, leaning to rest my chin against it. "Yes. You have a wardrobe full of gowns to wear."

"Why?"

"Would you rather parade around naked?" My fingers curl into a fist at the thought, and I lift my head before slapping my palm on the armrest. "Just get dressed, Mercy."

"I can't get dressed with you sitting there staring at me."

"Try."

She glares at me for a beat. "So the line is completely broken, then."

The line.

The thin fucking line between authority and abuse.

"Get dressed."

The same defiant look she had when she leapt into the tub and buried herself beneath the water touches her features. Without warning, she drops her towel, her bewitching eyes locked on mine. I force myself to hold her gaze, though my eyes beg to drop. She stares for what feels like the longest time—as if she's testing whether that fucking line still exists between us—before finally letting go. With a sneer and a frustrated huff, she shakes her head before turning toward the bed and reaching for her clothes.

I cover my mouth to conceal the heavy, heated exhale that rushes from my lungs, swiping my fingers over my short beard.

"I'd rather be put to a swift death…" I hear her mutter, and I don't know whether she intended for me to hear it.

"Speak up if you mean to be heard."

Her head snaps and her eyes meet mine again so sharply that I feel knocked back in my seat. I clutch the armrests. "I said that I'd rather be put to a swift death than be tortured by you this way through the end of my days."

I'm surprised she said something; I'm surprised she met my gaze. Naturally, I'd assumed she'd humble herself when I called out her muttering. But instead, she met me with heat, raised her voice, and spoke her truth.

She's a sinner, I remind myself.

She's a sinner, she's a sinner, she's a sinner.

I know she's a sinner, yet her unearned self-pride pulls a smile through my lips. "Mercy Madness, you've yet to know torture."

I shove to my feet and stride across the room to meet her. My body moves me into her space against my will, against my better judgment. I watch myself step closer and closer to that line.

I turn toward the bed and she turns with me, and when I press closer still, she tries to step back…only the bed is behind her. She drops to sit, her chin tilting skyward to look up at me, her strange, beautiful eyes staying with me.

"I will make you a promise, though," I tell her.

"A promise?"

I bend, dipping so low that my forehead practically touches hers as I slip two fingers beneath her chin. Her sweet lips part, probably to protest my nearness, but I speak before she can. "A promise for you and the twisted morals that seem to rule your life. You will know what torture is before you meet your end."

Her eyes narrow on me. "My twisted morals?"

"Those are the words you choose to question?"

I've made a promise that she'll meet torture in her numbered days, yet she questions my assessment of her morals—it's baffling.

"Those are the only words in your statement that I don't understand."

"What don't you understand about them, sinner? Your morality presents with as much madness as your namesake."

"If you think it's mad to run from a man who chases after you with the intent of setting you on fire, then yes, call me mad."

My gaze drops from her eyes to her lips. "Are you referring to me or to Hyatt Price? I assure you, my intent was also to set you on fire when you ran from me in the forest."

I shouldn't have said that.

I shouldn't have thought it.

I'm mad myself—mad with impulses I needed to have served.

"And you did," she whispers.

My ribcage opens up, letting my heart drop heavily and sink in my gut.

She blinks and turns her head, quickly breaking the connection between us—a connection that shouldn't exist.

I step back, straightening to my full height. "Get dressed."

This time, she obeys, rising to her feet and turning her back on me. I stand and watch as she dresses quickly, and when she pulls the gown up her body, I reach for the zipper on the back of her dress. I don't waste time, though I'm tempted to graze her spine with my fingers. I zip it up quickly, then turn on my heel and storm toward the door.

"Go where you like within the Homestead, but if you try to leave the manor alone, you will be stopped. I'll come later and retrieve you for dinner."

Without sparing her another glance, I pull open the door, step out into the hallway, and slam it shut behind me. I stride down the hallway with no direction, simply moving away from the temptation of her as quickly as I can.

chapter thirteen

Mercy

I HEAR THREE knocks against the bedroom door; three dull thuds that somehow sound exactly the way I'd expect Arlo to knock.

"Come in."

It feels strange to extend an invitation. I'm certain if I'd said, "Don't come in," or "Go away," he would have rejected the protest and come in all the same.

The knob turns and the door swings open wide, revealing Arlo centered in the entryway. I'm perched on the very edge of the armchair across from my bed, my head turned toward him, and there's a beat where everything within me feels so light and weak at the sight of him that I worry I might topple forward onto the floor with so much as a gentle breeze.

He's dressed all in black, his clothes pressed in sharp lines and severe edges. His button-down shirt is open at the collar, hinting at curls hidden beneath. The waistcoat he wears has a silver chain draping from the second button to the small pocket stitched across its side. His sleeves are rolled up to his elbows, exposing the lines and sinews of his forearms, which draw my eyes down to his closed fists.

He stands with potency, his feet planted in a wide stance and his arms at his sides. It's the tan length of rope looped through his gloved and fisted fingers that makes my words catch in my throat.

"What...Why do you have that?"

"Come here," he commands.

I'm on my feet and moving across the room before a single thought of protest has a chance to fly through my mind. I think it must be fear that compels me to obey him without a thought. I don't feel fearful, though…not truly. Not in the way I've felt real fear through so many nights of service—shaking through my soul and quaking in my bones.

I come to a stop in front of him, my head bowed slightly as I fixate on the rope in his left hand.

His right hand floats toward me, and his knuckles lift to tap beneath my chin. "I don't need to bind you, do I, Mercy? I know you're a sinner, but I also know you're capable of compliance when it benefits you."

Compliance is such an ugly word.

Compliant is what I've been for far too long.

It wasn't until recently that I realized how blind compliance to a doctrine—one that didn't even make sense to me anymore—was dangerous. But he's not wrong; I am capable of compliance since that's what keeps servants alive. It was my rebellion that put me here, after all.

I shake my head, causing him to drop his hand. "No. You don't need to bind me."

His eyebrows twitch, casting an odd shadow over his bright eyes that brings a look of disappointment. I step back when he steps toward me, but then he stops.

"You only need to give me one reason to wrap this around your neck and lead you like a dog." His voice is calm and cool, as if his threat is nothing more than polite conversation. "One reason, one step out of line. Do you understand?"

I huff, not in anger, but in exhaustion. I'm so damn tired. I'm tired and hungry and too drained to fight. I nod, understanding what he's telling me, though that understanding doesn't lessen my confusion over what's happened to my life.

Nothing makes sense anymore.

I don't understand what we believe.

I don't understand the god we worship.

I don't understand why running from service is a sin.

I don't understand any of it, nothing at all.

Arlo's shoulders loosen and relax as he watches me, and something in his features soften. Then he turns, moving to stand beside me, holding out his left arm for me to take.

"I'm glad we understand each other."

The rope remains tight in his grip, dangling between us. I watch it sway for a moment before slipping my arm through his. With our arms linked, he pulls me closer to his side, and I feel the end of the rope brush my leg through the thin silk fabric of my crimson gown.

I flinch at the touch of it, but not in a fearful way. It's almost like being touched by him, like the rope is an extension of his hand, and he's just grazed my thigh. I push out a slow breath through my nose, trying to steady myself as he leads us into the hallway.

"Where are we going?"

"To dinner. I told you I would collect you."

"I wasn't sure you would…" I trail off, realizing I have no interest in making it known how much I doubt his words—how much I doubt every word…how much I doubt everything around me.

"If I tell you I'm going to do something, you can rest assured, I'm going to do it."

I don't respond.

We reach the staircase, and he leads me down. He's careful, as if he assumes I'm wearing the ridiculous high-heeled shoes I found in the wardrobe, but I'm not. I'm wearing my black boots beneath the elegant gown.

I smile to myself, thinking of it as a small, though insignificant rebellion. Trivial, yes, but it has meaning all the same. It returns some sense of pride to my heart, pride I need to get through dinner with the Control.

The voices of men carry from the foyer as we descend, and I spot a few of them standing on the starburst pattern beneath the golden chandelier. Killian and Ryker glance in our direction, and I feel the weight of their appreciative glances—glances that would indicate their interest in using me in service. I know they won't touch me outside of a full moon, but I don't feel any safer. I don't feel any less devalued and objectified.

We reach the bottom of the steps, and I see Theo enter the foyer, moving toward us from a dark hallway across the sunburst. His hands are tightly fisted at his sides and a furious, fearful look darkens his features. He spots me and stops abruptly, catching my eyes and holding for a beat. I see the movement of shadow from behind him—two forms shifting into view before emerging from the dark hall at his back.

Park steps into the meager light from the chandelier, the dim glow bronzing the shade of his tawny skin and making his black hair look even darker.

And then I see the ripple of black fabric as a servant steps forward, moving into the dim light beside Theo, who casts her a sideways glance.

"Mercy," Park says with a smile and a tilted head, "it appears you'll have a companion during the trials."

Delle Carter stands beside Theo, her face awash with equal parts determination and outright fear. It takes me a few moments of deep confusion, fueled by my unwillingness to accept what's standing right in front of me, to work out the scene.

Delle is here, and it can only mean one thing...

She's volunteered to participate in the trials.

I open my mouth to speak, to protest, to scream at her, and beg to know why. Arlo's arm unhooks from mine and lassos around my back instead, sensing my rising agitation. He opens his hand around my side to grip me, smashing the rope between my stomach and his palm in silent warning.

He bends and puts his lips to my ear. "Give me one reason, Mercy."

A warning.

My heart is torn between fear for myself and fear for Delle. *What was she thinking?*

What has she done?

She's too young and naïve to make a decision like this, and I don't understand how they can allow it. She's sixteen years old. She spent *one* night in service. They can't really be thinking of allowing this.

I ignore Arlo's warning, shake myself from his grip, and charge across the space to Delle. "What are you doing?" I ask her, then look at Theo standing at her side. "You can't let her do this."

Theo's eyebrows stitch together over his brown eyes. "She has the right to make this choice."

"She doesn't understand the choice!" I shout.

I reach for Delle, placing my hands on her cheeks as she blinks at me through tearful eyes. "What were you thinking? What are you doing? Why? Delle, *why?*"

"I didn't...I couldn't..." she stammers. "After that service, I couldn't bear the thought of doing it again. Never again."

"This isn't the answer; this isn't a solution. Do you understand that no one has ever survived the trials?"

"I know." She nods, her delicate hands landing on my wrists. "I know, but there's a chance, right? There's a chance I'll pass, a chance I'll survive, a chance for something better than service. I have to try, Mercy."

A sob breaks free from her chest and she drops her hands, moving against me and wrapping her arms around my waist. I hug her tightly, wishing I could hug her tightly enough to take all the pain of this life away.

"You don't have to do this," I whisper. "You can survive a life of service. Some...some find joy from it, peace in doing God's work." I swallow hard because my words don't feel right.

They've never felt right.

"It's already done." Delle releases me and takes a small step back, turning to face away from me. She tugs her hair to the side, revealing the back of her neck. Seven fresh cuts still spill droplets of blood at the base of her neck.

They've already marked her for the trials.

"No..." The syllable falls from my lips in defeat.

It's already done.

chapter fourteen

ARLO

THE CLANG OF knives and forks touching ceramic dishes echoes through the silent dining room. I wouldn't say it's unusually quiet, but the silent energy is certainly different.

There are two women present for our nightly meal—two servants, no less. It's not that their presence is bothersome, just that it's different. I think we all feel a sense of duty to curb our usual nightly chatter in favor of presenting ourselves properly with the weaker sex present. It's no matter that they are sinners, servants, trial participants...we must always hold ourselves to a higher standard than they hold themselves.

The round, wooden table we sit at is dark—nearly black—and Mercy sits rigidly in the seat to my right. A gold and crystal chandelier serves as the only light source in the room, and it casts a spotlighted glow on the center of the table beneath it. The central illumination casts shadows all around us, darkness shrouding the space behind our backs. I can see my brothers in God where they're seated, but it's black as night behind them.

Delle sits to my left—a new ward I'll be required to take care of for the trials. I feel uneasy about her presence. Truthfully, her decision to participate doesn't sit right with me. By all accounts, she's a sinner as much as Mercy is for running during service, but it was her first night and she is so young. We had elected to give her another chance, and in doing so, she had a choice.

She chose poorly.

She chose sin over learning and growing from her mistake, and now she'll be put through the Trials of Dissension.

Mercy clears her throat, and it draws my attention. I look over as she shifts in her seat, straightening her spine, and reaches forward for her glass of wine. I watch as she draws the goblet toward her mouth. The glass touches her soft, pink lips and my gaze is stuck there, trapped at the way they part, allowing the liquid to slip past them as she takes a sip.

I have a sudden vision of her bewitching me with her sinner ways, draining the blood from my body, and sipping it from a glass just like that. I wait for the repulsion of such a vision to take hold of me, to steal my appetite, but instead, I feel the weight of it sink inside me. My thighs tense as I feel a heaviness between my legs, my cock thickening inexplicably.

Sweet sin.

I don't know how I'll make it another month managing the impulses I should have purged. I need to be careful in how I handle Mercy Madness.

"We should discuss the first trial," Killian says, his voice cutting through the silence so unexpectedly that it nearly startles me. I turn my head away from Mercy to look at him across the table. "The Elders sent over their documents of the last three trials, and it seems there's some room for creativity."

I feel the shift in energy at my left and right, both Mercy and Delle raising invisible shields.

"Creativity?" Ryker asks. "How so?"

"The purpose that each trial serves is set," Killian explains, "but the means by which they are carried out leaves some room for us to decide. It ensures that no two sets of trials are the same."

"The first trial is Service of the Flesh," Theo says from where he sits on the opposite side of Delle. His jaw is tense as he speaks.

"What purpose is that meant to serve?"

"As it's written in the Impulse Edict," Killian explains, mentioning the written religious law that governs Ember Glen, "servants must openly and eagerly offer the use of their bodies to the men of Ember Glen during nights of service. Under the full moon, their physical forms must be given entirely to performing acts of service that allow the men of Ember Glen to satiate their perverse sexual desires effectively, such that the domestic women of our community may continue to live their days in peace without fear of unwanted sexual acts being committed against them." He recites the edict from memory, as all members of the Control would be able to do.

Mercy sets her wineglass down on the table too hard, and some of the crimson liquid—which matches her gown—sloshes out, spilling onto the table. "Damnit," she mutters.

She lifts her white cloth napkin from her lap and works to wipe up the spilled liquid, though I notice her hands tremble. The rest of the room is silent as we all watch her dab at the red wine. The ways she trembles does something to me—twisting in my gut, making me feel uneasy. I don't enjoy watching her fumble and twitch through her nerves.

"Stop that," I tell her, reaching over and grabbing the cloth napkin and pushing her hands away. Dabbing with her napkin, I finish mopping up the spilled wine. I glance up when I feel the eyes of the room upon me. "Don't mind me." I nod. "Go on."

Killian blinks at me with a curious expression, but then continues, "Service of the Flesh is meant to be the ultimate act of sexual service."

I'm so utterly aware of Mercy's every breath, every twitch of every muscle, every slight movement in anxiety. It unnerves me for some reason, and I need to get control of it immediately. As soon as I finish cleaning the spilled wine, I remove the length of coiled rope where I looped it over the back of my chair. I push back my seat and swivel my body to face her squarely.

"What are you—"

"Shh," I hush her quickly as the conversation continues around us.

I grab hold of her wrists with one hand and tug them toward me. Before she can protest, I wrap them, circling coarse twine around both her wrists, looping and tugging it between. Around and through, and over again. Surprisingly, she doesn't squirm, she doesn't fight. I think she's in shock and it's frozen her in place. Once her hands are bound in front of her, I drop them in her lap.

"And how has this trial been delivered in the past?" Owen asks.

My eyes catch Mercy as she gapes at me, her wide, wild, silver-blue eyes blinking at me. She opens her mouth to speak, but I quickly lift her wineglass to her lips and tilt it. She can choke on it…or she can accept my kindness in taking control of her nervous actions.

A fierceness washes over her features as her eyebrows straighten to frame her narrowed and intentional stare. Closing her parted lips around the rim, she lets me tip another sip into her mouth.

My heartbeat doubles its pace as I watch her swallow, her throat working as she takes down gulp after gulp, nearly draining the glass.

"Once, there were three participants," I hear Killian explain, though his voice seems fainter than before, "and they were made to serve the entire village for a night." I strain to listen, but everything is fading around me as Mercy manages to draw my full attention. "Another time, there was only one servant, and she was made to…" His voice fades entirely to the background.

I watch Mercy drink, and when she's nearly drained the glass, I pull it away and set it on the table. I take my clean napkin from my lap and use it to dab at the corners of her lips. For good measure, I swipe my finger—covered by the cloth—across her bottom lip, intent on catching the wine that slipped out when I pulled the glass away.

But then I swipe again, even though I don't need to, noting the way the center of her lip has an extra tuft of plumpness that dips in the center to create that beautiful, sweeping curve.

"Arlo," Owen says, snapping me back to life.

"Yes?" I twist turn from her, placing the napkin on my lap.

"You're the warden for the trial participants," Owen says. "Do you wish to have a final say over the manner in which the trials are carried out?"

Yes.

No.

On one hand, I want that level of control over Mercy's fate—though I know that would be dangerous to my own suffering self-control. Furthermore, whatever is imposed on Mercy is imposed on Delle, and there's something about her participation that feels...bothersome.

"No," I decide. "I think we should decide collectively, as a group."

"I have a proposal," Ryker leans back in his chair, nursing a devious grin as he locks his fingers together behind his head and stretches back.

"Go on," Killian encourages.

"Perhaps the seven of us can come together to trial their ability to serve." His gaze shifts between Mercy and Delle. "Seven men for seven hours."

"Do you mean one per hour?" Park asks.

"Perhaps. Or perhaps not," Ryker leans forward. "If we're meant to push the boundaries of service, wouldn't more than one man at a time achieve that end? Given that a normal night of service allows for only one man per servant at a time."

"Seven men in seven hours." Park's expression indicates consideration. "I suppose that does have a nice ring to it. It feels like poetic justice."

I glance at Mercy without turning my head, curious to see her reaction to all this discussion happening right in front of her. Though she has no right to speak on any of this, I still find myself hoping this will provoke her, and I don't know why I hold that hope.

Perhaps because the thought excites me.

Perhaps that's precisely why I'm a danger to myself and everyone around me because I didn't purge.

In any case, she's seething at my side, her bound fists balled in her lap, and the corners of my lips twitch to smile.

"Seven in seven," Killian says. "I like the sound of it. But Ryker is right, one at a time certainly doesn't push the boundaries of service. It's a trial, after all, so we'd need to think on that."

My hand snaps to the side and I wrap my fingers around the rope coiled between Mercy's wrists. Lifting them above the tabletop, I drop them down without warning, and her fists collide with a *thud* that draws everyone's attention, as I meant it to. She huffs at me, but I ignore her.

"What if I string her up?" I offer. "Put her on display for a day inside the Homestead? Her body can be used by any one of us as we see fit. One at a time or multiple—she'll be helpless for seven hours."

"*Them*," Killian corrects me with narrowed eyes. "You said *her*, but of course, you mean *them*. You speak of one participant, but don't forget there are two."

My fixation on Mercy is evident, and I can't allow that. I need to get control of myself, lest I be judged for lack of self-control.

I clear my throat and ensure I'm turned squarely toward the table. "Yes, forgive me."

"I've seen the way Arlo binds women when he purges," Wesley says. "I think that could be an effective trial, to be left and used for so many hours."

"Let's put it to a vote," Ryker says. "All for seven in seven, say aye."

"Aye," the sound of the single word rings out in chorus.

"All opposed, say nay."

Silence.

"Give me fourteen hours," Mercy mutters.

I look over to find her head dipped slightly, her fierce eyes looking up through her eyelashes to stare across the table with a slow burning kind of fury.

Ryker grins with amusement. "Excuse me?"

"Give me fourteen hours and leave Delle alone. Let her skip this trial. Let me take the burden for her."

Sordid chuckles carry through the space, but the sound doesn't include my own. My stare is locked on her, humor evading me as I see the honest determination in her expression. She's serious. She would actually endure double the necessary time to spare Delle.

Ridiculous....intriguing.

My heart thumps an odd extra beat as I feel something I can't explain. It couldn't possibly be admiration or respect because I have no capacity for those feelings when it comes to sinners like her. And yet, those are the only words that come to mind describing the feeling.

There's a strangeness that vibrates through me, like dissonant chords being played simultaneously.

The laughter fades and dies.

"No," Killian says plainly.

"That's not how this works," Ryker follows.

Mercy lifts her chin and tilts her head, looking across the table and speaking with unearned authority. "And why not? It seems as though you're making up the rules as you go. You said it yourself... there is room for *creativity.*"

Sweet fucking sin.

This woman knows no boundaries. It fills me with fury, but oddly, it's only for the way she creates risk for herself. She has no concern for self-preservation. She understands no one has survived the trials and the likelihood of her own survival is equally low. Maybe knowing that her days are limited makes her bolder and more daring than she ought to be.

"No." Killian doubles down, harshly emphasizing the word. "And just for that ridiculous request, I think we ought to let Delle complete her trial first."

Mercy shoves to her feet, the legs of her chair screeching as they scrape across the floor and tumbles over backward. "Over my dead body," she spits.

"That can be arranged," Killian says, and the others chuckle.

I quickly slip on my gloves before standing, reaching out to grab the short dangling ends of the rope attached to her wrists. I tug on them, forcing her to spin away from the table to look at me. Our eyes catch for a heated beat, and I see rage swirling there, like a gray storm whirling around her irises.

It's rather beautiful.

I speak without looking away from Mercy. "If you'll excuse me, brothers, I need a moment to handle my ward."

"Please do," Ryker huffs.

"I'll be back for Delle," I add as an afterthought, nearly forgetting she's also my responsibility now.

"I'll see her to her room," Theo offers, and I nod without looking.

With a tug of the rope, I walk away, pulling Mercy along behind me.

chapter fifteen

Mercy

ARLO DRAGS ME behind him like a pet, and I don't think I've ever been so furious. But the way he charges forward down the hall and into the foyer makes me think he feels the same way, though I can't for the life of me figure out why.

I plant my feet when we reach the center of the foyer and stop on the starburst beneath the chandelier. I jerk back on my arms to stop him, and he halts and spins to face me. I'm ready to speak, to tell him what I really feel, but he beats me to the punch.

"What is it going to take to get you to understand your place in this life?"

Stepping forward, he invades my space in such a way that I'm forced to take a step back, but once I do, I refuse to take another, and I hold my stance.

"What life?" An honest question.

"Are you not concerned about the fate of your soul?"

I blink, my head tilted to the side. "There was a time when I was, but I'm no longer convinced I want salvation for my soul when the means to achieve it are so vile."

His eyebrows shift and lower as he narrows his eyes, not in judgment, but in grave concern. "You're lost. So lost, sweet Mercy."

I swallow the weight of his words.

They're true.

I am lost...I have been lost for so long, but it doesn't matter anymore. I'm a sinner; I'm beyond redemption.

I shake my head lightly. "And what does it matter now? I'm damned in this life. What difference does it make if I'm damned in the next?"

He steps impossibly closer and I lean away, my back arching. His hand snakes around me, his palm splaying across the small of my back to hold me in place. "You don't have to be damned in the next. Your soul can be redeemed. Yes, your fate in this life is sealed, but God will forgive you in the next life through your ultimate acts of service in the trials."

My breaths quicken at the touch of his fingers on my back, at the way he holds my stare with intensity and sincerity. "Why do you even care?"

His forehead wrinkles and he huffs a heavy exhale through his nose. "Because I'm your warden. It's my role to meet your needs, and that includes spiritual."

I scoff, "None of my needs are being met."

"You're clean, you're dressed, you're fed. Please tell me which of your extravagant needs aren't being met."

"Peace, comfort, friendship, compassion..."

"Those are wants, not needs." His finger twitches against my back, sending a jolt of electricity through my spine.

"I need them; Delle needs them. They can't be met here, not in this manor, not in Ember Glen, not with our vicious doctrine—"

He tugs me tighter against him as his free hand slaps over my mouth, silencing me with leather. He turns his head, glancing around us. "Watch what you say."

It doesn't matter what I say.

Not anymore.

I'm already doomed.

He spins me in his hold, turns us toward the staircase, and urges me forward. He releases me and I move immediately, climbing the staircase with stomping feet and swift steps. Jogging up the stairs, he quickly catches up with me, then lassos his arm around my side as he slows to match my pace.

He leans into me sideways and whispers, "I don't care what your fate is, Mercy Madness, but you will not be blasphemous to our faith. I won't allow it."

His words freshen my fury. I twist and jerk myself from his hold, then charge quicker up the staircase. When I reach the landing, I stop, whipping around to face him. "I won't be silenced any longer. If I'm meant to meet a torturous end, then so be it, but I will ensure the women of Ember Glen know the truth."

He laughs as he steps onto the landing. Creeping toward me, he holds my gaze, even while his hand drifts forward to wrap around the dangling ends of the rope attached to my wrists. He continues to walk right past me, tugging on the ropes until my arms are tautly drawn in front of me, and I'm forced to walk to avoid stumbling.

He drags me behind him as he moves down the hall. "Truth is our way of life. Truth is the Impulse, the urge, the need of men to purge the worst of their humanity—"

"Upon women who don't deserve it, who never asked for it."

"On women who were chosen by God to serve those needs." He stops in front of the room he says is mine, and he turns to face me. "You rejected God's favor when you turned and ran into the forest, when you hid in that tree, when you ran from *me*."

He unlocks the door and shoves it open, then his hand wraps around my elbow before he forcefully drags me across the threshold. Flinging me forward into the room, he releases me unexpectedly. My weight pitches forward and I stumble. I catch my balance and turn to face him as he closes the door and locks it.

Then he charges toward me, his intense stare scaring me enough to make me step back as he moves into my space. The force of him shoves me until my back hits the far wall across the room. He slams his palms against it on either side of my head to cage me in between his arms.

I can smell the mint on his breath as he glowers down at me, breathing out fire like a demon—like a man who needs to purge. Fear rises in my chest as my eyes widen at the way he watches me. While fear rises, sin descends, an unwanted clench of a forbidden feeling tugging desire low into my core.

My body remembers the warmth of his pressed against me, the touch of his fingers as they moved inside me, the overwhelming sinful sensation of coming at the touch of another's hand.

All the air escapes my lungs as he dips his head, bending closer. "Do you still want to run from me, sinner?"

"Yes," I breathe, and though I intended to speak honestly, it feels like a lie.

His plump lips part with a sigh as his forehead touches mine. "And if you did run from me again...would you want me to catch you like I did in the forest?"

"Yes." And that's the truest I've ever spoken.

It feels like the most blasphemous thing I've ever wanted, ever thought, ever said out loud. It's blasphemous to want my warden, my controller, my eventual executioner to touch me the way he did during a night of service.

I want it now.

I want it badly.

I want him to sin with me...and I don't understand the feeling at all.

It's perhaps the most shameful thing a servant could do—to admit such things to a man outside of the full moon and tempt him in that way when he's not allowed to act upon it. Yet I can't control the arch of my back as my body is called to his, as his warmth beckons me.

"You're a sinner," he whispers, his head rolling against mine.

"You're a sinner and you want to take me down to the depths of hell with you."

"I want no such thing." My hands rise between us, curious fingers reaching out for him, though I don't know where to touch. "Not for me, not for you, not for anyone."

He solves the confusion over where my hands want to be as he sways forward, moving into me, crushing them between us.

"Liar." He drags in a deep breath and forces it out again, his chest rising and falling against me.

"What are you doing?"

"Be quiet."

"I need you to hear—"

"*Silence*, Mercy. I didn't purge and you're tempting my urges..."

"You didn't purge?" I ask in disbelief.

"Your sins stole my attention under the last full moon."

Indignation wrinkles my forehead at the way I'm blamed. "I did nothing but run from flames that threatened to consume me."

I feel his breaths, quick and shallow, nearly panting. "You made your presence known to me, and that was enough."

I don't know how to respond, so I say nothing. I wiggle my fingers and they graze the button on his waistcoat. Absently, I grab hold of it, my hands fidgeting as a result of my anxiety in this heated moment.

"Your hair smells like wildflowers..."

My heartbeat quickens as he shifts forward, his body kissing mine.

He's on the brink of immorality—closer than he should be to that edge—and dangerously near sin.

My first instinct is to push him back, to remind him of his faith, to encourage him to stay right and true, and to wait until the full moon to seek service for his needs. But something stronger than that takes hold of me, something warm and wild, like sparks threatening to ignite.

It feels wrong.

It feels dirty.

It feels good and necessary.

A true sinner's thoughts.

I try to swallow my desire, but there's something stronger within me, something evil that wants to unleash and take his soul, blend it with what's left of mine.

I dare to speak the words that should only ever be spoken in service. "How can I serve you?"

He pulls back with a snap, his head jerking to look at me as his arms drop from the wall and fall heavily to his sides. "What did you just say to me?"

"I asked how I can serve you?" Shame wells in my gut for offering service here, now, with *him.*

"It's not a full moon, and you're no longer a servant. You're a *sinner.*"

"Then perhaps it's not a sin to purge with me."

What am I saying?

I'm out of my mind with this begging sensation that lies heavily between my legs. "If I'm not a servant, and I'm not a domestic, then I'm really not anything, am I?"

He flinches, and I hang my head, feeling overcome with guilt, shame, disgust for losing myself within a moment's lust when I should be fighting, demanding forgiveness for myself...for Delle. I should be focused on the reason why he dragged me from the dining room in the first place. I should be focused on fighting to save Delle if my fate is already sealed.

I let my eyes flutter shut to block out my senses, to try to recenter myself. Yet as soon as I see darkness, I'm swept up, arms wrapped around my back, body dragged away from the wall, and lips landing heavily on mine.

Lips.

Soft, but bruising lips...

My eyes snap open.

Arlo Rainn is kissing me?

I lift my bound hands, press my fists to his chest, and shove. He stutters backward, catching himself on the arm of the chair behind him as he quickly lowers to sit. His hand comes up to swipe across his short beard as he watches me with disbelief.

Before I can think, before I can process, my feet move, stepping toward him. As I move, so does he. We crash somewhere in the middle of the space between us, and our lips collide with furious, sparking passion. His tongue presses to the seam of my lips, begging me to open for him, and in service, I do.

He needs my service, and I want to give it to him.

I never wanted to give my service—I always gave it with reluctance and out of necessity for my own survival.

So why do I want to give it now? To Arlo?

What is happening to me?

My tongue is timid where his is eager, swiping across mine, tasting me fully as his arms close around me again. It's like he forces desire into my mouth with the swipe of his tongue, and I swallow it down, letting it sink heavily, making my stomach clench and my back arch as my body sways against him.

He shoves me back against the wall, breaking our kiss for but a moment to grab my bound wrists, to lift them high above my head and slam them to the wall before descending again.

I gasp into his mouth at the shock of his force—shock that he's kissing me, touching me at all. This is beyond inappropriate—especially for a man in his position—and the rumbling voice of the servant that's still buried somewhere deep within me tells me how wrong this is, that he's misusing his position of power, that he's doing something he should be condemned for.

But my rebellious spirit is strong, engaged, eager for this connection with a man I only know in passing...eager for so much more.

It's wrong.

I'm wrong, he's wrong, wanting this is *wrong*.

Yet I part my lips and taste him as much as he tastes me.

If this is the flavor of sin, then let me be gluttonous for it. Let me burn in hell for the taste of it. Lust has me in its grips like a demon, sinking its claws into my skin and burrowing deeply.

His lips move, catching the corner of my mouth, my cheek, along my jaw beside my ear. "Your madness is spreading," he whispers. "I can feel the way you spark sin within me."

His hips shift and I feel his hard length press against me. I nuzzle desperately into his cheek as he kisses beside my ear. "It's not the spark of madness you feel, Warden Rainn…" I feel him tremble as his body moves, rocking into me. "It's—"

Sanity. Clarity. Divine.

Those are the words I mean to say, but he interjects with his own interpretation.

"It's the Impulse. It's because I didn't satisfy those urges when I was meant to." His mouth moves down the side of my neck, catching me off-guard with a wave of pleasure that causes me to whimper.

I find myself disappointed at his interpretation, but I know I shouldn't be surprised by it. It's what he believes; I used to believe it, too.

"Then satisfy it now," I pant.

He pulls his head back and regards me with a desperate expression. I see the self-control flicker across his bright blue eyes, but that control is lost completely when my hips roll forward unintentionally, desperately seeking the same relief he does.

"Sweet sin," he mutters.

He releases my hands and his drop to his pants, working with haste to unbuckle his belt. My eyes fall to watch as his long fingers work—the same long fingers he buried inside me and brought me to pleasure with. I sink without his body against mine, my back slipping down the wall as I bring my hands down between us.

This is wrong for both of us.

Yet the sound of his aching breaths, the sight of his trembling hands reaching to free his cock, the heat in his blue stare, and the pained expression of lost self-control as his lips part swirl around me.

He fills every sense, intoxicating me with his suffering.

It calls to me.

No matter how much I rebel, no matter how much I want to be free, no matter how much I question our doctrine and defy my unwanted role, there's still a desire within me to please, to serve.

As much as I hate it, I want to serve him. I want to serve Arlo Rainn for the way he overwhelms me, the way his presence consumes my rational thoughts and steals them, making me a desperate servant willing to drop to her knees and *serve*.

Why him?

How does he do this to me?

Guilt and shame threaten to grip me, to take hold of my mind, but I force them away. I can't bear it. I don't *want* to bear it at this moment. I want a moment's freedom from heartache, from the melancholy and fear and pain. Sharing this sin with my warden is the only way to find that freedom.

My bound hands reach out for his cock, but he slaps them away.

"Let me serve you," I say, my nipples hardening beneath my dress, breasts swollen and aching for touch as my chest heaves with each longing breath.

"Don't touch me," he growls.

He reaches for my hips, his hands latching on with a firm grip that nearly aches. He spins me around and slams me forward to the wall. I try to bring my hands up to catch myself, but they only get caught between my chest and the wall as he pins me in place with his body. I feel how hard he is as his bare cock presses forcefully against my ass.

"Warden Rainn…"

"Quiet, sinner."

His fingers are gentle as he runs them beneath my long hair, tugging it back over my shoulder and laying it softly down my back. His hands fall to my arms as his cheek slips along mine. He turns his head to press soft kisses on my cheek, working them back to my ear. The quick switch to gentleness has me stunned, immobile, and it has wetness dripping between my legs.

For a moment, I feel wanted.

No one has ever kissed me sweetly, softly.

No one has ever given me an erotic moment of gentleness and peace.

Then his tongue paints a wet, hard line across my skin, dragging up the spot behind my ear all the way to my hair line. I shiver.

"Do you want me?" he whispers.

My head nods, though it's turned, my cheek pressed to the wall in front of me. "Yes."

"Why?"

"I-I don't know…"

"I don't know why I want you, either."

His hands glide down my arms, dropping to my hips. He grapples with the fabric of my dress, his long fingers working to inch it up my thighs. His hips press, and he slowly grinds against my bottom, hissing his relief as he tries to let go of his waning control. "I should be repulsed by you, sinner…but you bewitch me."

His cock moves from behind me, and suddenly, I feel it sliding along the side of my hip, slipping across the silky fabric of my gown. My eyes dart down and my breath hitches to see his excessive thickness rubbing along my hip, watching as he works to wrap my dress around it.

He leans heavily, pinning me to the wall, crushing my hands between my breasts, and nuzzling his face into the crook of my neck.

He works his hips, slowly thrusting, stroking his cock along my hip wrapped in the fabric of my dress.

I want this so much it aches. It aches between my legs, but it also aches in my heart, in my conscience. I shouldn't want this with the man who controls my fate, the person set to put me through the trials that will more than likely end my life.

But I think I need it right now.

I need to be touched, too.

"May I—"

I only manage to squeak out those two words before his hand wraps around my body, grips one of my wrists, and forcefully shoves my hands down. He moves them until they're between my legs.

"Do it, sinner. Show me your depravity and come with me."

His words lasso around me and tug everything to my center. My body sinks with the ache in my belly, the sick desire that makes me curl around it. My face scrunches with the pain of need, and I stretch my fingers, their tips grazing over my underwear. I whimper.

I need more.

My fingers stretch and bend, trying to reach the pulsing throb in my clit, but I can't with the way I'm pinned.

"Please..."

Arlo groans, hips thrusting, his cock slipping along my side. His thrusts push me harder to the wall, but if I shift my hips just right, the pulses make my clit slam against my fingers. Each thrust sends a wave of pleasure ripping through my body, and each beat between makes me more desperate.

His lips are on my neck, rubbing over my skin, parted and slick, and his breaths pant heat in their wake. The heat spreads and lowers, sparking something terrible, vicious, and truly depraved within me—it sparks a madness I can't control.

"More," I beg. "Harder. Faster."

Teeth nip at my skin as he groans, as his body curls, and his thrusts along my side hasten and grow in strength. "Sweet fucking sin…Sweet *sin*, Mercy."

He pounds against me from behind, one hand curled around the silk wrapping his cock, the other gripping my hip. His fingers dig into me painfully. He steps closer until the entire front of my body aches from being pressed so hard to the wall.

The ache is exquisite.

With the angle of our hips and the way he pins me to the spot, my fingers can finally reach and circle that throbbing nub. Puffs of breath escape me as we work fast and hard, chasing release together.

His nose nuzzles my neck, drifting back, and I feel it brush against my hair. He inhales deeply, and a moan escapes me as he whispers, "Wildflowers and starlight." His hand leaves my hip, and suddenly, it's wrapped around my hair at the base of my neck. He jerks back on it, and I whimper as my neck cranes, chin lifting skyward at a beautifully painful angle. "This is mine." He rubs his face in my hair.

Hair he called the color of starlight.

Hair he said smelled like wildflowers.

I don't think any part of me has ever been compared to such beautiful things.

In service, I've been called names—cunt, whore, slut—and parts of me have been referred to as fuckholes, and were used as such. I've been told my hair was good for pulling; I've been told I smelled like a good little bitch.

To have a part of me compared to wildflowers and starlight in the midst of such sinful lust…it's a sentiment more incredible than I can even begin to describe. Emotion swells in my chest, a deep, longing ache for more of that feeling overwhelming my heart as his body touching every part of mine overwhelms my senses.

"Come," I breathe. "Come for me, please. I want you to." I really do want him to—something I've never wanted for a man before. I want him to feel pleasure for the joy he's just sparked inside me. "You can use me. Any part of me. I won't tell a soul."

His grip on my hair tightens as his thrusts sharpen. I feel it swell as if he were inside me because every pulse of him along my hip pulses through my clit just the same. I'm so close, so quickly—quicker than ever before—and more powerfully than ever before.

He thrusts. He pants. He groans.

And as my climax looms, my clit swelling and aching, he shoves me over the edge with a whisper, "Come for me, starlight."

A sob escapes me as I come—as he comes with me—and he swallows it with a deep kiss over my shoulder. The pleasure peaks and my body trembles, quaking in waves that ripple out and back, out and back.

He groans into my mouth as his hips falter in their rhythm, turning him frantic. He bites my bottom lip as a strangled moan chokes him—and it chokes me, too. I feel like I can't breathe.

His hips surge forward at the peak of his release, and then he stills, his chest rising and falling heavily against my back as we pant together, as we come down from the high together.

Stay.

Stay in this moment with me.

Stay with me.

Arlo can't hear my silent pleading for him to remain in this bliss for just a little longer. He releases his grip on me slowly, gradually loosening. I feel him pull away, and I allow my gaze to fall to my side, watching as he drags his cock away, letting it slip through the silk, and wipe the remnants of his release all over it.

My body slumps as he steps back fully, and though he's still panting from exertion, I hear him already working the buckle of his belt, already leaving me alone in my bliss, and preparing to steal me from it entirely.

Slowly, I turn, pressing my back to the wall, slipping down until

I sit on the floor, legs stretched out before me. Glancing down, I see my dress is ruined beyond repair. I lift my chin to look at Arlo, terrified of what I'll find in his expression. He's already put himself together again so quickly, tucked and fastened, looking as sharp as always…except for the red flush around his gorgeous lips from kissing me and the way his thick hair is tousled from our movement.

His head inclines and he watches me for a beat as he catches his breath. Then he steps over me, straddles my legs with his feet on either side of my knees. He crouches to his haunches so abruptly that it makes me gasp.

He pulls the leather glove off his right hand. I hadn't realized he'd still been wearing them while he fucked my silky dress. His blue eyes flicker across my face, and I stare into them deeply, watching as he processes something in his mind.

What is he thinking?

With his gloved hand, he reaches out to lightly lift my chin. With the other—and without looking away from my eyes—he reaches down to the smeared, stained fabric and swipes his thumb down, collecting some of the white residue.

He lifts that hand, his eyes darting to my lips as his tongue sneaks out to swipe across his own. Then he touches his thumb to my bottom lip, pressing in, slowly swiping his cum from one corner to the other.

A puff of breath escapes my parted lips at the feel of it and the way he claims me. At least it feels like he's claiming me, though I know that could never be the truth.

"Don't tell a soul, sinner. Promise me this will be our dirty little secret, and perhaps we can sin again."

His words are abhorrent. He knows what we did was wrong; he knows consequences would find him for this. I should tell…I should shout it down the hall and let them end him for this.

But, as sick as it is, I don't want that.

I *want* him to sin with me again. They could punish him for this, but it won't change my fate. If they insist on putting me through the trials—insist on ending my life and sending me to hell—then at least I can take his corrupted soul along with mine.

I nod slowly, feeling degradation and sin settle inside me for wanting anything from him so much that I would lie for his sins—when he isn't man enough to lie for mine.

He leans forward and presses a kiss to my cum-covered lips, then pulls back and licks them clean. Heat flashes through his eyes, sparking a fire within me that burns so bright and hot that it forces my shame to creep from the darkness and flee from the inferno.

I'm a sinner...I am.

And now, I'm a lying whore, too.

chapter sixteen

ARLO

WHAT HAVE I done?

I leave Mercy's room and go to mine, slamming the door behind me and locking myself in.

I used a woman; I purged my impulse with her. I wiped my cum across her lips.

Sweet fucking sin.

All the worse I asked her to keep the secret.

All the worse, she agreed.

My chest feels tight with the sinful pride of it.

Where is my self-control? My discipline? How did I lose it so easily?

I could blame her for my transgressions—Mercy fucking Madness. She is the sinner, and I could say she corrupted me, influenced me with her wicked ways. I could say she brought me into sin with her. But even I know that would be a lie because I *wanted* it. I wanted her, more desperately than I've ever wanted anyone or anything in my life. I wanted to sink inside her and feel her warmth wrapping around my cock.

I don't know what to do from here. I don't know how to control myself, but I must get myself under control.

I cross to my desk and sit, unlocking the drawer and pulling out my leather journal. I remove my gloves—which I'd left on while I fucked the fabric of her dress—and thumb open my journal to the next blank page before picking up my pen. I press it to the paper and within a minute, my hand moves, quickly working to scribe my mind's racing thoughts.

Light of the universe,
starlight in human form.

Celestial beauty and the scent of earth,
like the meadow and sweet mountain air.

Wildflowers and starlight.

She shines like the heavens,
and I am deceived.

She's born from hell.
Stars burn, and so does she.
Her light born from hellfire, lit from the spark of madness.

Wildflowers and starlight.

She ignites me, a falling star colliding with my soul, setting it ablaze,
spreading like wildfire.
She incinerates me with passion.

Intoxication from her heat burns my blood,
rushing it low with the swell of desire.
I'm overcome with the impulse to ravage, relief promised in her warmth.

Wildflowers and starlight.
Starlight and hellfire.
Hellfire and lust and sin.

I lose myself in the sin of her, yet in that sin...
I'm found.

    I sit back in my chair, reading the words on the page—blasphemous words of lust that shouldn't be on record. I tear the page from my journal and crumple it into a ball as I stand and cross my room to the fireplace. I draw my hand back, prepared to toss it into the fire, but the flame catches my attention and stills my hand. The dancing orange flickers with shimmers of white light that remind me of the stars—of starlight, of *her*.

Her starlight hair will be the death of me.

My grip on the crumpled page loosens, but I can't seem to let it go. I can't bring myself to burn the words that ring so true.

I unfold the page and read the words again.

I lose myself in the sin of her, yet in that sin…
I'm found.

I've never written with such ease; I've never written with such cadence. She's a muse as much as she is anything else.

She's also a sinner, a demon of lust who wants to possess me. And she did possess me for moments as we came undone, and I have no doubt she could do it again. She *will* do it again if I'm not careful.

I need discipline.

I need self-control.

I need to punish myself for this transgression.

I drop the crumpled paper on the carpet. I take the candelabra from the mantle and tip it toward the flames, dipping the wick of the candle into the fireplace until it catches. I pull it out and carry it to my desk, setting down the silver candle holder before lowering into my chair. I lift the long ivory candle from the holder and reach toward the flame, the tip of my finger hovering beside the dancing glow.

I revel in the anticipation of pain, the preemptive, knowing ache of my skin as I await the searing burn. I inch my finger closer, tempting the heat, yearning for the pain that reminds me why I need to control myself…Because if I don't, I will burn in hell, and this is the pain of the flames I'll feel for an eternity.

I push my finger toward the flame, but it twitches before it touches, and it gives me pause. The pause makes me feel weak, and I can't be weak—not with myself and especially, not with Mercy.

I drag in a deep breath and move my hand above the flame, hovering above the flickering tip. I force fear from my mind, and I lower my hand quickly, dropping it so the center of my palm falls into the fire.

I hiss as it burns my skin, groan as the ache deepens, as I let it heat my flesh and hope that it adds another scar. I remove my hand while the pain is still intense, knowing I will have burned too deep and deadened the nerve endings when the pain ceases. My hand is shaking as I turn it over and witness the red blistering flesh in the center of my palm.

I'll remember this mark whenever I think of Mercy as anything more than a sinner and a trial participant…whenever I think of her whimpers, her flesh, her starlight strands of hair.

This mark is for her.

This mark is *because* of her.

It's a reminder of the pain that awaits me in death if I let her drag me into sin with her.

But somehow, I already know it's a pain I'd welcome.

chapter seventeen

Mercy

IVY JANE'S CHARRED remains are on display in the center
of the village square. It's bleak and gray today, a soft breeze cutting
through the air. Arlo leads Delle and I to the black mass of servants
kneeling in their dark clothes facing Ivy in rows. The villagers are
gathered behind them, hands clasped and heads bowed in reverence.
Arlo directs Delle with gentle gestures to the end of the front row
of servants, indicating she should kneel beside the last servant there.

He doesn't show me the same gentleness.

His gloved hand lands on my shoulder and firmly grips me,
twisting my body before shoving me down. I drop to my knees
beside Delle and land hard on gravel, tiny rocks pushing against the
fabric of my burgundy gown and pressing into my kneecaps.

I try to ignore the way Arlo broods at me as he backs away. He
hasn't said a word to me since we...since we sinned together days ago.

I glance over my shoulder and spot Ellary and Cambria in the
row behind me. I press a small smile through my lips, but it's not
returned. They quickly avert their eyes, Cambria bowing her head
and Ellary looking forward. Pieces of my soul crumble and fall with
how they turn from me.

Though, I understand why they turn away. I understand what
they think of me now. I'm no longer their friend; they can only see
me as a sinner. They think I'm wrong, that I'm bad, that I'm going to
hell. They think I betrayed their trust and sullied our friendship with

my actions against service. I can accept why they would believe that, and I don't fault them for it, yet the evidence of their swift detachment still cuts through my chest like a blade, piercing my heart.

I could cry right now for the way it hurts me, but I don't. I don't want to give everyone the satisfaction of a sinner's tears. I take a deep breath that hitches with a begging sob, but I swallow it down and force my gaze to Ivy's dead body, reminding myself that if I hadn't run—if I hadn't *sinned*—I might've been lying beside her right now.

Worse, I might've been alive, suffering excruciating pain for the burns Hyatt Price had threatened to inflict upon me.

Ivy's once smooth skin is red and blistered, and she's been embalmed to preserve the sight of horror—yet surrounding the horror is beauty. Her body is laid flat on a raised platform that's covered with a pure, white cloth draping down the sides and delicately dusting the ground. Wildflowers in shades of violet and garnet have been plucked from the meadow and laid around her body, encircling her form on the platform. Her beautiful ebony hair has been brushed and pulled out around her head, creating a halo. She looks angelic in her white gown, aside from the tragic burns and blisters that mar her skin.

The gloomy day surrounds her with appropriate melancholy, and though I wasn't close with her personally, sadness for the loss of her swells within me all the same. She was a servant—a sister—and she died the way I was meant to.

Wesley steps away from the rest of the Control, who stand in a line behind the platform where Ivy's laid to rest. A breeze whips around us, kicking up the black skirts of servants in a dark, ominous way.

Somberly, Wesley begins, "We've gathered in remembrance today. Ivy Jane gave her life in an act of service, and she deserves our honor, our praise, and our gratitude. She served the Impulse with dignity and grace. She served willingly and with pride for her God-given duty. She was honorable in this life, and though we will find peace in knowing she's found paradise in the afterlife, she will be missed. She'll be missed by her fellow servants. Remembered by the villagers as they go about their peaceful days—peaceful because of Ivy's sacrifice in serving the Impulse. She'll be held in reverence by the authority of Ember Glen. Her life will not be lost in vain. Let us take a moment of silence in her honor."

Silence settles quickly and uncomfortably, amplifying the sound of the wind as it rustles through the trees at the outer edge of the village square. I look beyond the Homestead in front of me to the mountains behind—I wonder if heaven is found at the peak.

My hair tickles my cheek as the wind catches it, blowing it sideways across my face with an unusual chill that makes goosebumps prickle up my arms. I turn my gaze and find Arlo's brooding expression—he's staring right at me. His gloved hands are clasped in front of him. I hold his stare as my eyes narrow, confused by the attention when his head should be bowed and he should be thinking of Ivy.

Perhaps he is thinking of her as he looks at me. Perhaps he's thinking how lovely she is for her sacrifice...how wonderful and honorable it was for her to step into the fire and ask to be burned. Perhaps he's thinking of how much I disgust him for running from the same flame, for refusing to serve when service meant pain beyond comprehension and almost certain death.

I sneer as I stare back at him, wondering why I haven't told anyone about our indiscretion yet.

Because I'm a sinner, and no one would believe me.

Because I don't want to tell anyone.

Because I want it to be our secret.

A heavy sigh escapes me, and I tear my gaze from him. Bowing my head, I turn my eyes to the ground.

"*Malo mori quam foedari,*" Wesley says, ending the moment of silence.

"*Malo mori quam foedari,*" everyone repeats in a chant...except for me.

I only mouth the words we use to end our prayers. They roughly mean death before dishonor, and Ivy Jane took them to heart. There's a pinch of shame in my stomach because she died to evade dishonor, and I was unwilling to do the same.

Wesley steps back into line, and Killian steps forward. He holds his arms behind his back and paces in front of Ivy. "Ivy Jane's remembrance comes at a time that forces further reflection on our lives here in Ember Glen, on our doctrine, the Impulse Edict, on God."

I lift my head as he speaks, feeling indignation rise at the tone of his voice. There's something about the way he keeps his hair long, pulled back into a knot at the back of his head, that makes him look pompous and arrogant. Perhaps it's just because he *is* pompous and arrogant that I think he looks that way, too.

"As Ivy stepped forward and offered her body to the service of a man's impulse, another servant fled from the very same fate. As we revere Ivy Jane's strength and pride in her role, we must reflect on the dishonor and shame Mercy Madness has brought to our community. As we mourn the loss of an honorable servant in Ivy Jane, we must equally mourn the choice of Delle Carter to dissent from the will of God." He points an outstretched finger at us. "These two have brought dark days upon Ember Glen. They've brought anger, sorrow, and reminders that demons lurk within the shadows, able to overcome anyone of us. But we will not let that destroy us. We will win this fight against sin and the sinners who commit them."

Against my will, my gaze lifts, seeking Arlo, though his gaze is already upon me.

"The Trials of Dissension will purge them of their demons, grant them absolution from their sins if they prove themselves worthy, and will rid Ember Glen of the darkness they've brought upon us."

I force a breath out through my nostrils, my chest sinking heavily, anger making it rise again sharply. Arlo's tongue slips out to wet his bottom lip before his brow furrows, narrowing his stare on me.

I want to look away from him.

I don't want to look away from him…I can't.

I don't hear the rest of Killian's righteous tirade. I'm locked in, my attention held, trapped in the way Arlo watches me. My pulse quickens as moments pass, as Killian's voice fades to a muted rumble, and the wind sounds like a roar as it flicks my hair across my face.

Wildflowers and starlight.

I can hear his voice in my mind, and the sweet words drop through me like a lead ball in my gut. My fingers curl over my knees, nails digging into my flesh as I watch the flicker of bright blue in his eyes, as something in him calls to me, compelling me to stay locked in.

It isn't until the service has ended and Delle stands beside me that I'm pulled from the trance. I gasp, feeling like I haven't taken a breath in minutes. Sound returns and voices mutter around me.

I glance over my shoulder as Delle says, "Mercy?" I see everyone is standing except for me, the villagers returning to the village, the servants hugging and chatting quietly.

I stand and pat Delle on the arm reassuringly. I turn quickly before Arlo can catch me and make my way over to Ellary and Cambria, who are locked in a sorrowful embrace.

"Ellary." I tap the brown tresses that hang over her shoulder.

They release each other and Ellary turns to face me, expressions of discomfort and judgment greeting me.

"You shouldn't be speaking with us," Ellary rushes. "Go back to your warden."

"I just wanted to say hello…" I peek around her to Cambria, "to see if you were healing okay."

Cambria crosses her arms and her brow furrows. "You can't speak to us anymore. It's not right."

"It's not— What do you mean, I can't speak to you? You're my friends. I need you."

Cambria leans forward. "For heaven's sake, Mercy, you're a sinner. We can't be seen talking to you." She glances around warily, looking at the other servants before she lowers her voice. "People will talk. They'll think we're sinners like you."

"I'm not a..." I know there's no use in arguing my virtue. It's what everyone believes, and I can't change their mind. "I just want to know you're okay."

"We're fine," Ellary clips, her features soft though her voice is sharp. "We take care of each other. But we don't wish to speak with you anymore. We're so disappointed in you. You—" Her voice breaks and I feel it in my chest. "You broke our hearts."

I press my palm over my heart, rubbing over the aching, pounding muscle. "What?"

"You always had a different way of thinking, a different view of things, but I never would have thought you would sin this way," Cambria says quietly. "I never would've thought our best friend would condemn herself for eternity." Cambria breaks into a sob, and I feel my heart stop beneath my palm. Ellary slides her arm around Cambria's shoulders, pulling her into a side hug.

"You've brought this upon yourself," Ellary tells me. "We fear for you...we do. We pray for you every night. We pray you'll find absolution for your soul through the trials. But darkness and demons plague you, Mercy, and we won't risk corruption. We can't speak to you anymore." Tears well in her eyes, as they do in mine. "It hurts too much."

"It hurts to speak to me?" My voice cracks against my will as teardrops slip from the corners and run down my cheeks.

Ellary nods sadly as Cambria begins to cry.

"I'm sorry." Though I don't know what I'm apologizing for, I mean it.

I *am* sorry.

I'm sorry we were born in Ember Glen.

I'm sorry we were chosen for service.

I'm sorry my self-preservation hurt them.

I'm sorry we don't see our world the same way.

I step backward, not because I want to, but because I feel the weight of their disappointment drop between us, shoving me back.

"We'll keep praying for you," Ellary mutters. Her arm tightens around Cambria, and they turn away.

I take another step backward as I watch them walk away from me, and my tears fall like a river down my cheek. I close my eyes and let them fall, clutching my dress over my heart. My world has become so sad and silent.

The touch of leather against my cheek startles me. My eyes snap open as Arlo traces the trail of tears with the tip of his gloved finger.

"You're pretty when you cry, sinner," he whispers from behind me.

Sadness turns to anger, and I let go of the fabric at my chest to swat his hand away. "Don't touch me."

He snatches me by the wrist before I can bring my arm down, and whips me around to face him, bringing us chest to chest. "Are you finally seeing the full impact of your sins? Friends turning away from you?"

"They don't know what they're saying."

"I think they know exactly what they're saying. Your actions have consequences for everyone you care about."

I look at him squarely. "And what consequences will those you care about face when your sins come to light?" My threat of exposing our dirty secret is idle for now but reminding him that I could expose him is the only power I have in my life right now.

His jaw tenses and his eyes turn sideways, looking to see if anyone else is near enough to hear. "You haven't told anyone." It's a statement more than it is a question.

My shoulders sag. "No. I haven't."

"Good choice."

"No one would believe me."

"Probably right."

"And they wouldn't care if they did."

"You're very insightful for a sinner."

"Is that all I am? From now until the day I die? I'm no longer a person, only a sinner?"

He clicks his tongue. "There's that golden insight of yours."

I look at our hands between our chests, realizing only then that his gloved palm has slipped from my wrist to curl around my fingers. He holds my hand so tightly that I can't pull away—and I'm not entirely certain I want to. I look up at him and he sucks in a breath as our eyes meet, then he blinks and releases my hand.

"Come along now," he says. "Delle's already gone back to the Homestead, and I'd like to check on her."

I rise on my toes to look over his shoulder, spotting Delle climbing the steps behind Theo and Park. Suddenly, my attention is drawn to her and the need to protect is overwhelming. I don't wait for Arlo's lead; I move around him and stalk across the square at a quick pace. It's only a few steps before I feel his hand on the small of my back.

"I don't need you to lead me. I know where I'm going."

I twitch my hip, arching sideways and trying to shrug him away. His hand only slides around the side of my waist and grips me.

"Don't be ridiculous, Mercy. If I wanted to lead you, I'd place a collar around your neck and attach it to a leash."

I stop abruptly and look over at him. "I may be the sinner, but there's something *deeply* wrong with you, Warden Rainn."

He stares at me, blinking his bright blue eyes. "Just as there is with you, Mercy Madness."

He doesn't elaborate, nor does he wait for a response. He drags his hand across the small of my back, fingertips grazing in a way that's almost sensual as he drags his hand away. He gives me a quick smile that sets off a flurry of feeling in my stomach.

And much like a leash, his aura tugs me, dragging me up the stairs behind him.

chapter eighteen

Mercy

BACK INSIDE THE manor, I catch up with Delle at the top of the staircase. "Delle."

She stops on the second-floor landing and turns, waiting for me to climb the last few steps to meet her.

"Are you okay?" I ask her.

"I suppose." She absently runs her hand down her straight, ash-brown hair. "Are you?"

I sigh as I reach her and drag her into a hug, mostly because I need one, though I know she needs one, too. "Of course not."

I pull back and smile before releasing her, comforted briefly when she returns my smile with a weak one of her own. We walk down the hallway side-by-side toward our bedrooms—hers is the room next to the one I've been given.

"I saw you talking to your friends," she says. "What did they say to you?"

I sigh. "They're unhappy with me."

"I'm sorry." Her regret for me sounds genuine, and her head dips. "I was too afraid to speak with my friends."

I nod in understanding. Her friends probably feel the same as mine, or maybe they feel worse. Delle wasn't forced to participate in the trials; instead, she *chose* it. She chose to dissent for a practically non-existent chance at a life outside of service. As awful as it is, they probably hate her for it, and it makes my heart hurt for her.

"Well, I suppose we'll just have each other." We stop in front of her door and I give her a quick smile.

She grins, but there's no joy in it—only fear and misery. She glances over her shoulder, then lets her face fall slowly. She exhales fully as her head bows, and she lowers her voice. "I'm worried I've made the wrong decision."

Oh, Delle.

"Come with me." I take hold of her arm and drag her into her bedroom. I push the door open and pull her through behind me. I motion to the armchairs in the corner which face the foot of her bed, and she moves to take a seat, gradually and with heaviness in her steps.

I move to the bed, lowering to perch at the foot of it, pressing my palms on either side of my hips. "Talk to me."

"I don't know what to say. I...I don't really think I've made the wrong decision because I know I can't live as a servant. I *won't*. I refuse to. But I don't understand why...why we have to live this way."

I hear the heartache in her breaking voice, the sorrow of her soul. I know this deep soul ache that she's feeling. I felt it for months during my first year of service. Not to say that it ever really went away, but eventually, service felt normal—at least, as normal as it could be.

"I don't understand it, either. Refusing to understand and believe is why I'm here facing the trials and an almost certain death. It's why my life is over, Delle. I never would have wanted you to make this choice."

"I didn't want to make it either, but what was I supposed to do?" She begins to cry, and it claws at my soul.

I cross the room, quickly dropping to my knees in front of her as she drops her head into her hands and cries. Her pain swirls around me, encapsulates me in heartache so strong that it threatens to tear me in two.

I know how hard the transition to service is when you're sixteen. Though our training over the years gave us an idea of what our role would be, there is no understanding the depth of it until you're thrown into your first night of service. And Delle is like me, which makes it all the worse.

She thinks.

She questions.

She wonders.

And all those lead to rebellion.

We're warned about it, of course. We're preached to, repeatedly, about the pain that awaits us in the afterlife for rebelling against our servant role. The mere desire for something different is seen as a secret sin—one that will bring you to hell after death, though no one would know about it if you didn't speak it. We're taught that the only way to live a godly life is to find joy and pride in our role. It's perplexing how all the others seem to find a way to do it.

Unless...

Unless they're all living that secret sin and simply unwilling to speak it. The hand we've been dealt is a losing one, and there is no exchanging cards.

The only thing I know is that I would do anything to take this poor child's pain from her, to spare her the trials, to fight against the impossible and grant her the domestic life free of service that she deserves.

I think my aptitude for self-preservation is entirely lost as ideas for saving Delle run rampant through my mind. I'm meant to die in these trials; I'm the reason they're holding the trials at all. My fate is sealed.

But if there was a way to spare Delle the same fate...

I gently tug on her wrists to pull them away from her face. I wait until she lifts her head to look at me, trails of tears streaking down her pinkened cheeks. I reach up to brush my thumb across and swipe the drops away.

"Delle, is a domestic life what you really want? Is that the reason you volunteered to participate?"

Her voice is quiet. "I don't want to die, Mercy. I want to live, but I...Not like *that*...I can't live the life of a servant. How have you survived that life this long? How have you done it?"

"Truthfully, I don't know. I've just done what I have to do to survive."

She swallows hard and pulls her shoulders back, bringing her hands to her thighs. She sniffles before forcing a determined expression. "I don't want to do it. I don't want to serve, not ever again. If it means I die in the trials, I have to at least take that chance. I have to—" Her voice breaks as fear cuts through the determination and widens her hazel eyes.

I watch as the realization hits her, as the reality of her decision takes hold, as the thought of death and what that truly means strikes her. Her breaths quicken and sharpen, and her fingers move restlessly against her thighs.

She's not prepared to die—of course, she isn't.

"Mercy, I can't—" She takes in a rasping breath as she falls into a panic.

"Okay." I reach for her calmly, grabbing hold of her wrist and tugging her gently forward. "It's okay, come here."

I guide her down to the floor in front of me and wrap my arms around her, hugging her fiercely as she breaks apart. My breath catches in my lungs and tears spring to my eyes, but I force my emotions away, swallow them deep into my soul.

I stroke her soft ashen hair as she sobs, as we both drop from our knees to sit on the floor, and I cradle her against my chest. I let her release. I wait until her tears have all been spilled, until her breathing slows and steadies, until she starts to come back through the panic.

I don't know how long we sit like this. I only know it feels like an eternity that I have to force my own fears and pain and heartache away so she can release hers in the safety of my presence.

"I want to ask you a question," I say calmly, stroking her hair.

She nods against my chest, and I feel her tug away. I let go of my hold so she can pull back and sit up to look at me.

I give her a small, comforting smile. "If there were a way…" I hesitate in my words, not sure how to frame them, not yet sure whether they're worth anything. I tuck her hair behind her ear in my pause. "If there were a way for someone to take on this burden for you…if someone could take this pain away from you and allow you the chance at a domestic life without going through the horror of the trials…If someone wanted to do that for you and offered it, would you let them?"

Her forehead wrinkles in confusion, and I know I'm not being clear, that I'm not making any sense.

"What do you mean?"

"If someone else could go through the trials for you and give you the chance at a domestic life, would you allow them to do it for you?"

"Mercy, I don't understand what you're asking me."

"I just need to know, Delle. If there were some way I could bear it all for you, would you allow me to do that? Would you promise me you'd go on and live your happy domestic life after it's all over, after I'm gone, without shame or guilt?"

"How could I ever answer a question like that?" I see tears fill her eyes again, but the way they flicker with the possibility of living without this fear tells me exactly what I need to know.

I shake my head. "Never mind." I don't want to force an answer from her. I won't make her say it when I already know what it is. "It's an impossible question."

But maybe the answer isn't impossible.

I was sentenced to this, and she chose it. She was braver than I ever could have been, and that should be enough for her. It should be enough for her to be given the domestic life she deserves to have. I was given no choice, and I don't think I would've been as brave as Delle to choose this if presented with the opportunity. But I can find my bravery in her honor now; I'll meet her courage with my own and fight for the impossible.

I LEAVE DELLE tucked in her bed—she was so exhausted that I insisted she climb into it and get some rest for a few hours before dinner. Closing the door behind me, I run my knuckles beneath my eyes, catching and dragging what's left of my tears. I let out a heavy, shuddering breath before finding the strength to move.

I enter my bedroom one door down, and head directly to the bathroom. Looking into the mirror above the sink, I note that my eyes are a little red and the skin beneath them is puffy from crying. I can't go to Arlo looking this way. I need to convince him to help me, and to do that, I need to appeal to him.

I need to tempt him.

If I can tempt him to sin with me again, then perhaps I can hold it over his head, blackmail him into helping me convince the Control to let me save Delle. Even with his help, it's unlikely they'll let me do the trials twice to spare her the burden of going through it. Even if they allowed it, I'd probably die before I'm able to complete them and save her.

The odds are stacked against me, as close to zero as they can be. I don't even know if blackmailing Arlo would work. I truthfully don't know that any of his brothers in God would care if I told them he used my body outside of service—or if they would even believe a sinner like me. But I don't know what else to do, and I have to try something. I couldn't live with myself if I didn't try something, anything, to spare her.

This is the only thing I can think to do. It's the only plan that I have.

Tempt him.

Make him sin.

Keep the secret in exchange for his help.

My life already has an expiration date, and my soul is already damned. I may as well take my warden to hell with me.

chapter nineteen

ARLO

I FLING OPEN the door to my bedroom to stop the insistent knocking. "What?"

I'm taken aback at the sight of Mercy standing before me, her fist raised mid-knock, encased in her overwhelming aura of wildflowers and starlight. I expected it was one of my brothers with the persistent rapping at the door. If I'd had any inkling she would be calling on me unexpectedly, I wouldn't have answered the door with such indecency. My shirt is unbuttoned, hanging open at my sides, exposing my chest and torso.

She drops her hand as her eyes land on me, skimming down my front. My head inclines with curiosity to watch her scan me so boldly. She blinks a little too long before raising her chin a little higher, forcing herself to meet my eyes.

Her jaw is set, expression taut. "I'd like to speak with you."

"Then speak."

"May I come in?"

My pulse thrums at the request, both with anxiety and anticipation. It's a dangerous game she and I have been playing, yet I want to play it. I return her appraising gaze to drink her in, instant frustration tightening a knot in my stomach at her maddening beauty.

Her white-blonde hair cascades in perfect, tumbling waves over her slender shoulders, and even though her crimson dress is plain and hangs somewhat loose on her frame, she looks like an angel—a fallen angel, but an angel, nonetheless. She's a thing of beauty, once from heaven, though she's fallen from grace to rule in the kingdom of demons.

Against my better judgment, I step back, sweeping my arm to welcome her into my room. I watch as she breezes past me, her fingers twisting nervously in front of her as she moves across the room. I shut the door as she turns to face me, then leans back on the sideboard against the far wall. She curls her fingers around the edge at either side of her hips.

If only her fingers curled around me the same.

I move forward a couple of steps, then stop and cross my arms over my chest. I tilt my head, looking at her expectantly, and wait for her to speak.

"I've come to an unfortunate realization," she says, her eyes are downcast, staring at a spot on the carpet.

"Oh?"

"I can't win." She looks up at me, and the silvery blue of her eyes sparkles. "I refused to accept it before, but I accept it now. My life is going to end in these trials, and I can't go on pretending there's a chance I'll survive."

My arms fall to my sides as an odd pang strikes my chest. "What made you come to this conclusion?"

She regards me with a piercing stare. "I'm capable of reflection. In any case, I'd like your help, if you're willing to give it."

"I'm your warden; it's my role to help. But what exactly is it you want my help with?"

She swallows. "Finding absolution for my soul."

My breath catches.

I want absolution for her soul, too.

The thought of her burning for an eternity causes an ache I can hardly bear.

"I want that for you, too, Mercy."

"And I want it for Delle."

"She'll find it in the trials."

Mercy shakes her head, starlight brushing over her shoulders. "No, she won't." She pushes off the sideboard and takes a slow step in my direction. "She doesn't understand the choice she's made. If she could take it back, she would."

"What's done is done. She made the choice, and she has to live with the consequences."

"It's not right, Warden Rainn."

The way she recognizes my authority stitches a thread of desire through my gut.

"She's a child," Mercy goes on. "She made her decision out of fear. Her first night of service was rough…it was rough on all of us servants. Ivy Jane lost her life. Can you imagine one of the servants losing their life on your first night of service? It would make any first-timer fearful."

"You're not meant to be fearful. You're meant to have pride in your work."

"Pride takes time." She nudges closer. "It takes time to understand the benefit of our work to the community."

I slip my ungloved hands into my pockets and huff out a breath. "Now you're singing an entirely different song, Mercy Madness. I thought you had no pride in your role; in fact, you outright rejected it in sin. Your words are contradictory to your thoughts and actions."

She nods and grants me a tight smile before looking down. "I know." She looks up at me from beneath her eyelashes and the flash in her bewitching eyes tugs on that thread of desire, pulling it tighter. "But you and I are singing the same contradictory song, aren't we? You and I have sinned together, Warden Rainn."

I breathe out slowly, letting my chest sink as her eyes hold mine. "What do you want from me?"

Her head rises and our gaze locks squarely. "I only want your help to save a lost child from a life of misery and eternal damnation."

I chuckle, but it's humorless. "Oh? Is that all?"

"What do you want from *me*?" She dares to reach out her hand and press it to the center of my bare chest.

My reaction should be disgust at her obvious attempt at seduction, at her sinful promiscuity. Yet my reaction is one of sin—a clenching low in my stomach, a spreading warmth from my center, the twitch of my blasphemous cock.

I force myself to take a step back. "I want to save your soul, Mercy."

She takes a step forward. "And I think there's a way for me to save Delle's soul, too."

"Her soul will be saved through the trials—"

"No. It's not right, and you know it. If there were another way to repent, wouldn't you want that for her?"

"I want to follow the Edict…God's word."

Mercy shakes her head. "No, you don't."

She steps closer and I pull my hands from my pockets, reaching up to grip her shoulders and push her away…only I don't push. I grab and hold on as the front of her body kisses my chest and torso.

"I know you don't want to follow the Edict. If you'd wanted to, you would've purged that night in the forest. You wouldn't have fucked the fabric of my dress the other night in my room. You wouldn't allow me to be alone with you in your room." Her hands press to my chest, spreading warmth across my skin. "You're *indecent*, Warden Rainn."

Indecent.

The word drips from her lips.

It makes me hard.

It makes me desire indecency with her.

Squeezing her shoulders, I push her back, walking her quickly until her back slams to the wall behind us. I release her shoulders and slap my palms to the wall on either side of her, caging her in. I lick my lips as my eyes drop to watch the rise and fall of her chest.

My lips creep up into a cheeky smirk. "And you desire my indecency, don't you, sinner?"

Her expression is odd—a mixture of determination and temptation. The look of sinful wanting in her eyes is clear, but it's as though she fights against it.

Why fight it when it's so clear what she's trying to do here?

"You want to drag me into sin with you," I tell her, because it's obvious.

But I don't expect her response. "Yes, I do."

She reaches up to touch the sleeves of her dress and nudges them down her shoulders. The ill-fitting gown slips too easily from her body, revealing the tempting silk chemise she wears beneath. I stifle a gasp at the sinful look of her nipples peeking through the thin fabric, at the truly indecent way one of the thin straps slips down her shoulder.

I should step away.

I should demand that she leave.

I should call upon my brothers to save me from this temptation, but instead, I inch closer.

"Tell me why. Is it because you think you'll get what you want from me if I become a sinner like you?"

Her lips part as her eyes move around my face, searching for a place to land, the determination in her expression waning. "It's because it feels so good to sin with you." Her eyes finally land, fixing on my lips.

There's no hint of deception or dishonesty in her words, nor in her expression. In fact, the honesty rings so true that it punches through my heart, delivering a lightning strike to the good and righteous part of me, forcing it into a shock that renders it temporarily useless. That moment of shock is all it takes for her demon claws to reach into my chest and sink into my heart, delivering a poison of lust straight from hell.

I clutch her face and I dip to kiss her, but then she speaks, halting me. "I want to endure Delle's trials as her proxy."

What?

I'm already gone, lost in sin, so I ignore her, pressing my lips to hers and forcing a kiss that she eventually succumbs to. A pleasure-fueled whimper vibrates through her as I push my tongue between her lips and taste her—taste every drop of sin from her soul.

We devour each other for moments before the need to taste her flesh consumes me, and I leave a trail of kisses across her cheek, along her jawline, to her neck.

"I mean it," she whispers, her voice breathy and desperate as her body arches into mine. "She regrets the choice. I'll endure my trials and hers if the Control will allow me."

My hand trails down her body, moving from her shoulder over her chest, down the mound of her breast. Her hands touch my cheeks, and she lifts me away from her neck, pulling me into another shattering kiss. My palm squeezes her breast as her tongue dances with mine.

This is wrong.

This is sinful.

Yet it feels more divine than prayer, more righteous than atonement.

I let myself sink into the depravity. The weight of my desire for her is so heavy that there's no sense in fighting it. Fighting it will only make me sink faster.

I comb my fingers through her starlight tresses. When they catch on a tangle, I wrap my fist around the length and jerk sharply to the side. She whimpers but lets me pull, exposing the bare expanse of her ivory neck. I lick from nape to ear, tasting her fully and filling up on her sin.

"Will you help me, Arlo?" she pleads softly as her hands brush down my neck, my chest, fingers grazing the lines of my stomach until they hit my belt.

My hips rock forward against her touch. "Help you?" I pant against her neck. "How?"

"Convince them to let me do each trial twice. Once for myself, and once for Delle."

I stiffen at her words, confusion overtaking me. I lift my head to look at her. "What are you saying?"

"I want to win her a domestic life." She tugs at my belt. "I'm damned, we both know that. I want to sacrifice for her. If I complete all my trials, and hers, would the Control consider giving her a domestic life for my sacrifice?"

I release her all at once and take a step back. "You aren't making any sense."

Her chest heaves with heavy panting, and I can hardly breathe, watching the swell of her breasts lifting and lowering.

"One of the ultimate acts of service is sacrifice, isn't it?"

"It is…" I run a hand over my scruffy beard as my brow furrows, still trying to understand her through the pounding of my heart.

She pushes off the wall and steps toward me. "The Trials of Dissension are meant for the participant to perform grand acts of service. Sacrifice is a pinnacle act of service. I want to make a sacrifice to prove myself, and in honor of my sacrifice, I want the Control to spare Delle the fate she chose impulsively."

Her fingers toy with my belt buckle, and I drop my chin to watch her hands as they work.

"She made a mistake one time," Mercy continues. "She's not like me, and I think you all know that." She looks up at me and I meet her eyes. She unbuckles my belt as she speaks, holding my gaze. "I'm a rebel…always have been. My thoughts are blasphemous, and my actions are sinful. I understand why I have to participate in the trials, but Delle is different." She unbuttons my pants. "She's just a child who made a mistake…a misguided child who can find her way back to God." She tugs down the zipper and slips her hand inside before I can protest, wrapping her small hand around my cock and making me gasp. "I've always been a sinner, Arlo. Let me suffer twice and spare her. Let me suffer twice and give her a peaceful life."

She squeezes, and it feels like burning in hell—only the fire feels good searing my flesh. I wrap my hand around her wrist, squeezing tight to still her stroking palm.

"Do you deserve to suffer, Mercy?"

I feel the quickening beat of her pulse through her wrist as she nods, her gaze holding mine steadily, hardly blinking.

I bend and press my forehead to hers. "Then you will suffer greatly."

"I…I'll accept that."

I jerk her hand from my pants and bring it up to her chest, pinning her arm between us as I press in closer. "Yes, you will. You have no choice but to accept just how much you'll suffer in the first trial."

"I know."

"Oh, you have no idea."

"Tell me."

I let a grin touch my cheeks, then I tilt my chin and draw her into a consuming kiss. Grabbing her shoulders, I shove her down until her knees buckle beneath her, and she drops. She looks up at me, a sinner on her knees, prepared to sacrifice herself.

I grip her chin and brush my thumb along her bottom lip, so viciously tempted to press my cock against it. Instead, I drop to my knees before her, wrap my arms around her, and take her down to the floor. I force her onto her back as I stretch out above her.

"My brothers will want your pleasure in the first trial." I press a kiss to her cheek. "But you're not going to give it to them."

"I don't understand." Her fingers curl around the open sides of my shirt, pulling me down against her.

"If you want me to try to convince them to let you do this, then you're going to do something for me in return."

"What?"

I bend to whisper against her ear. "Denial, starlight."

She shudders and I feel it vibrate through me.

"Denial of what?"

"I know I'm the only man who's given you pleasure before, aren't I?" I kiss her neck. "That night in the forest when you came on my fingers…it was the first time by another's hand, wasn't it?"

"Yes."

"And I'll be the only man who gives you that until the day you die."

The haughty sound of her chuckle awakens something playful within me. I tear her hands from my shirt, lock her fingers between mine, and stretch them out above her head, pinning them to the carpet.

"Do you think there's any way I would ever find pleasure in being forcibly fucked by seven men?"

"Of course you would, sinner. Because I'll be there to make sure you don't forget the way you feel stretched out beneath me."

I roll my hips forward, and her legs part naturally, trying to make more room for me between them. The movement inches the short chemise up her hips, and that's when I realize she's bare beneath. I squeeze her hands in mine, let my weight fall a little heavier on top of her, aligning every inch of me with every inch of her.

Sweet fucking sin.

She sighs as her lips part, beckoning me to taste.

I dip my head, bring my lips to hers, and let them brush as I speak. "Promise me your pleasure belongs to me, and to no one else." My hips shift, grinding her down to the floor. "Promise me your sins belong to me, your flesh, your moans, your desire. Let it be for me, and I'll try to help you."

She tilts her chin, trying to steal a kiss, but I don't allow it. I drag my head back and let go of one of her hands, bringing mine down the side of her neck. I brush my thumb over the hollow of her throat, relishing the way her muscles work as she swallows against my touch. I slip my palm higher, stopping at her jawline to rub my thumb across her bottom lip. She puffs out a whimper that threatens to undo my self-control entirely.

"I promise," she whispers, and there's nothing but sweet, sinful sincerity in her gray-blue eyes.

"Promise me you won't tell a soul about this, about us…and I'll grant you that pleasure now."

Fuck, I'm losing control.

I'm not losing it…I'm letting her take it.

Am I going to hell for this?

"I promise, Arlo." Her voice begs sweetly, and her hips lift from the floor—and I believe her. "Please."

I groan at the word, at the way it slithers inside and coils around my desire, wringing out every last drop of lust to pool deep in the pit of my stomach. My head falls as my body drops its full weight onto hers, pinning her entirely. I bury my face in the crook of her neck, kissing and nipping with my teeth.

"Say it again, starlight."

"Please, Arlo. *Please.*" Her voice trembles, as does her body beneath mine.

Fuck absolution.

Let me burn in hell with her.

I slink down her body, my lips and tongue tasting her everywhere, down her throat, along her chest, over the swell of her breast spilling out above the silk.

She tenses and squirms beneath me as my mouth works its way down her body. I kiss the satin fabric over her stomach, turning my cheek to run my nose down her belly, sniffing my way down to the apex of her thighs.

My palms grip her hips, my fingertips wrapping around to splay across her bare cheeks, and I squeeze. She whimpers as she raises her hips, bucking against nothing to seek relief.

"Please...please," she continues to beg and all the goodness within me dies.

Her voice is angelic as she begs—contrite and needy. There's nothing even remotely sinful about the way she needs me. The way she needs me is spiritual, holy, *divine.*

In this moment, I am God, and she prays for me to grant her pleasure in mercy.

Sweet Mercy.

I grab the hem of her skirt, working quickly to shove it higher above her belly button. I press onto my knees to look down at her and see her bare, exposed, slick, and ready for me. I sit back on my heels, pressing my palms to my thighs so I can admire the perfection between her legs as she draws them back, bending her knees and spreading wide for me.

She's wet, glistening, so ready for my touch.

I didn't expect that, and the sight of it sends a pulse of dark desire through my veins that I can no longer deny.

Mercy rises onto her elbows, her pink lips parted, eyes hooded with desire. She doesn't speak a word, she just watches me with a silent plea in her eyes—a needy plea that calls to me.

I want to give this woman pleasure until it breaks her.

And I want to break her slowly.

chapter twenty

Mercy

THIS DESIRE IS maddening.

I feel out of my mind, yet perfectly settled in my soul.

Arlo runs a hand across his lips as he gazes at my aching center. I'm exposed and open to him in the most intimate way—it's what I wanted, what I planned for. My intent was to lure him into wanting me, to seduce him into sin, and convince him to help me. I got what I wanted already, but now I want more.

I need more.

I ache for more.

"Touch me. Please," I beg him, watching as his broad chest rises and falls.

He licks his lips like he wants to taste me, and I want him to. My skin burns for it. Rising onto his knees, he shoves his pants and the elastic of his underwear down over his hips, and I watch with wide, wanting eyes as his thick cock springs free.

He leans forward with a snap, and I sigh, sensing relief coming. He wraps his arms around my waist and hoists me up, pulls me against him where he kneels. He shifts to sit as he settles my weight across his lap, positioning me to straddle him. He holds me close, palms splaying across my lower back, making me arc my chest forward.

His lips are aligned with my breasts, and his eyes flicker with anticipation as he scans the swell of them above the fabric. He presses a soft kiss between them, which hits me with a swirl of relief and stronger need all at once. My head drops back as he kisses his way across my chest.

I wrap my arms around his neck, but I don't need to hold myself up. His hold on me is strong and sure, heating me from the inside out.

One of his hands slips up my back, slowly working up the center, between my shoulder blades, then over my shoulder. One finger plays under the strap of the silk chemise, nudging carefully until it slips and drops down my arm.

My fingers creep up the back of his neck, sinking into his wavy hair. It's thick and soft, and the feel of it in my grip is empowering… like I have a hold on him.

I exhale in a heavy rush as he toys with the silk over my breasts, easing it down, steadily exposing my flesh until he's freed them. The cool air breezes across my nipples, but his gaze upon them is warming.

"How can a sinner look so divine?" Arlo whispers, almost as if he's speaking to himself. He presses a soft kiss to the hardening peak. "So heavenly, so angelic?"

Another soft, almost sweet kiss, and then he runs the flat of his tongue over my nipple, sending a cascading swirl of pleasure down my center.

My lips part as I pant out a moan, and I struggle to speak through breaths of ecstasy. "Maybe…maybe divinity isn't what you think it is."

He kisses the hollow of my throat, trailing a line down my breast with a smug grin. "And I suppose you'd like me to entertain your sinner thoughts?"

"You're already entertaining them." I draw my hips back and rock them forward, my slickness spreading along his cock.

What am I doing?

What am I?

I feel wanton and flesh-hungry, as if perhaps I am the sinner he claims me to be.

He groans, his hands splaying across my back as he hugs me closer, burying his face in my chest. He takes in a shuddering breath, and I feel the way he fights against himself. I feel the tension as he tries to hold himself still, gripping me like his sanity depends on it.

Slowly, he lifts his head, gazing up at me with an odd softness in his blue eyes—an ethereal glow that looks like a cloudless sky, clear and vibrant, open to the heavens.

His gaze is heavenly.

His hold on me is spiritual.

The raw touch of our intimate parts is sacred.

To have him inside me would be divine.

I untangle my hands from his hair, slipping them back so I can cradle his face in my palms. I drop my forehead to meet his, holding his eyes with mine, breathing with him through this unexpected moment of connection I know I'll treasure for all my days.

I've never felt connected this way—engaged, wanted, needed. His eyes tell me a million different ways that he needs me, though he doesn't want it to be true.

He doesn't want to want a sinner.

I let the tiny ball of shame sink in my gut, let it roll through the coiling desire and mix with lust into a kind of need that feels filthy and wrong.

It's wrong, but I like it.

It's wrong, but I want it.

"I won't tell a soul," I promise him, and I think I mean it.

I shouldn't mean it. I shouldn't want to keep this filthy secret for one of the men set to ruin my life, but I know I will keep it for a moment like this.

"Please," I beg him for the millionth time, and a fire ignites behind his eyes.

Shifting, he reaches between us with one hand, fisting his cock. We both look down between us, watching as I lift my hips, as he angles the tip and brushes it through my folds. We pant through the tease, our breaths growing heavier and more desperate as we slip and shift into position.

And when he sinks inside me, the gates of heaven spread wide open and welcome us in glorious light. Our embrace tightens as we revel in stillness and the bright white light of pure and holy pleasure.

As a moment's relief gives way to greater need, my stomach tightens in dark knots of lust, and our bodies start to move. He encourages it when his hands fall to my hips and squeeze. I rock with him inside me, holding him close.

He groans with all the filth of a demon, and suddenly, we're cast out of heaven, forced back through the pearly gates before they're slammed shut to lock us out.

I don't mourn the loss of heavenly light as we're dropped down into darkness. My pace quickens as need builds. As his chest heaves and his lips part against my skin—as pleasure sinks us into the darkened depths of depravity—hellfire rises to greet us, and we welcome it with pure carnality.

Thought is lost.

Reason has fled.

Caution and fear have caught fire and burn to smoldering ash all around us.

"Oh..." My head falls back, and I moan, a sound I've never heard myself make before.

I've never found pleasure with a man—not until Arlo first touched me in the woods. And even that pales in comparison to the pulsing and tingling between my legs now.

His lips and tongue are on my breast, licking over the mound, swirling around the hard pink bud, and sucking it into his mouth. My body sinks, twitching around my center as warmth spreads and ecstasy builds through this ethereal sin.

"Yes," I encourage, the first time I've ever used that word in sex and meant it.

I want more, harder, faster.

I want every dark plea of my senses to be filled by him, fueled by him.

He tenses around me, his grip tightening, his lips falling away from my nipple as he takes in a rasping breath. "Come for me," he groans. "Punish me with your pleasure, starlight."

His fingers find my hair, curling and fisting a lock in his grip. He tugs my head back sharply, and I whimper as my chin shoots toward the ceiling. His thick lips brush lightly across my throat, the soft touch contrasting the rough way he keeps my head angled with the ferocity of his grip.

"Come, Mercy…" He trembles against me. "Now. Come now."

This would be the moment I'd fake it in service—not that it's common for men to want the pleasure of the women who service them, though sometimes they like it. But the way Arlo commands it—*no*, the way he *begs* for it—lassoes around me and tugs deep through my core. Leaning back, rocking my hips in this steady rhythm, forces him against a perfect spot inside me that pulses and swells, making me feel like boiling lava slowly rising inside the mountain.

His thumb sweeps softly over my nipple before pinching it in his fingers. He rolls it as he flattens his tongue, running it heavily over my skin from the hollow of my throat to the tip of my chin.

It sets off the explosion within me, and I erupt from my center, waves of heat pulsing through me as pure bliss ripples between my legs. My lips part to gasp through the wave of ecstasy. I barely notice the pain of him tugging on my hair harder, craning my neck deeper.

I can feel him swell inside me, and the thought of him coming with me touches my cheeks through a smile as my pleasure breaks. "Come with me," I whisper toward the ceiling as my twitching body stills.

He releases my hair so fast that my head wobbles, but he steadies it quickly with his hand, cradling the back of my head in his palm as the other grips my hip. He lowers me to my back in a rush, and I turn my gaze to him, trying to meet his eyes, suddenly excited, hopeful, somehow even wistful at the thought of him taking me this way…at the thought of him taking control to spur his release.

But his eyes don't meet mine, and his cock slips out. The sudden absence feels as overwhelming as if he'd torn a piece of my flesh from my body just to watch me bleed.

He drags himself away, scrambling unsteadily to his feet, cock still hard and proud, with a bead of liquid settled at the tip in anticipation of release.

He doesn't come back to fuck me.

He doesn't do anything to relieve himself.

Instead, he forcefully shoves his rigid length back into his pants, zipping and buckling with the most pained expression I've ever seen on a man.

"Arlo?" I don't understand what he's doing.

"Quiet. Don't speak another word to me, sinner."

Sinner.

The moment has passed.

The play and the pleasure are gone.

A deep ache settles in my chest as an unexpected longing to return to passion with him washes over me. I'd felt some peace in his arms, in the way he consumed every sense. And now the peace is gone, replaced by misery, heartache, and the dreaded fear of how limited my days truly are.

My climax was a lie.

The peace was deceptive.

He's one of the righteous collective, and I'm only a sinner to be used.

I press my legs together as he crosses to a dresser and pulls open a drawer. I shove my skirt down to cover myself and slowly sit up, then I climb to my feet. I collect my dress from the floor and hold it against my chest.

"I'll go," I mutter, moving toward the door as I pull up the straps of the chemise to cover myself.

"Stop," he hisses.

I turn to face him, but he's not looking at me; he's too busy sifting through the contents of his drawer.

"Go sit in that chair at my desk."

Shame rains down on me like a storm, and as I move to obey his command, I fear I may drown in it. I do as he asks, smoothing out my dress before lowering to sit on the wooden chair. I have a good view of the walls and the windows that frame the two sides of the desk—I almost wish I could see the view beyond them, but the curtains are drawn.

I hear him move around me, behind my back. My heartbeat quickens as he walks past me, going into the bathroom. Moments later, he returns, coming over to where I sit, stopping at my back. I can't seem to steady my breathing, my chest heaving out of control.

I hear him sigh as he lets out a heavy breath, and it's like an ancient monster breathing fire over me. When I feel his bare fingers gather the strands of my hair, the heat dissipates as a frigid breeze of warning combs through them.

His breaths are heated and heavy, blowing out a mixture of residual longing, prolonged aching, and rising anger. "You've gotten inside my head, sinner. You've made me lose control of myself, and it's time I take it back."

chapter twenty-one

ARLO

EVERY INCH OF me is screaming in pain, and I welcome it.

After losing myself to this dark demon of lust disguised as bright white light, I need the ache of denial. But fuck, how I want the release. I want to bend her over the bed and destroy what's left of her, then put her back together with mind-numbing pleasure.

Sweet sin, the way she came undone.

It did something to me—something that must be undone immediately.

She's a sinner, and she's meant to die.

I slowly comb my fingers through her white-blonde hair, taking my time to loosen the tangles my fisted grip created. I'm so intently aware of each shuddering breath she takes as she sits as still as a statue in the very chair where I sit to write my poetry—where I sit to write poems about *her.*

I begin to plait her long, luxurious hair. She turns her head in confusion to ask me what I'm doing, but I stop her.

"Face forward."

She stills, forcing out an anxious breath.

"There's something dangerous about you, Mercy. Something bright and dark all at once."

"I don't understand—"

"You've brought me into sin with you. I can accept my failings. I'll suffer the pain of denial and beg God for forgiveness for my loathsome indulgences outside of service. And I'll be forgiven because you tempted me, because you're a servant and you drove me to this. In the eyes of God and my community, this is all *your* fault."

"You're a hypocrite," she mutters. "All of you are."

I give a sharp tug on the end of her braid, eliciting a yelp. "So says the sinner. You've always been rebellious."

"Why will your sins be forgiven and mine won't?"

I tie off the end of her braid with a short length of twine that I pulled from my dresser drawer. The view of the coarse rungs wrapped around her starlight hair sends a shudder through my spine that makes my cock painfully throb. I stifle a groan as I work to loosen the braid at the base of her neck, flattening out the strands.

"Because your sins were your choice, and your temptation brought me to mine."

"You're unbelievable!" she snaps, trying to rise to her feet, but I shove her back down in the seat with a firm hand on her shoulder. "You *chose* this as much as I did. You let me fuck you, commanded me to come."

I tug on her hair again, forcing her chin up, craning her neck back far enough that she can look at me when I bend over her. "Because you *knew* I didn't purge and came here with the intent to tempt me anyway. Don't lie to yourself and pretend you didn't know exactly what you were doing. You used your body to get what you wanted, to spare Delle."

Her cheeks flush pink with fury as she fumes at me, nostrils flaring. But I've successfully managed to shut her up. I release her, and she whips her head forward with a huff.

"This...these starlight strands of hair...you must have been colored by demons, painted bright white to mimic the heavens as a lure for men. This temptation is too great."

Her chest heaves with fury, but her voice is lowered to a harsh whisper. "And now you blame my hair for your failure."

I pull the scissors I had collected from the bathroom from my back pocket. An unexpected tremor shakes through me as I grip them and open them, prepared to cut. She's not even aware that I'm holding them. Not even aware that I'm going to cut her fucking hair because it calls to me like a siren's song.

I bring the scissors to the base of her neck where I've loosened and flattened her braid. I spread the scissors open wide and hover them over the strands. I take in a steadying breath and shut my eyes for a beat as indecision washes over me.

Yet, I know I have to do it.

To save my tempted soul, I have to do it.

Snip.

I cut a chunk at the base of her neck.

She gasps, startles, tries to turn as her hands fly up to her skull. "What're you—"

I place my other palm on the top of her head to keep her still, and with forced determination, I *snip, snip, snip* my way across the line of her shoulders. Each snip echoes, slicing through the quiet room, a horrifying sound I feel rip through my chest, cutting me with regret.

Yet, I continue.

"Stop!" She wiggles, fighting against my grip which presses down on her head.

I cut all the way across, from shoulder to shoulder, and her braid drops free, tumbling to the floor in a heap.

"No!" she cries as I let go.

I bend to grab the fallen braid as she leaps from the seat, whirling around to face me as her hands reach behind her for the hair I now hold as a severed braid in my hand.

"Why did you *do* that?" Her expression is a mix of sadness, shock, and horror—you'd think I'd cut off a limb by the look of her face.

And it kind of feels like I did.

"If temptation is brought to man outside of service, the temptation must be removed," I quote the Impulse Edict, the documentation of the doctrine we follow in Ember Glen.

"My hair…" she gapes at me, "you cut my hair."

"I removed a temptation."

"You haven't removed *anything*!" She stomps forward, pressing into my space. "You're *horrible*," she spits. Her hands slam to my chest and she shoves me back. "You're *disgusting*. I hate you!"

I'm struck by her words. They physically pang as they hit my heart, forcing me to take another step backward. I swallow an odd lump that rises sharply in my throat.

She turns from me and stomps toward the door, and though I could let her leave—*perhaps I should let her leave*—I know I can't. I won't. I refuse to let her walk out that door right now, lest she do something phenomenally stupid. She might be hurt enough in this moment to break her promise and share our secret sin.

I slam the scissors and her braid down on my desktop and charge after her. I reach her just as she reaches the door. I circle her wrist with my hand, then tug and twist her around before slamming her back against the door. I pin her with my body, my cock aching, my heart hurting.

Looking down at her, I see tears in her eyes and note that the beauty of her hasn't relinquished at all with the length of her hair gone. I cut it just above her shoulders, but the choppy line of what's left still shines like starlight, still begs for me to touch its silky smoothness.

She holds my gaze with anger for a moment, but then a sob overtakes her, and her chin drops.

I don't know what to do.

Before I can decide, my arms move to encircle her, pull her away from the door, hugging her close. She pulls back, fighting against my arms, but I tighten my grip. I hold her until her fighting relents and she lets go, shedding her tears, burying her face against my chest. Her tears coat my bare skin, and I swear it feels like they're boiling, burning my skin…

It feels like the punishment I deserve.

No.

She's the temptation. She's the sinner.

I grip her shoulders and turn, pushing her backward as I rush forward with her to the dresser. I open the top drawer and remove a length of rope I normally only use on servants during nights of purging.

"No," she cries as I turn to her, gripping it in one hand and wrapping it around my palm. She takes a step back as I rush her, but she's not quick enough. "Don't!"

I shove her back toward the bed and force her to sit on the edge. I grip her wrist and lasso the rope around it, quickly tying a solid knot to secure it firmly. She swings her free arm at me with a closed fist, punching cleanly into the side of my stomach. Her fist pounds painfully into my flesh and I flinch, my body jerking away.

She stands, trying to make a run for it. Though the hit took me off guard, and my hand slips down the length of rope, I quickly recover, clamping my hand around the coarse twine and tugging. Her tied arm jerks back, dragging her entire body with it, and she tumbles into me. I grab hold of her and toss her onto the bed. I reach for her hips, twisting her body until she's laying back on the pillow.

I keep one foot planted on the floor as I lift the other knee over her body. She thrashes beneath me, bucking against my still hard cock, sending painful shockwaves throughout my entire body. I grit my teeth against the desire I still hold for her, my jaw tensing as I fight my lust.

God help me.

Tugging the rope, I tie the free end around the bed post. I manage to secure it entirely while she fights me. Once it's secured, I shift my weight back and huff out a breath of exhaustion from the struggle. The moment I take that pause, she reaches up with her untied hand, and slaps me across the cheek.

My head turns against the impact, hair falling across my brow. I snatch her wrist and slam it to the pillow above her head, then do the same with the other, thankful I left enough slack to be able to do so. Her now short hair fans out behind her head, the platinum strands looking more like a halo than the remnants of my temptation.

Yet the temptation still exists.

It's when she spits at me that the demon within her reveals itself. I feel it taking hold of me as my cock thickens dangerously. I can nearly envision her seductive tresses re-growing before my eyes in the way the tattered strands fan out around her. I can almost see them lifting ethereally from the bed and wrapping around me, taking hold of me, forcing me to devolve in depravity.

But the vision is only in my mind. Beneath me is just a sinner—a broken woman possessed by some demon of the mind, who twists her thinking and forces her to take everyone around her to the depths of hell in her seduction.

Not everyone around her…*just me.*

She's crafted from sin, born of the deviances and temptations I've struggled with since I was old enough to purge, since the age of sixteen.

She's my own personal demon...and I think I deserve her torment.

BY THE TIME I've taken the coldest shower of my life and willed my throbbing cock to deflate, Mercy has calmed herself to stillness, though she still huffs with seething breaths. I forcibly tugged the covers from beneath her and tucked her into my bed before climbing in beside her, leaving ample space between us.

I need a good night's rest, and so does she. Rest will give us both some clarity over what occurred here tonight. I need the clarity because I have no idea what has transpired between us or why it's happened.

Moments of frustrated silence pass in the dark as we both lie on our backs, staring up at the ceiling.

"I'll try," I tell her quietly.

I hear her head move against the pillow as she turns it in my direction. "What?"

"You wanted to take on Delle's burden, and I'm telling you that I'll try. I'll bring it to my brothers and let you make your case. But it's not the nature of the Trials of Dissension to allow one to take on another's burden, especially when she chose to participate. It defeats the purpose entirely. Don't get your hopes up."

She's quiet for a minute before she asks, "Why would you do that for me?"

"Perhaps there's a part of me that thinks Delle should be forgiven for choosing so impulsively. That maybe she should be given guidance and redirection, rather than endure this torture for a chance at a life that's really no chance at all."

"Is there any part of you that thinks I should be forgiven for my impulsive decision to run?"

Maybe.

I harden my voice, though my instinct is to speak softly. "After what transpired here tonight? No. You're the worst kind of sinner, Mercy. You're the kind of rebel who inspires rebellion in others."

"Are you saying I inspired you to rebel?"

"I'm saying you inspire sin."

"Call it rebellion or call it sin, but either way you say it, it's admission that you and I were the same for a moment tonight."

I bring my hands up, linking fingers behind my head, elbows jutted out and resting on the pillow. She's not wrong. It's bothersome that she's right, because it makes me like her—even if it was just for weakened moments, even if it was her fault for inspiring my desire with her sinful intent.

"A moment of weakness isn't a pattern worthy of punishment," I tell her.

She scoffs, tugging against the rope around her wrists—I'd had to secure both to the bedpost—and the wooden headboard creaks. "A man's moment of weakness should be as equally punishable, and it's disgusting that it's not."

I can't help but chuckle. "What the devil *are* you, Mercy Madness?"

I hear her sigh, and she speaks calmly. "I don't know what I am; I don't know who I am. But I know I don't belong here in Ember Glen."

"There's nowhere else for you to be. Ember Glen is the only safe place in the world."

"Then perhaps I should be glad I'll be dead soon."

The resignation in her voice is alarming, and it creeps over my skin with the vibration of warning bells. Truly, I don't know how else I would expect her to view her impending doom—it's just the clarity in her acceptance that stabs between my ribs, slicing right through my aching heart.

There's nothing else to say. There is no logic or reason I can counter her statement with. Perhaps she should be glad she'll be dead soon because it's so clear she doesn't belong here—and there's truly nowhere else in the world for her to go.

But what's most bothersome is the fact that I'm not glad for it. I'm not glad that this sinner will meet the fate she deserves. And that's a fact I can't reconcile in my mind.

chapter twenty-two

Mercy

"DELLE DESERVES ANOTHER chance," I plead my case before the members of the Control and the Elders on screen in the dark courtroom. "As the authority of this community, you should be guiding our youth, especially those who serve. Her decision to participate in the Trials of Dissension was impulsive, made after a particularly brutal first night of service. Her decision was a mistake. Not one of you here is above making mistakes. You may think I'm different because I'm a sinner, but at the end of the day, we're all human."

I don't know whether my words hold meaning to them, whether they'll understand my thoughts and their intentions, whether their minds are capable of the same level of rationality and compassion that I pride myself in having. I know they all think my thoughts are irrational, but they're wrong.

I know they are—they must be.

The heat of the spotlight shining down on me makes sweat break across my brow. The Control sits in a semi-circle in front of me, hardly visible as they're shadowed in darkness behind their black table. The courtroom is bleak, black, dark to inspire fear.

And it works.

Owen speaks first through the shadows. "No one forced Delle to volunteer to participate in the trials. In fact, we discussed her fate and whether she should be *forced* to participate at the same time we decided your fate, and we chose to spare her. We've already granted her leeway, and I find the tone of your argument to be presumptuous against our compassion for the people of Ember Glen."

"Agreed." Killian leans forward and folds his hands on the dark table. "I find it presumptuous and offensive. Our concern at all times is the well-being of the members of this community. It's the reason why sinners like you must be put on trial."

Wesley crosses his arms over his chest, leaning back deeper into the shadows that further darken his already dark skin. "This is a waste of our time." He turns his head, looking at Arlo at the end of the table. "You've got your hands full with these mouthy wards."

Arlo glances at Wesley, giving a small smirk from the corner of his mouth, though it falls away quickly. He says nothing, then turns his attention back to me, watching quietly.

"I've said this from the beginning," Theo speaks up, "Delle deserves another chance. But even I can't deny the fact that she *volunteered* to participate. No one forced her hand, Mercy. It was her choice, regardless of whether it was the right one."

"It was the wrong choice," I speak boldly. "It was her moment of weakness. That night of service where she ran was brutal. A servant died. Any new servant would be terrified of serving again."

"It was brutal," Owen says, "I'll give you that. But every full moon brings the potential for that level of brutality in service. It's the entire point. We purge our impulses when the moon is brightest and we're all at our celestial worst. Delle knew that before she served. She was trained."

"But you can't train the humanity from a person." My voice rises in agitation, and I take a deep breath to calm myself. "No sixteen-year-old girl can be truly mentally prepared for that. And she's certainly not mentally prepared for the trials. She doesn't understand what she's volunteered for. She doesn't *want* to participate. She was scared, she saw a way out, and she took it." We all know it was never really a way out, but who could've expected Delle to understand that? "I want to take the burden for her. Let me right her wrongs. Double my burden, and let my efforts absolve her of her sins."

"Mercy," Clyde speaks from the projection on the wall behind me, and I whirl around to face the three Elders, anxious for turning my back on the collective Control. "I'm sure you realize how absurd it is that you're standing here before us, asking for a favor. You're not in God's good graces, and we don't hold you in ours."

"Absurd, indeed," Edgar agrees on screen. "We could've burned you at the stake like your mother, but we've granted you this chance at absolution from the compassion within our hearts. And here you are, standing before us, asking us to change the rules because you think you understand something about humanity that we don't?"

"We hold the secrets of God as the Elders of this community," Clyde says. "We are the keepers of the Impulse Edict. We know what God wants for Ember Glen, and you know *nothing*."

Chair legs scrape against the floor behind me, and I turn to see Killian slowly stand, buttoning his black blazer. "I think we've all heard enough from you, Mercy. You had your time, now kindly leave us so we can pretend to discuss your ridiculous request."

I have to try one more time. "I just want to—"

"*Enough*," Killian snaps and it startles me. He stretches his arm toward the door, pointing his finger. "Out."

I glance at Arlo, our eyes catching for a moment. Then he leans back in the chair, shrouding himself in shadow, hiding from me. Defeated, I nod slowly, then make my way to the door.

I WAIT IN the foyer, pacing across the starburst-patterned tile for another fifteen minutes before they've finished their meeting in the courtroom. I know it didn't go over well, and I don't expect they'll return a result in my favor, but I still have hope. I had to try.

I stop my pacing abruptly, landing perfectly on the center of the sun, as I hear the courtroom door click open from down the nearby hallway. The sound of male voices filters out and moves closer.

Killian is the first one out, and he pauses for a moment as his eyes land on me, the corner of his mouth quirking up with a sneer that makes me feel terribly uncomfortable. His eyes scan me from top to bottom before he moves again, crossing from the hallway into the foyer and heading in my direction.

Wesley and Owen follow close behind him as they all move toward me. They hardly veer as they approach, and my shoulders tense as I pull my arms close to my sides, shrinking myself to take up less space. But they still come in far too close as they brush past, heading for the staircase at my back.

"See you soon, sinner," Killian mutters, his shoulder bumping mine as he passes.

"Looking forward to that first trial," Wesley says at the same time.

Park and Ryker aren't far behind, sharing their whispers of warning, which make anxiety wash over me. All their words whirl around me like a tornado of dark promises for the upcoming trial, and suddenly, I worry that standing before them today has prompted them to hate me all the more. Their hatred will, in turn, prompt more brutality when it comes to the trials.

Have I just worsened my fate while trying to spare Delle's?

Five of them are on the staircase and climbing when Theo appears from the hallway. He comes close and stops just beside me, moving in so the front of his shoulder touches the front of mine.

The softness in his brown eyes catches me by surprise before he leans in to whisper, "Thank you for trying. I mean it." He looks sad—sadder than I've ever seen. Yet the gratitude he has for me is humbling…heartwarming.

He and I haven't interacted much outside of service, but we've spent enough time during those purges that we grew something akin to friendship—however shallow it was, it existed, nonetheless. And he was always happy, always joyful and enthusiastic. I sense none of that now as our gaze meets, and it aches in my chest for him.

He gives me a tight smile before walking away, heading up the stairs behind his brothers. I sigh as he passes, but when I raise my eyes again, I see Arlo coming toward me.

My pulse quickens, and though I want to believe it's from the anxiety over waiting to hear what they've decided, I know it's not. I know it because I feel that swirl of wanting through my belly as my eyes drop to take him in.

The black sleeves of his button-down are rolled up to the elbows, revealing the lines of sinew in his forearms that draw my gaze to his large, gloved hands. His fingers clench and unclench, mirroring the anxiety I feel. I almost feel like the sinner they claim me to be when my eyes sweep lower to see the outline of his length beneath his perfectly ironed black slacks. When we meet in the center of the sun, my heartbeat stops altogether.

I blink up at him expectantly, tucking both sides of my newly shortened hair behind my ears. "What did they say?"

"The answer is no," he says flatly, his blue eyes scanning my face, "which was to be expected."

My chest sinks as I let out a drawn-out breath, feeling deflated, defeated. My head drops, knowing that I tried, but I failed. I failed to save Delle.

Arlo's fingertips tap beneath my chin, lifting my head and forcing me to look up at him. When I do, he moves his fingers to tug the hair from behind my ears. It's a clear assertion of his authority over me, a reminder that he cut my hair, that he controls me.

"I think there's something to be said about the fact that you tried," he says quietly, almost a whisper. "Perhaps absolution will find you yet."

He says the words with such earnest that they breeze right through me, blowing gentle embers of the fire from within him to brush against my soul, threatening to spark a fire I can't control. I hate the way it feels because of how much I love it, how much I crave it, how much I need it.

My head tilts against his fingers lingering beside my ear, and for a moment—just a brief, perfect moment—he opens his palm to cradle my cheek. And for that moment, I feel comforted.

But the moment is gone just as quickly. He blinks, eyes flickering and drawing him back to reality. I see the remembrance of who we are and where we're standing rush back in to the flush of his cheeks as he jerks his hand away and steps back.

"Come," he says, brushing past me toward the stairs.

Though I know he only means for me to follow, the alternative meaning of the word in the context of our heated moments of sin rushes shameful wetness to my core.

I follow behind him, lifting my long, red skirt so I don't trip. "What now?"

"I need to gather some things from my room, and then we're going to take a walk."

"Where?"

"You'll know when we arrive."

"Arlo, please…tell me what's going on."

He stops suddenly on the landing, and the abruptness makes me stop just a few steps beneath. I quickly grab hold of the railing to steady myself as the sudden stop unbalances me.

His eyes narrow on me. "Warden Rainn."

I can see the distress he holds within that single look, and it seems overwhelming. He wants formalities in front of the others… maybe he wants formalities all the time.

"Warden Rainn," I start again, "what's going on?"

He turns away and starts moving down the hallway. I hasten, jogging up the last few steps and chase after him. I want to grab his arm and stop him physically, but Ryker and Park stand only a few feet past, chatting casually, and Theo is near the end of the hall, knocking on Delle's door. So, I continue to meet his pace without reaching out to touch him.

I long to touch him.

"We've wasted too much time already," he says, still walking away from me. "It's my job to prepare you—both of you—and we don't have any more time to hesitate."

"I don't understand. Will you please tell me what's going on?"

"We're going to be away for several hours," he says. "Take five minutes to attend to your personal needs, and I'll come to collect you."

Before I can say another word, he rushes to unlock his bedroom door and hurries inside. It closes behind him, and the lock engages, effectively shutting me out. The sound of another door opening draws my attention, and I turn back to see Delle's door swing open, Theo pushing past her to enter her room.

What is he doing?

He shouldn't be alone with her. He's twenty-seven years old—the same as all of the members of the Control—and she's only sixteen.

Turning on my heel, I charge after Theo. I reach Delle's door just before it shuts, slapping my palms to the wood and shoving it wide. I nearly tumble through the entry in my haste.

"Mercy?" Delle says as I move toward them.

"What are you doing in here?" I ask Theo as he turns his head to look at me.

"Not that it's any of your business, but your warden asked me to retrieve her." He then turns his head again to look at Delle. "You have five minutes to take care of your personal needs. Then we're heading out and we'll be gone for a while."

Delle looks back and forth between us. "Where are we going?"

"You'll know when we arrive," Theo replies.

"That's what Arlo said," I confirm.

"Well, that's what he told me to tell you," Theo says to Delle, then looks at me. "Does she know what you did for her? What you tried to do for her?"

Tried.

Tried and failed.

Delle looks at me. "What?"

I shake my head pointedly. "No, she doesn't. I wasn't going to say anything, Theo."

He gives me an appraising look and it nearly feels like acceptance. He nods slowly, and though it looks like he's going to say something, he just reaches out to pat my shoulder with a tight smile.

"Okay," he says. "Five minutes, both of you."

Theo turns to leave, but not before casting a sideways glance at Delle, giving her a much more genuine grin before leaving us alone. The door clicks shut behind him.

"How often does he come to you?" I ask her. "You don't have to let him in, Delle. He has no right to be alone with you."

"Not often," she replies, her eyes fixed to the door behind my back. She blinks and looks at me. "He's been kind, and I—"

"Delle, you can't trust any of them. Do you understand me? Not even when they're kind to you…*especially* not when they're kind to you."

"I know." She nods and casts her gaze to the floor. "I know that."

"They're not allowed to touch you outside of service. Don't let them."

"No one's touching me, Mercy." Irritation shades her tone as she lifts her head to look up at me, crossing her arms. "That's why I'm here. It's why I volunteered to participate. I don't want *anyone* touching me ever again. I'll take death before I allow it."

All of them will touch her for the first trial—whether she allows it or not. My blood runs cold at the thought, and a shiver tremors up my spine. Yet I understand what she's saying—she's chosen this fate rather than be forced to serve.

"Okay," I say softly. "I just want to make sure you're okay."

She nods a little, though I still see the frustration in her expression—teenage defiance that was once a hallmark for me before months and months of service dulled my affect. I almost want to smile at it, recognizing my former self within her. Perhaps that's why I care about her so much. Caring for her almost feels like caring for my younger self.

Fighting for her feels like fighting for me.

A few moments pass as she relinquishes slowly, bringing her arms down to her sides. "What was Theo talking about? What you tried to do for me?"

I wave my hand dismissively. "Never mind. It doesn't matter. It didn't work, anyway."

"Mercy, did you...The other day you were asking me about whether I'd let someone take the burden of the trials from me... whether I'd choose differently if I could go back. Did you try to—"

"Don't worry about it, Delle. Unfortunately for the both of us, nothing has changed." The reality of my failure strikes me hard in the chest as I speak the words out loud. It threatens to knock me down, and I step back to avoid stumbling over my emotions. "Five minutes," I remind her. "Whatever it is Warden Rainn has planned for us, it sounds like we'll be together. It will be okay."

I smile at her before turning away, and my face drops immediately, our situation sitting heavily on my shoulders.

I tried to save her, and I failed.

I tried to save myself, and I failed.

I fear the outcome of the trials will be no different.

chapter twenty-three
ARLO

I KNOCK ONCE on Mercy's door as a courtesy before letting myself in. She stands at her window, gazing out at the mountains. The first hint of sunlight I've seen all day peeks out from behind the cloud cover, shining through the window and striking her as if she had called upon it herself.

She turns her head over her shoulder to look at me, her shortened hair whipping around her face like sparkling strands of shooting stars. Cutting her hair didn't lessen the draw of her starlight tresses, it only gave them more freedom to move and draw my attention.

Yet I quickly lose sight of her hair as it falls away, the strands framing her porcelain face, blushed cheeks, and pink lips—but more than that, my gaze is drawn to her gray-blue eyes which are glassy with the sheen of tears, glistening in the sunlight which sweeps across her face.

I should remain in place, let her feel whatever it is she's feeling without interference. But the messenger bag I packed drops heavily from my shoulder to the floor, and I stride across the room before I can stop myself. She turns her head as she brings her knuckles up to swipe beneath her eyes. I stop at her back, my arms aching to reach out for her, but I clench my fists to keep them at my sides.

"You tried," I quietly tell her. "It's more than most would do in your position. There's something to be said for that."

Her hair shakes with her head. "It's not that. I mean, it *is* that, but not *only* that." She turns and starts to brush past me. "Never mind. I'm fine."

I reach out and wrap my palm around her bicep, pulling her in front of me. "You're not fine."

She sniffles and blinks and a strained tear slips out from the corner of her eye. "You said five minutes. I'm ready to go—"

"Pretend I said ten minutes. Talk to me."

Her expression flickers, eyebrows dipping toward her delicate nose. "Why?"

"Because it's clear that you're going through something, and you need to talk about it."

Her head jerks back and irritation creeps through her features. "Going through something? Obviously, I'm going through something. I'm going through *everything*. My life is over. It's coming to a close and all for what? Because I've questioned? Because I've wondered? Because I ran to avoid a painful death? It's all wrong... everything is wrong, and I've never felt so afraid—" her voice breaks. "I've never felt so alone. I've never felt so lonely."

Her tears break free, and she brings her hand up to cover her mouth as she tries to hold them back, but the way it strains through her body to resist the purging of her emotions is something I can feel throbbing in my chest, in sync with the beating of my heart.

Before I know what I'm doing, my arms encircle her and tug her against me. Her hands land on my chest and push, but I tighten my embrace, holding her against me until her sob breaks free and her body goes limp in my arms. And then she cries, dropping her face against my chest, her hands fisting my shirt.

My heart pounds, pulse races, breaths quicken with the swirl of emotions that sweep into a tornado within me. Holding her while she cries makes me feel equally vulnerable and safe—like I'm home and free to exist in my feelings without the mask of authority I'm always expected to maintain.

A sinner shouldn't make me feel that way.

I sigh, allowing myself a moment to relinquish control and feel her. I know immediately it's a mistake...because she feels like something I'll struggle to let go of.

And I know I'll have to let go of her.

I count to twenty in my mind, granting us both that much time to exist in this state. And then I let go, steeling myself, hardening my shell, separating myself from her emotions.

Why do her emotions feel like my own?

I clear my throat, release her, and turn away. I walk toward the door and bend to pick up my messenger bag. "Dry your eyes, sinner. Let's go."

"Where are we going?"

"Somewhere I can prepare you for the first trial."

I COLLECT DELLE and Theo and lead them all back to the courtroom downstairs. Inside the dark room, there's a concealed doorway, hidden behind the table where the Control sits for judgment.

I lead Mercy, Delle, and Theo through the door—one that all the Control knows about—and down the hidden staircase. The first set of steps are wooden, and they creak as we descend. At the bottom, our feet touch stone, and on our right is another set of steps. These are carved from stone, created from the natural bedrock that lies beneath the Homestead. This is where wooden, man-made structures disappear, and natural rock supersedes.

I light a torch at the stone landing before leading us down the next set of steps—a long staircase that takes us down, down, down into the depths beneath the Homestead. At the bottom is a long, narrow pathway, and I lead us through the twisting corridor. The ceiling is low and rock walls surround us with dark, damp grayness as we make our way deeper into the darkness.

"Is this safe?" I hear Delle ask from somewhere behind me. "Where are we going?"

"Somewhere that we won't be interrupted or watched."

"Or listened to," Theo adds from the rear of our line. "Somewhere with privacy."

"Privacy," Mercy echoes him with a sarcastic tone. "I haven't known privacy since I was brought here."

The torchlight casts an orange glow around us, leading us with flickering light and heat.

"We're granted privacy for the purpose of trial preparation," I tell them. "It's in the Impulse Edict."

"A serious question for you, Warden Rainn," Mercy says. "How would one know it's in the Edict?"

"The Elders tell us." They're the guardians and interpreters of the Impulse Edict, and we rely on them to guide our community based on the written word of God. What we know of the Edict is what has been told to us by each generation of Elders. The only fully documented version of the Edict is in their care.

"And you just presume that the Elders always tell the truth?" Mercy asks.

"You're quite bold for a servant trapped in a cave," I tell her.

She chuckles. "I'm not a servant; I'm a *sinner*."

A smile spreads across my cheeks at her banter, as she throws my own words from previous conversations back at me.

"Is that where we are?" Delle asks. "In a cave?"

"Nearly," Theo says. "These underground tunnels lead to a cave system that runs through the mountains."

"We're going to the mountain?" Delle asks with a hint of childlike wonder in her tone.

I remember the first time I was brought through these tunnels and shown the caverns. It was shortly after I moved into the Homestead my first year as a member of the Control two years ago.

I was filled with wonder, too, and my mind overflowed with poetry depicting the beauty of the Earth. I was filled with awe over God's creation, and the fact that I was chosen to be one of the few to bear witness to it.

Perhaps I should feel bad that a sinner is allowed to see it now, except I don't. It somehow feels okay that she sees it, it feels right. Perhaps a part of me hopes that seeing it will trigger her sense of awe and return her lost reverence for God and his creation.

A ten-minute walk through winding tunnels brings us to a wide open cavern. Towering high above our heads, stalactites hang from the ceiling as pointed cones of natural rock pointing down at us. The solid rock beneath our feet creates a flat, winding path through the same coned rocks that jut up from the ground surrounding us in rows and clusters of stalagmites.

Between the points of hanging stalactites and rising stalagmites is vast, open space, and it's filled with nothing but echoing darkness. It's eerie and ethereal all at once, and it never ceases to take my breath away.

"Oh…" Mercy breathes out the sound of wonder on a sigh, and I somehow feel relief in knowing she sees the same beauty I see here.

"This is incredible," Delle's small voice echoes with excitement.

"It is," I agree.

I lead us along a flat, narrow path of bedrock that years of men traversing have flattened out neatly between stalagmites. The flat path leads us across the open cavern to another tunnel, and a sharp turn to our right stops us in front of a large boulder.

Only the boulder isn't real.

I hand the torch to Theo, grip the false rock with both hands, and easily slide it sideways. Behind it is an opening to a space I've often retreated to be alone with my thoughts.

"Follow me," I tell them, taking the torch back from Theo and ducking my head to creep into the short tunnel.

A few steps take me into the grotto, a carved-out space as large as my bedroom and as dark as night. My torchlight sets a glow that allows me to circle the space, finding the three torches I'd fixed to the rock walls a long time ago, lighting each in turn. Two at the sides, one at the back, and a fourth spot at the front wall where I place the torch I carried in with me.

The space is dimly lit from the firelight with a shadowed, flickering glow. As Mercy makes her way inside, turning to reach behind her to help Delle through the small opening, her short tresses still shine as brightly as the stars.

What demon is within her that calls to me so loudly?

I drop my messenger bag and crouch to my haunches to open it, pulling out several lengths of coarse rope and drop them heavily onto the rock floor.

"What's that for?" Mercy asks behind me.

I stand and turn to face her. "Preparation. It's the reason I've brought you here." I look at Theo. "The reason *we've* brought you here."

Mercy's head inclines as she looks at me pensively. "Preparation for the trials?"

"The first trial," I confirm with a nod.

Staring down at the rope, she fidgets with her hair, dragging her fingers through the ends as if she could still stroke the phantom length I cut. Then she hugs herself, her eyes telling me that she's trying to retreat. Delle sucks in a quick, shaky breath just behind her, and it snaps Mercy from her retreat. She lets go of herself and reaches her arm back, turning her head over her shoulder to find Delle's hand and grabs hold of it.

It's bewildering the way the demon in her mind relents and allows her compassion for Delle. Perhaps Mercy's compassion is simply so strong that no devil or demon could overpower it. The thought stirs a flurry of extra beats through my heart.

I clear my throat and pull back my shoulders to stand a little taller. "I've been tasked with binding you for the trial. I think it's fair that we have some practice with what that's like beforehand."

Mercy takes a step back, pushing Delle behind her as she moves. "We're not meant to endure a trial twice. I won't allow you to bind us here."

"You will allow it if you want to be prepared." I try to appeal to her protectiveness of Delle. "You'll allow it so Delle will know what to expect and won't panic in the moments before her trial begins."

Mercy watches me discerningly, her eyes scouring my form from top to bottom, as if she can assess all my intentions—good and bad—with a single glance. Perhaps she can, but she'll find no bad intentions here.

"Tell me your plan then," she says carefully. "What do you mean to do to us here?"

"I mean to bind you with rope, to show you how you'll be bound for use in the trial, and give you a chance to prepare your mind for endurance through limited movement and the inability to escape of your own free will. I mean to help you prepare, as I said."

"And why is Theo here for this?" she asks me. "You're our warden."

"That's something we need to discuss."

"So discuss it, then. I assure you that you have our attention."

"To avoid exhausting my brothers, you'll be participating in the first trial simultaneously."

Her nostrils flare with a touch of anger. "We most certainly wouldn't want to exhaust your brothers while they defile us."

Something like a whimper escapes from Delle, and the small sound makes something resembling shame tick through my heart for a beat. It passes quickly with the next beat, though, because I know my God—I enforce His Edict, and I will do His will in these trials.

"Collectively, it's been decided that you'll be placed in two separate rooms to ensure the validity of your experiences."

Mercy stares. "You're going to have to explain that one to me."

"The trials are an individual endeavor, and this one is meant to try your ability to endure the passionate needs of men with your flesh. On your own, and without support or encouragement. You should consider this to be a good thing, Mercy. You won't have to witness Delle's trial."

"And I won't be able to support her, now, will I?"

"Tell me when you've ever supported another servant on a night beneath the full moon. Service relies on the individual—"

"And the collective," she interrupts me. "Without my sisters in service, there wouldn't be enough to fulfill the needs of all the men in Ember Glen."

"True, but this trial doesn't require you to serve the needs of *all* men. It requires you to serve the needs of *seven*." Slowly, I step toward her. "In a way, you've won your case with my brothers."

Creases form on her brow in confusion. "What do you mean?"

"They're angry with you, Mercy. They were already angry with you for your sins and your pattern of rebellious thinking over your years of service. Perhaps it's my fault for letting you speak your case in Delle's favor today, but they feel insulted by the speech you gave asking to take on her burden. And the way they speak about taking out their aggressions on you in the trial, the way they speak about giving you what you deserve, means that their time and attention will mostly be focused on you."

I watch her face fall as I speak, fear creeping through her features, though she tries to force a determined expression to hide it.

"With your trials taking place simultaneously," I continue, "they'll give you their worst, and Delle will be an afterthought. The anger you inspired in them today may very well have spared Delle the worst of them in this first trial."

Even in the dark, I can see her throat bob as she swallows, quickly steeling herself as her shoulders pull back. "Good. Fine. That's what I wanted."

"Is it?"

She hardens her expression. "Yes. I wanted to take Delle's burden, and I'll take as much of it as they'll give. Let them be angry with me if it should spare her their depravity."

I nod, crossing my arms. "Good. Because they'll give you a mountain of depravity in your seven-hour trial, which will take place a few days before the next full moon."

"And you think you can prepare us for that?"

I drop my arms to the sides. "I can't do anything to prepare you to fulfill the lustful desires of my brothers, as sexual acts are forbidden outside of service." I cast a wayward glance at Theo, a natural movement of my eyes as I feel caught in a lie—no one can know of the things I've done with Mercy. "But I can mentally prepare you to endure the entrapment of being bound for hours and hours." I take a step forward. "Now, will you let me help you?"

Mercy blinks, holding my gaze, and though the light is dim and constantly flickering, I can see the thoughts swirling behind her eyes.

It's Delle who speaks, looking over at Theo. "Why are you here? What do you have to do with this?"

"The Control have decided that Arlo has his hands full with Mercy. They're concerned about her continued rebellion and what she might inspire in others during the trials. They don't want Arlo's attention divided, and they asked for another volunteer to be your warden," Theo says. "I volunteered."

Delle's eyebrows lift. "You're my warden now?"

Theo nods, shoving his hands into his pockets. "Yes. It means I'll be responsible for you during your trial—binding you, suspending you, adjusting the ropes to ensure your safety. I need to learn from Arlo. I don't want to hurt you, Delle. That's why we need to practice this. It's why I'm here, to learn."

"Okay," Mercy says, "then prepare us." She looks squarely at Theo. "But please remember that Delle is a *child*. I don't care what the Edict says about her age and her ability to serve, you will mind her with care in this preparation. Do you understand me?"

"I understand that you're a sinner, Mercy, and your words hold no meaning here. What you need to understand is that I have no intention of harming Delle. I don't have to be here; I don't have to learn how to bind her safely. I don't have to do any of this. So, if you think for a second that my intentions with her are malicious, then you're *wrong*. I volunteered to help her."

"I don't trust anyone's intentions, Theo," Mercy replies quietly, "not even yours."

"You don't have to trust me," he replies, "but maybe you should trust her to speak for herself."

Mercy looks at Delle over her shoulder, who meets her eyes and gives her a small smile and a grateful nod. "It's okay, Mercy. I chose this, remember? And I want to try. I know you think it's hopeless, but I want to try to pass these trials. I need you to let me do that."

I can feel the conflict within Mercy pulsing from her soul. She wants to protect Delle, but I think even she knows that she can't—not really. She bobs her head in understanding and side-steps away, letting Delle step forward beside her.

"All right then," Mercy says. "Let's prepare."

chapter twenty-four

Mercy

IN AN UNEXPECTED act of kindness, Arlo lays a soft blanket on the floor for each of us. I watch as he spreads them out and backs away, curious for all the unknown thoughts in his confusing mind.

Every time I think I have him figured out, he changes my mind. Sometimes—most of the time—I hate him. He's my warden, the man who judges me as a sinner, the same as the rest of Ember Glen. He's the man who cut my treasured hair as punishment for stirring lust within him. He's a man who will never understand me.

But other times I look at him and my heart skips a beat, my stomach clenches in shameful attraction, and my fingers twitch with the ache to sink into his hair. He confuses me, and though it's frightening, it's also exciting.

"Kneel," he says, turning away to grab rope from the rock floor, untangling a stretch of it and handing it to Theo.

Delle complies, moving to the center of the square blanket laid out in front of her and lowers to her knees. Her compliance is a learned behavior. Regardless of the fact that she ran from her duty on her first night in service, the same as me, her entire life leading up to that moment had taught her to obey—submission is what we were trained for.

A memory sweeps through me, capturing me in a trauma I'd rather tuck back into the dark corner in my mind. Interacting with Delle has brought me so many recollections of my teenage years.

Here in the darkness of this cave, the recollections come so vividly, taking me back to one of my worst memories when I was only fourteen years old.

The Control entered our classroom unexpectedly that day and stood before our rows of desks at the front of the room in a menacing line. I remember them standing with such authority, dressed in tailored clothes that matched the sharp, pressed lines of their expressions perfectly.

Back then, the seven men who made up the Control were older. Arlo and his cohorts only came into authority two years ago, when they were twenty-five. When I was fourteen, the men comprising the Control were forty-six, nearing the end of their reign. Their age and experience only served to make them more intimidating.

When the Control stood before our class, one of our three teachers announced that they had come to assess our progress. I was surly as I leaned back, slouching in my chair, arms folded across my chest with an angry stare.

I didn't want to be assessed. We'd been learning about the male anatomy and the tenants of oral pleasure over the last several days, and I was disgusted by it, indignant that I should ever have to put my mouth on that part of a man. I couldn't comprehend why they would want such a thing if they could use my cunt just as easily.

One of the Control, whose name I can't remember, stepped forward. He was a forty-six-year-old man with silver strands streaking his thick black hair. He asked who would be willing to demonstrate their learning by serving him.

I'd scoffed, but every girl in the room shot their hands up high and fast into the air. They were eager to serve, eager to please, eager to serve God in their duty before their time in service even began.

Slowly, I'd lifted my palm and held it just in front of me. I didn't want to raise my hand at all, but I knew if I didn't, my teachers would scold me and beat me. My bottom was still red, welted, and sore from the last beating I'd taken for my attitude.

I'd turned my gaze away from the Control, disturbed by their wandering eyes and darkened gazes as they looked at my sisters. My stomach had turned in sick knots, and I'd prayed I wouldn't be called upon that day.

Relief came when another name was called.

Relief fled when I realized who it was.

They'd called Cambria.

I dropped my arms and straightened in my chair while nerves prickled anxiety through my veins. I hadn't been surprised she was chosen because Cambria was the most eager. She'd practically been bouncing in her seat with her hunger to serve as her arm stretched high in the air, her fingers wiggling in excitement. She was so excited about her role in life and that she would be an honored servant of Ember Glen.

She'd found pride that she was chosen to become a servant and was eager to please God in her service.

I remember her walking to the front of the room and the way the man watched her with thirst in his dark eyes. He'd commanded her to kneel, and her excitement had been palpable as she lowered to her knees. It was the same level of excitement that had rippled through the classroom and the girls who watched with wonder and whispers and innocent giggles.

They were all eager to see their sister perform well in service, to see the flesh of a real-life man rather than just the mannequins built for our practice—all because they'd been taught this was good, that it was wonderful, that it was Godly to kneel and serve the men of our community.

I'd searched the room, hoping my eyes would land on a single girl showing any attitude other than enthusiasm. I'd found no one—only me.

I'd wondered what was wrong with me, whether I was possessed or born from hell. I'd wondered how I could become better and whether I would ever be able to find joy in service. I'd tortured myself, wondering why I couldn't just be like everyone else.

The man at the front of the room revealed himself, sending a ripple of nervous whispers through the classroom. It had sent a ripple of nausea, stress, and fear through me. Then anger flushed out the anxiety, and it took hold of me. It possessed me, and I shoved to my feet.

"How can you be doing this now?" I'd demanded as the room fell into abrupt silence. "There is no full moon. You're only meant to purge on a full moon."

I recall the way the man stared me down with heat and fury, and the way it made me want to shrink away. But it had been the look Cambria gave me that filled me with guilt. Her look was one of annoyance, a pointed reminder that I should be quiet—and I'd known the look well. Truthfully, I wondered almost daily back then why Cambria and Ellary had remained friends with me given all the times I'd gotten myself into trouble.

"Come here," the man demanded of me, and the silent room held stagnant.

I hadn't dared a glance at my teachers. I didn't need further direction—a member of the Control had given me a command, and I had to obey above anyone else. I'd stepped out from behind my desk and slowly walked to the front of the room.

"Kneel." His hand was around his jutting erection, holding it out in front of Cambria, and I'd felt terrified at the sight of it. "Put your hand at the back of her head," he said to me, "and hold her in place. She'll want to pull away when I gag her, but she must learn to stay in place, all in the name of pleasure for the man." He looked down at Cambria. "You want to learn to do it properly, don't you?"

Cambria nodded eagerly. "Yes, of course."

"Good." He looked to me once again. "You. Do what you're

told or face consequences by my authority in Ember Glen."

Rebellion had leaked through the odd mixture of fear and anger flowing through my veins. If he'd cut me open just then, I would've bled with dissent-tainted blood. I wasn't going to lay a hand on Cambria to help this man touch her with that monstrous appendage.

"No," I told him boldly.

And in an instant, I was overcome.

The Control encircled us, lifted me from the floor, and carried me outside. While Cambria was left kneeling in the classroom to demonstrate her knowledge of oral pleasure, five men stood shoulder to shoulder and surrounded me as the sixth took my virginity outside. He fucked me against the outside wall of the school building until I bled.

That was the day I learned to keep my mouth shut.

That was the day I learned it was best to kneel.

That event, and too many others that followed, helped tame the rebellious spirit within me before I officially began service at sixteen. But over the years since then, that rebellious spirit has grown bigger without me realizing it. She grew so big that she burst at the sight of Hyatt Price and his torch chasing after her beneath the full moon, and her return made me run, made me sin.

It's not a sin.

I'm not a sinner.

Regardless, I want this preparation. I don't want to go into these trials blindly. I want to know what to expect. I want to know what it's going to feel like to be bound by Arlo Rainn.

My pulse quickens as he turns toward me, and I step forward, gripping my skirt at my knees and lifting it so I can bend. I kneel at the center of the blanket, and though the fleece fabric is soft against my skin, the hard rock beneath is instantly painful. Arlo steps in front of me, and I cast a sideways glance to observe Delle watching Theo step toward her all the same. Her eyes are downcast, palms pressed to her thighs as she takes in shallow breaths.

"It's okay, Delle," I murmur. "I'm right here with you."

She glances at me, nodding with a weak smile before taking in a steadying breath. I return my attention to Arlo and the aching rhythm of my heart. Stepping closer, he drops the rope beside my knees, then works to roll up his shirt sleeves.

"We'll start simple," Arlo says as he exposes his forearms, taut tendons drawing lines to his hands. "You'll be suspended for the trial, but we'll work our way up to that."

I lift my chin to look up at him. "You took off your gloves."

His head is still dipped as he works on his sleeve, but his eyes raise for a moment, meeting mine from beneath his lashes. The fleeting moment of connection is intense, swarming my insides with a flurry of butterflies' wings.

He doesn't offer an explanation for why he took off his gloves, though I can guess it's because they restrict his dexterity in tying rope. I wish he would speak because the way he holds my gaze without a word as he rolls his sleeve is overwhelming.

I swallow anxiously and blink, dragging my eyes from his stare before taking a deep, steeling breath. I rub my palms over my thighs, looking down at my hands as though they're interesting enough to steal my attention.

Nothing is interesting enough to steal my attention from Arlo.

"There's a stark difference between what will happen here in our preparation and what will happen to you both in the trial, and I want to be very clear about that." He pauses, his arms falling to his sides. "Here, you're in control. If you want us to stop what we're doing or untie you, we will. But for preparation's sake, I'll encourage you to push yourself past what you think is your breaking point. Because you'll have no control in the trial; none of my brothers will stop if you ask them to. No one will untie you if you demand it. The more you can push yourself to withstand excessive time in bondage, the better prepared you'll be."

Quiet settles for a moment with the weight of his words. This trial will be much like a night of service, except for the fact that we'll be bound and suspended. My choice, my will, my self-control will all be lost in a much more significant way than it ever has been in the forest. I lift my palm, absently smoothing it down the side of my shortened hair—another symbol of my lost control.

Arlo steps forward and my downcast gaze lifts slowly, grazing up the length of him so close to me, until my head is lifted high to look at him staring down at me. "You may keep your clothes on if you wish, but you'll be naked in the trial. At some point you'll want to take the opportunity to know what the rope will feel like digging into your bare flesh."

Bare flesh.

There's something sultry in the way he says the words, as if he's saying them to me, and only me…speaking them like poetry.

Inexplicably, I wish we were alone.

My lips part as he reaches out and touches my cheek with his bare hand. Skin to skin, flesh to flesh, his touch is striking against the embers of desire that linger from our last encounter.

"What will it be?" he asks.

"I won't remove my clothes, not tonight," Delle says.

The sound of her voice seems muffled, far away, too quiet to compete with the roar of my soul as Arlo's fingers slip down the side of my neck.

"Brother," Theo snaps, and his voice is loud enough to break us. "Mind your hand."

I blink from the enchantment of Arlo's touch and look over at Theo. His eyes are narrowed where Arlo's palm touches my skin before he tugs his hand away sharply.

"I know you didn't purge," Theo says to him with righteous anger in his tone, "but there is no full moon tonight. You know better than to touch a woman like that outside of service…even a sinner."

Arlo clears his throat and takes a step back. "You're right. Forgive me."

I look up at him again, but the moment is lost. He bends to grab the rope, and he doesn't meet my eyes again.

Theo's warning reminds me that Arlo has already stepped across the thin line to abuse his power with me. I should have turned him in before…I should turn him in now, though we both know the Control would deny me and believe I was lying if I did. They would side with Arlo, and not just because he's one of them—it would be because they hate me, too.

It doesn't matter because I know I wouldn't tell them, anyway. It wouldn't change my fate. And if I wasn't aware of it consciously before, I am now—the sins of the flesh we committed together gave me the only moments of true peace and pleasure I've ever known.

And I want more of it.

Wrong as it is, if I'm sentenced to die, I'll keep his secret if it means I can share a forbidden passion with him until the very end, because I want more of this overwhelming need.

I'll take this secret to my grave just so I can revel in these sinful cravings a little longer.

chapter twenty-five

Mercy

A LITTLE MORE than two weeks of preparation in bondage have passed. I've spent every third night with Arlo, Theo, and Delle in the caves, and they have been nights of abject misery with Arlo's grazing touches and secret glances.

Otherwise, he's stayed away from me, avoiding me as much as he could. I've felt the distance he puts between us. He avoids me in the hallways, and he certainly doesn't come to my room. When I go to his, he speaks from the doorway and sends me away discourteously. He ignores me at meals, his words cold and curt.

But then we go to the caves where he binds me, and I *feel* him. His essence is braided into the ropes he coils around my body. I've come to feel freer when I'm bound by him than I've ever felt running through the forest or walking among the wildflowers in the meadow.

The anticipation of it is thrilling.

Of course, the thrill is always subdued, limited by the presence of Delle and Theo.

Tonight is different. I don't know where Delle and Theo are, and Arlo leads me through the secret door in the courtroom. The two of us descend the stone steps alone and traverse the winding tunnels through the caves.

He leads me along a different path than we usually follow, taking us through corridors that require us to dip our heads from low-hanging rock, and side-step through narrow openings. Some paths we travel are frightening in the dark, but I keep my eyes on the flame of his glowing torchlight, letting the flickering orange guide me through dark shadows that threaten to close in all around me.

We duck beneath a naturally formed stone archway, then step forward. He stops, and when I try to take another step to move beside him, he sharply throws out his arm, effectively stopping me from taking another step forward.

"Careful," he says, holding his torch out ahead of us with an outstretched arm. "It's a long way down."

I lean forward, gazing out in the direction of his light. Looking down, I see the rock beneath our feet drop off into a vast darkness just a few steps ahead. When I realize how close we are to falling off the edge, it startles me, and I scurry backward toward the arched stone opening we came through.

I look over at him with confusion, and a sudden fear punches through my chest, shocking my lungs, quickening my breaths into anxious panting.

Why did he bring me here?

Why did he bring me here alone?

I look over my shoulder, but all I can see is black without the glow of the torch. I can't run from him. Even if I could see, I don't remember the path we traveled, and I'd never find my way back. I'd be lost in these tunnels forever. My palm jumps up to press over my heart, willing the pounding muscle to steady.

In the glow of his torchlight, his dimples crease as a grin I haven't seen in weeks spreads across his scruffy cheeks. "Mercy. I didn't bring you here to push you over the edge…at least, not in the way you think."

"Are you trying to frighten me?"

"I'm not trying to frighten you. There's no reason for you to be frightened. Though, I will admit, my intention is to spark adrenaline."

I blow out a breath through rounded lips. "You've succeeded."

"Good."

Arlo takes a step toward me, lifting his torch and placing it on a bracket fixed to the rock wall beside me. He drops his messenger bag and reaches out his gloved hand to me. I swallow the lump of residual fear and slowly lift my hand from my chest to drop my palm on top of his. His hand closes around mine, and he gently tugs me toward him. I take a careful step as he guides me closer, my eyes glued to my feet.

"Do you trust me?" His free hand floats up to tuck a wayward strand of hair behind my ear, and it sends a cold shiver down my spine.

"I don't know," I tell him truthfully.

"I'll need you to trust me during your trial."

"Why? It's my trial, not yours."

"It's your trial, but I'm going to look after you."

"I don't need you to...you should look after Delle, if anyone. I don't know how she's going to get through this."

"She's much stronger than you give her credit for. In any case, Theo will look after her. It's you I'm worried about."

There's a flurry of feeling in my belly, an odd sense of pride that he has concern for me at all. Then I wonder if that means he thinks I'm weak, and my brow furrows in scrutiny.

"Why are you worried about me? You don't think I'm strong?"

"I have no concerns about your strength. I've seen firsthand how powerful your mind is over the past several weeks. Your strength is impressive. It's your grit and your tenacity that worry me because you're the sinner my brothers truly want to punish. You've been so concerned over Delle that you haven't really prepared yourself for the fact that she's secondary in this. I don't want to frighten you, but you need to understand how my brothers speak of you."

"How do they speak of me?"

"With great anticipation to defile you. They have no respect for you. All you are to them is a sinner on her way to the grave." He takes in a shuddering breath. "They see you as nothing more than a shell of a human, fallen from God's good graces, a body they're meant to desecrate in His honor."

As he speaks, my heartbeat crescendos, and I imagine I can hear the sound of it echoing through the empty space in the cavern, each beat bouncing all around us. I watch the blue in his bright eyes swirl in the glow of firelight. I look for deception, for any trace of warning that he's only trying to frighten me. I see nothing but truth…truth and concern.

I'm suddenly overcome with awareness of how I've neglected myself, which was only partly intentional. I chose in many ways to put Delle's well-being ahead of my own because I'm so fearful for her and all she's going to face in these trials. I've focused on her to spare myself from fear. But I don't feel regretful about it, not in the least.

Yet I'm overcome with emotion by the reality of how I'm viewed by the Control. The truth is harsh spilling from Arlo's lovely lips in this strange, dark place. And being separated from Delle now, I can feel the weight of the truth I've been ignoring slowly lowering onto my shoulders, sitting heavily, and pushing me down.

A shell of a human…

Fallen from God's good graces…

A body they're meant to desecrate…

I draw in a trembling breath and all the emotions I've been shoving down for weeks come rushing out on the exhale. Tears well unexpectedly in my eyes, and when I blink, they slip down my cheeks as an echoing sob breaks free. I cover my face with my hands, trying to hide as the heavy reality tries to crush me with dread.

Then, Arlo's arms come around me, pulling me against his strong chest, embracing me as I cry. My tears stutter in their release at the surprise of him holding me, touching me, encircling me with warmth after enduring weeks of cold, lonely nights without companionship.

"Let me help you," he whispers.

I pull back to gaze up at him through a sheen of tears. His expression is somber, painted with compassion, and I hadn't expected it. I hadn't expected to see him looking at me the way he is right now—it shocks my heart. I nod slowly, agreeing to let him help me. Relief touches his eyes and I find it comforting.

His hands come up to grip my shoulders, and he dips his head, lowering his eyes to level with mine. "Will you let me bind you bare this time?"

I'd only gone as far as stripping to my undergarments in all our practice sessions before—not because I felt uncomfortable. Truthfully, I would have preferred to properly prepare myself for the first trial. I'd kept my underwear on because Delle and Theo were with us, because Delle was uncomfortable, unready, and I wanted her to feel safe.

Maybe I've done her an injustice in that way, neglecting to insist that she practice bare. She'll feel anything but safe in the trial, and now I worry I should've fought to prepare her more realistically.

And here I am again, neglecting myself in a moment Arlo has set aside for my own preparation. I close my eyes through a deep breath, letting Arlo's words float through my mind to remind myself that his brothers in God look forward to defiling *me*, not Delle. They only see me as the sinner who sparked Delle's rebellion.

A body they're meant to desecrate…

I shiver at the words in my mind, opening my eyes. I nod slowly, indicating that I will let him bind me in the flesh this time. I want to know what the rope will feel like on my skin when I wear it for seven hours in the trial. I want to be prepared. I want him to help me, and I have to let him.

Without saying a word, I reach behind to grip the zipper at the middle of my back, tugging it down to loosen my crimson gown. I push down the fabric at my shoulders, letting the long sleeves brush down my arms as they fall to my feet. Arlo's eyes lower to my chest as I unhook my bra, and my heart skips a beat at the way his light eyes darken—dark like the empty space of the vast open cavern beyond the flickering firelight.

I pull off the black bra, then bend to remove my boots before slipping off my underwear. As I rise, cool air swirls around me, and as it brushes across my breasts, my nipples harden into taut peaks. I find myself in sudden anticipation, wondering how it will feel to have him wrap the rope around my breasts, secretly hoping for a slip of his fingers brushing over the stiffened buds.

"Do you know how painfully beautiful you are?"

His words breeze past me, scattering in the darkness beyond.

He blinks and turns away before I can respond, moving to a spot on the rock wall a few steps away. I'm almost thankful that the darkness swallowed his words, that he turned away before I could reply. I don't know what I would say to that. I place a palm on my stomach, hoping to settle the flurry of pleasant stirrings in my gut.

I watch as Arlo takes a couple of steps toward the darkness, holding my breath in fear that he'll misstep and slip over the edge. He reaches up and my eyes follow his hands, stopping at the glint of metal as he tugs down a solid metal hoop. Lifting my gaze higher, I see there's a rock overhang there, like a ceiling from which the hoop hangs.

"I rigged it myself," he says, releasing the hoop. He's pulled it down far enough that it's visible in the firelight, the shiny metal reflecting the orange glow as it spins in a slow circle. "It's safe."

"What is it for?"

"Suspension. I'll put up a similar rigging for the trial."

I nod slowly, the darkness at the edge of the drop-off beckoning my glance, reminding me of a long fall with a painful death looming.

Arlo moves, stepping closer. "Trust me." He holds out his hand.

Mine is drawn to his like a magnet, my palm floating out instinctively to fill his. My skin tingles as my hand lands on his, and

I realize we're skin to skin—I hadn't even noticed him remove his gloves.

I've noticed the burns and scars, but I haven't asked him about them yet, and I'm not sure if I want to. I fear that knowing vulnerable details about him will grow too strong of a connection between us—a connection I'll have to let go of when I meet my death.

The connection I fear already exists.

He guides me until I'm beneath the suspended hoop, standing behind me and positioning me where he wants me with his hands on my shoulders. I lift my head to see the metal hoop slowly spin just above me. His hands leave my shoulders, and only moments later, he begins to coil rope around my body, and though it's the same as every other time he's done it before, it's entirely different.

We're alone.

I'm naked.

I'm lost in these dark caverns, standing on the edge of a cliff.

He drapes rope around my front and ties knots along my back. I knew the braided twine would be coarse against my bare skin, but I hadn't expected it to be quite as rough as it is. It's not painful, it's just a feeling. It's a feeling that makes my pulse race to pump desire through my veins.

He twists and tugs, each small jerk of the rope threatening to drag me backward against him. I move one foot slightly in front of the other to plant my feet, to keep myself rooted to the spot because I fear colliding with him and knocking him off the ledge. I also fear feeling his warmth against my back, which will knock me off a different kind of cliff.

"Where did you learn to do this?" I ask quietly, hoping that speaking will distract me from the flood of chemicals rushing through my veins.

"From a book," he says. "There's a small library of texts hidden away on the third floor."

"A library of books on how to bind women?"

"Not just binding women. It's…" he hesitates. "There are many books there about the impulses and desires of men and ways to satisfy them. Most of them I find uninteresting."

"But ropes were interesting to you?"

He grabs my arms and brings them behind my back, forcing my elbows to bend. My forearms touch as they draw parallel lines across the middle of my back. He ties me this way, and my breaths quicken as he shifts me from relative freedom to bound and at his mercy.

If I fall, I won't be able to catch myself with my hands.

"It's not the ropes that interest me."

His hands fall away, and he's silent through several pulsing beats. I can feel his eyes on my back, and they burn my skin.

I'm almost relieved when the ropes start to move again, as he continues to twist, loop, and tug. Each drawing of the braided twine whooshes as coarse fibers rub against coarse fibers. The dangling ends whip against my flesh, each grazing touch threatening to startle anxiety and trigger another rush of adrenaline.

"It's the artwork of it that I find alluring." I feel the touch of his hand against my thigh before the rope coils around it. I look down, turning my head back to see him on one knee behind me, nimble fingers twisting a knot. "The way it twists and coils, the way it lays across tender flesh is a thing of beauty—true beauty." There's a pause. "I don't think I could ever dress another creature in bindings as beautiful as this, as natural as the way you look right here and now. The way you submit to it, with every inch of rebellion and every ounce of will that you have to fight…I'm overcome by your presence in front of me right now, Mercy."

The rhythm of his words excites me. Each panting inhale draws in a heated breath that sinks through my stomach, pulses between my legs, and slickens my cunt. Before I realize any time has passed, my thighs and ankles are knotted. I feel the heat of him move as he rises behind me, and his fingertips gently graze the ends of my hair, lifting a strand from the back of my neck.

"I mourn the length of your hair, starlight. But I'm not sorry that I cut it. I don't want any other man wrapping their hand around those perfect strands but me." He bends over my shoulder and his lips move closer to my ear. "I kept your braid," he whispers. "I couldn't bear to part with it."

A quake ripples down the length of my spine as he leaves me. He circles me, lifts a dangling end of rope that hangs from one of the many knots on my body, and reaches above me.

Looking down at myself, I find that I can see it—the artwork in his binding. The rope is so intentionally turned and twisted around my body, swooping across my chest and around each breast to cage them in, framing them as if they were paintings worthy of display. It's twirled beautifully down my stomach, spread across my hips, wrapped tightly around my thighs. I feel every inch of the crisscrossing along my back, and part of me wishes I could see it, because I understand what he means about it being beautiful.

And it isn't just in the rope itself.

Just as he said, I submitted to this. I stood still and let him position me, let him bind me in whatever way he wanted. All while standing at the edge of a cliff in a cavern so dark, I can scarcely see the opening through which we entered.

I submitted to Arlo Rainn.

I freely gave him reign to bind me, and in that, I gave him my trust.

Do I trust him?

How could I ever truly trust him?

"Ready?"

I look up at him standing squarely at my side, and though I don't know what he expects me to be ready for, I know that I am ready, regardless. With trust I didn't decide to give him—trust I'm not sure he's actually earned—I nod.

He tugs on a strand of rope at the center of my back that he must have fed through the metal loop above my head. I feel the pull of the binding as it shifts and scratches over my skin, and I yelp as my weight pitches forward with the lift. He tugs again, and I rise to my toes, calling out his name as the feeling of falling washes over me. His name echoes through the empty cavern as he works to fix a knot to hold me in place.

My body turns and sways as he works to do something, making my stomach lurch with nausea. But even the nausea draws a fear-induced desire down low in my gut.

My right leg rises as he tugs on a knot that's settled on the back of my thigh. Once my toes are off the ground, he bends my knee back, lifting my ankle from another knot placed there.

He secures me as I dangle with the toes of my left leg still dancing across stone, but then he lifts that leg, too. Within moments, my entire body is floating, suspended, laying parallel to the ground. I'm facing down and my knees are bent and parted, toes pointing toward the metal hoop that holds me up from the center of my back.

Arlo touches my hip, sending a shockwave through my body, but his touch only exists for a moment. He pushes, and I spin slowly. I make the mistake of looking out as I circle toward the dark abyss of the cavern, out beyond the drop-off. Panic overcomes me, burning through my veins like wildfire through brush, sweeping me into outright terror.

"I can't—" It's all I manage before my panicked, panting breaths overtake me.

I sense him moving, tugging, lifting, adjusting.

But all I feel is panic.

I want to clutch something, grab hold of something firm and stable, but I'm bound. The jerking feeling of suddenly falling hits me over and over again, and after several waves of it, I lose myself entirely.

"Take me down!" I shout, the eerie reverberation of my voice echoing back at me. "Take me down, I can't—"

I thrash in my bindings, trying uselessly to free my arms, but the movement only makes me swing and spin. I can't calm down, I can't relax. All I can think about is breaking free.

Then Arlo's palm lands on the back of my head, his fingers dig into my hair and grip it tight, lifting. He steadies my wriggling form with a single look as he bends to meet my eyes.

The look...

Blue fire glints in his steadying gaze, and the heat of it is unlike any earthly flame. It's something otherworldly.

Celestial.

The glimmering light of a burning star on the brink of explosion.

Eruption.

Corruption.

"Give in to the panic. Let go and give in to it, then let it be done. I've taken your control from you, and I'm not giving it back. Accept it. It's mine." He breathes out and tilts his head, narrowing his eyes with sinister, sexual, seductive intent. And with command, he speaks a truth I can't deny. "You're mine, starlight."

chapter twenty-six

Mercy

IT'S HIS TOUCH, his words, his breath against my cheeks. It's the whisper of acceptance from the shadows surrounding us that seeps through my skin, penetrates my bones, and settles me with perfect calmness.

Acceptance.

It's the peace that comes from acceptance.

I'm bound and immobile, suspended, and at his will.

I accept it.

I welcome it.

I embrace it.

Our gaze locks for moments as we share heat between us. I feel it burning from his eyes into mine and melting every molecule. It seeps through my insides and warms me deeply, sending a warm river of pleasure rippling through my core.

Arlo's grip on my hair loosens, then his hand strokes down the back of my head as a small but intense smile creeps up his lips—a smile filled with sinful intentions.

"You're mine," he says again, and I nod my agreement.

I am.

I am yours.

His fingers brush down my back, tracing over the lines of rope and slipping in between coils to touch my skin. He stops when he reaches the small of my back, his hand pressing to a flat expanse of exposed skin, rubbing a gentle circle. The ropes creak as they rock lightly in my suspension, though his hand keeps me steadily at his side.

"How do you feel?" he asks gently.

I pause, tasting my words and whether they're palatable enough to share before speaking. "I feel every molecule of existence. I feel like every atom in the universe is swirling beneath me, keeping me afloat."

He exhales heavily. "Sweet sin."

"Arlo…" I speak his name, but I'm not asking for anything.

Suddenly, I spin. His hands are on my body, turning me until I'm facing him. Then he reaches over me to grip two ropes that reach from the loop above to the middle of my back. He pushes on them, leans forward against them, and it causes my body to lift upward. He angles me so our gazes meet. His lips are parted and eyes are hooded as he lets them wander down my form.

"I've wanted to see you like this since I saw you hiding in that tree in the forest. Since the night you sinned, I've had images of you this way clouding my mind, stealing my peace, threatening to destroy my self-control. And seeing you this way now, in the flesh… it puts those images to fucking shame."

I don't know what to say, so I say nothing.

"I'm fighting sin, but, Mercy…" he pauses, leans close, and brushes his mouth over mine, "I want you to drag me to hell."

His lips are a flint sparking a flame between us, and I tilt my chin, capturing his kiss before he can steal it away from me. His pillow-soft lips press hard enough to bruise. His tongue is long and thick, sweeping past the threshold of my parted lips, tasting me with unburdened passion.

My arms twitch against my bindings, aching to wrap around him. As I wriggle uselessly, he palms the back of my head, gripping my hair and lifting my head away.

"No fighting," he pants, pressing his forehead to mine. "Be still. Practice endurance. I promise I'll give you everything your body is begging for right now."

"Touch me," I beg.

"Where shall I touch you?" he whispers, his breath hot as it breezes across my face. A playful smile touches his cheeks, tugging at the long dimples that draw such beautiful lines down his face. "Do you want my hand between your legs like it was in the forest?"

"*Yes.*"

"You'll have to earn it, then."

All at once, he drops me and steps back. I cry out with the rush of fear that grips me as I fall forward, my brain lagging in the knowledge that I'm suspended and secure, and not on the precipice of dropping into that dark abyss. The ropes snap me to a stop.

"How…how do I earn it?" I ask between panted breaths.

He grabs hold of me, stopping my body's sway. His hip presses against my side as his hands reach around my body and his palms find my breasts. I moan as he squeezes, kneading my flesh. "You earn it with patience."

I don't understand.

"Tell me how," I whimper.

His long fingers drag and dig before pinching my nipples, twisting, squeezing, turning painfully before releasing.

"Please…"

His touch turns soft, fingers grazing over the hardened buds and caressing gently.

"Stop begging." His voice is strained. "I know what you need from me without a word." His hands drag down my torso as he moves backward along my body, stopping to grip my hips to hold me steady. "But just as you'll be in the trial, I want you still and speechless right now. I want nothing more than your whimpers and moans, your acceptance of my touch."

I whimper, both as a natural response to his thumbs digging into my ass and to make it clear that I understand him.

"I'm going to touch you, Mercy." His voice trembles at this admission of his choice to sin with me. His hands drag heavily over the curve of my ass, tracing down the backs of my things. "I'm going to lick you, taste you, fuck you. I'm going to bring you to the brink of pleasure…" his hands stop at the bend of my knee and dig into my thighs, slowly pushing back up again, "over and over and over again."

His hands meet the crease beneath my cheeks and stop, fingers splaying, thumbs dipping between my legs and rubbing in small circles. "I'm going to bring you right to the cliff's edge of pleasure, and I'm going to pull you back every time before you fall."

"Why?" The single word slips out before I can stop myself.

One hand leaves me, then quickly finds me again with a sharp strike against my cheek. The slap reverberates through the darkness as it shocks me with pain, but the pain fades so easily.

"You will not give my brothers the satisfaction of your words in the trial. Do you understand me? Do not speak, do not beg for mercy, do not ask for more. If you can't control yourself, then I will gag you."

Why do I want him to control all of this? All of me?

Why do I want to give him that power over me?

He's as dangerous as any of the Control…perhaps even more dangerous for the fact that he can make me feel this way. I try to bring my shields up, to shut off the desire and lust which burns within me only for him. But trying to fight it only makes it burn deeper and hotter.

I resign myself to silence to please him, though I tell myself I'm doing it for me.

I feel him move behind me, his hands dragging down the insides of my thighs. Moments later, I feel his breath brush over the skin between my legs as he speaks.

"As much as I want to lose myself in you," fingers brush softly down my slick center, giving me a jolt of pleasure which forces a moan, "as much as I want to lose myself in this perfect pussy…*Fuck*."

His warm, wet tongue touches me quickly, licking me cleanly from end to end. "I have to control myself to prepare you for this trial." Two fingers spear me, and I cry out as he sinks them deep inside. "Sweet sin. From this day until your last, Mercy Madness, you come for no man but me. You *only* come for me, starlight…and only when I tell you to."

This is something I prayed for but never imagined could be real. It feels precious to be claimed by one man and one man alone, to be consumed by him, pleasured by him…someday loved by him.

Not shared by him.

But I will be shared.

Arlo's fingers twist inside me, as if he turns the dial on my loud thoughts and forces them to silence.

There is no tomorrow.

There is no thinking about what will come in the trial.

There is only the touch of this man as he claims me as his.

Stroking, his fingers curl, rubbing with perfect pressure against some spot inside me that feels heavy as it aches and throbs. It's a spot that seems to condense every pound of my weight to that single spot. It's like I can feel his touch over every inch of my body as his fingers stroke and thump in that perfect place inside me.

My ears are filled with the echoes of my wetness as his fingers move, the creaking of the ropes as my body sways, and the reverberating echo of it all in the empty cavern.

My head drops all the way down, my hair dangling toward the ground beneath me. When his thumb curls around to rub my clit, my head snaps up again with a jolt. I have to bite down on my lip to stifle my cry, because more than anything, I want to scream out his name and beg for more.

But he said I'm not to speak, and I want to obey.

"That's it, Mercy. That's what I want from you." His voice is heavy, hot, and panting. "Get close for me, come right to the edge for me."

His fingers are expert with the way they work me, inside and out, two fingers rhythmic against my inner walls, and his thumb circling, rubbing just right. His other hand is wrapped around my thigh, holding me steady, and his warm lips trail kisses along the inside of my leg.

I feel it coming; I feel it burning and building. I'm throbbing with each stroke, aching with heat and need. My body is tense and tight and begging for release.

I want it.

I need it.

He's going to take it from me.

I pant and whimper as his stroking takes me higher and brings me closer to the edge. And just as it swells, clenching through my belly, just as my breath changes and my body stills with the anticipation of onrushing release, he takes it all away.

He pulls his hand back, his touch leaving me entirely.

I'm dangling on the edge and leaning, but instead of letting me go…he pulls me back.

chapter twenty-seven

ARLO

"NO…" SHE WHIMPERS, her head dropping forward with the disappointment of lost release.

Sitting back on my heels from where I kneel behind her, I bring my fingers to my nose and inhale.

Sweet fucking sin, this woman smells divine.

I dip my fingers inside my mouth, pressing them down on my tongue and dragging them out slowly.

It's exactly what I would imagine a fallen angel to taste like. Something so sweet it could only be forged in paradise, but so sinful it must have been cast out. Whatever kind of demon she is, she's mine, and I've never wanted anything more than this.

Am I willing to burn in hell for her?

For the taste of her cunt and a moment of bliss spent inside her?

My head aches from the turmoil of this passion for a sinner who brings such corruption to me. I fear I can only find the cure for this ache between her thighs. A demon possesses her, but it must be within me, too.

"Arlo?" she asks softly, sweetly, her voice whimpering with an edge of begging.

I pull my hand away from my mouth and press my palms to my thighs, bowing my head to take several deep breaths as I work to steady the frantic beating of my heart.

"I won't allow you to come for my brothers," I tell her. "I need you to learn how to control your pleasure, and not just when I take it away from you."

"I won't come for them," she whispers.

I shoot to my feet, rounding on her. She lifts her head high to look at me as I move to stand in front of her, straining her neck as she fights to meet my eyes. They only reach as high as my chest in her suspension.

I loosen the buckle of my belt. "What did I say about giving them your words?"

She responds with silence, and her submission screams loudly through it. It calls to me, drawing me closer.

"They're going to take you from every angle, in every way they can. I want you to know what it feels like to have your breath stolen from you while you're suspended this way." With one hand, I bring out my throbbing cock, and with the other, I tap beneath her chin. "Open for me."

Her tongue runs across her bottom lip before she tugs it between her teeth, hesitation and the desire to obey fighting between her lips. I want to give her the space to come to submission on her own, but I'm in physical pain for the way I need her lips wrapped around me. I've never ached so much for relief but in her presence.

More than that, my brothers in God won't give her a moment of mental space to prepare for their assault. They'll take from her when she's not ready to give.

The thought of it has blood boiling in my veins.

Yet, I have to prepare her.

I twist my hand so I can pinch her cheeks. "*Open*," I demand, and as soon as her lips twitch to part, I push my cock between them.

She whimpers at my intrusion, but I press forward, keeping the pressure until I'm sunk inside her, and I groan. "Fuck."

I move my hand around to the back of her head, fisting her hair and holding her steady as I force myself deeper than I should. She gags as I reach the back of her throat, spluttering around me, but I needed that protest from her body to stop me and force me to pull back—I'm so fucking lost in my hunger for her, I can hardly control myself.

I pull all the way out and she coughs. I let go of her hair and her head falls, dropping low as she sputters.

I'm about to reach out and tilt her chin for me again, but she lifts her head on her own. Though she can't raise her eyes high enough to meet mine, I don't have to see them to know they hold the force of her strength. She opens her mouth for me and waits.

Sweet sin.

"Mercy, you're killing me."

Quite literally, the lust she stirs within me inspires me to sin in ways that could lead to my death. And she'll be put to hers because she ran—she ran from the same violence and lust she stirred within Hyatt fucking Price. Jealousy and a need to claim heat me. A firestorm swirls in my gut, clenches through my stomach, and rushes blood to my cock.

I need to fuck.

Gripping her, I spin her away from me, and she cries out as I turn her swiftly and unexpectedly. I force her to face the looming darkness beyond the edge of the drop-off. Slinking my hands between the ropes that suspend her, I wrap my palms around her hips, hold her steady, and slam deep inside her.

A cry of relief bursts from her, echoing like a fallen angel's song through the dark cavern. Heaven and hell collide in our connection, in the dichotomy of celestial reward and punishment that makes this feel right and wrong all at once.

Pain and pleasure.

Sin and sacrifice.

Bliss and fury.

Tightening my grip, I push her forward, then drag her back against me, impaling her deeply with the hope she feels it in her damned, rebellious soul.

She huffs out a breath as I do it again, as I rock her away, then drag her back. I push her so she sways over the edge, dipping her starlight hair in the looming darkness, and I feel the tremor rip through her spine as the fear takes hold of her once more.

But that fear heightens her senses. I can feel the way her muscles tighten around me, the way her cunt contracts around my cock and begs for release.

I'm not giving her release.

I'm taking mine.

Push and pull, sway and slam. My pace quickens and her journey forward shortens as I pull her back to my cock with shorter, faster thrusts. I fuck her recklessly, painfully, angrily.

I'm angry.

A fury awakens unlike any I've felt before, screaming through the beat of my heart, raging through my veins.

But why?

Sway and slam. Thrust. Thrust. Thrust.

"Arlo," she says, and I feel her there, embracing my cock, trying to corrupt me with the pure, hedonistic pleasure of it all.

She's fulfilling my every desire, strung up in a dark cave with danger lurking all around us. She's submitted fully to whatever way I choose to use and abuse her. I could fall for her...I could so easily fall into this trap she's set for me. Yet, the voice in my mind calls to me, reminding me of the truth.

She's a wolf in sheep's clothing.

A demon disguised by human flesh—flesh that perfectly matches my every dangerous desire.

God is testing me.

I fuck her harder and faster. I dig my fingers into her fleshy hips to hold her steady instead of swinging her so I can give her the full force of my furious longing. Grunting and sweating, I pound into her cunt.

"Arlo," she chokes on my name, "it hurts…"

A feral growl builds behind my voice. "It's what you've earned, sinner."

I don't exist within my body. I hear my voice and the words I speak, but I feel powerless to control them. I only want the release I should have taken from her that night in the forest. I want it to hurt her for the way she makes me hurt. The longing is unbearable, and I can't have her. She'll be dead soon, and I can't even have her now without shame for what she's made me become.

"It hurts," she whimpers again.

It's as if the demon leaves her soul and enters mine, because her plea only encourages me to fuck her harder. I want to fill her deeper.

Leaning forward, I wrap one arm around the ropes at her midsection and pull back to keep her in place as I continue to move inside her. Once I'm sure she's firmly in my hold, I drag my other hand down her crack, teasing the tiny hole that makes her flinch when I touch it.

Turning my thumb and lowering it, I sneak some wetness away from her cunt and drag it upward until I reach that spot again. I should warm her up, stretch her, prepare her, but her demon tells me to claim her ass without preparation. It tells me she doesn't want to be prepared. She wants to be taken forcefully, painfully.

She wants to be mine.

But she'll never be mine, and soon, she'll be dead.

I groan with the pain of my thoughts as I push my thumb inside that tiny hole with a sharp thrust, causing her to scream and flinch, but that doesn't stop me. I press in deeper and harder. I fuck her faster, pulsing and pumping as the most painful kind of pleasure gathers in the base of my cock and swells. It throbs and pounds and begs for relief.

Dear God, give me relief.

Let me come quickly. Let this sin be over.

As if God Himself heard my plea and spurred it to spare me this pain, my release spills inside her without warning. The most intense pleasure I've ever felt tears through my soul. I shout out my anger, my shame, my absolute satisfaction into the dark void. I hope it will swallow our sins and hide them in the darkness forever.

I pant as I fight to catch my breath, still buried to the hilt inside her. It takes me far too long to come down from the high, but her soft sobbing drags me from the paradise of pleasure into the darkest level of hell.

She's crying.

She's crying because of me...because I hurt her.

I used her, and there is no full moon tonight.

If everything I've done with her before has toed the thin line that stands between my power and my duty, then this moment has been the hand on my back shoving me across it.

I drag myself out of her slowly, giving far more care than I did in fucking her. My grip on the ropes loosens gradually, and I pull my thumb from her with the gentleness I should've given her on the way in.

I stumble backward, then bend to lift my pants, working quickly to put myself back together. Her body slowly turns in my direction, as if spun by an unseen force that insists I come face to face with the pain I've caused. Her head hangs, short strands of hair dangling around her cheeks as her chest heaves with her panting.

I take a step back, then another, my spine hitting the solid wall of rock behind me as I watch her on bated breath.

And then she speaks, her voice sure and clear, but shaken with fear, and perhaps, disappointment. "Thank you." There's a long pause after those two words that stab me like a knife. "I feel very well prepared for what your brothers will do to me."

chapter twenty-eight
ARLO

I CLOSE MERCY'S bedroom door behind me as I leave her. I brought her back from the cave, cleaned her up, and tucked her into bed. She let me, and I don't imagine a day will ever come that I'll understand why.

She didn't say a word to me after I defiled her, after I used her in a way a woman should only ever be used in service under the full moon. The only thing that feels worse than her silence is knowing she'll keep my sin a secret for me. I wish I had doubt about that, but it's something I can feel. She's a woman of her word, and whether her word is sinful or saintly, I know she'll hold true to it.

"Where have you been?" I'm startled by Killian's voice as he comes down the hallway. "Theo said you were working with Mercy." His hands are lifted behind his head, retying his long hair into a knot.

"I was." I turn and walk toward him, meeting him after a few steps.

"But Delle's in bed. He said she wasn't feeling well."

"Right. And that's why she and Theo weren't with us."

Killian's eyes narrow as his hands fall to his sides. He tilts his head to regard me with suspicion. "So, you were alone with Mercy, then? Where?"

A tight grin flattens my lips. "Is there a problem? Mercy is my ward. It's my job to take care of her between the trials."

He looks down with a huff of amusement, then steps closer. An accusatory smile spreads across his cheeks as he lifts his head to look at me. "How exactly have you been…taking care of her?"

I know exactly what he's accusing, but I play dumb. "I'm not sure what you're asking. I've been taking care of her in the traditional sense. You know, feedings, cleanings, meeting basic needs. The pets need fresh air and exercise on occasion, too, so I took her for a walk."

I'm lying openly, but worse than that, I hear myself as I speak of Mercy as if she were a dog. Speaking of her that way feels like a sin greater than tying her up and fucking her.

Killian's expression turns serious. "Where did you walk?"

"Through the forest."

"Really? So Wesley didn't see the two of you coming out of the courtroom? What were you doing in there?"

Caught in my lie.

"Intimidation," I rush to cover myself. "She was being unruly, so I brought her there to remind her of her place."

He presses his lips together and nods slowly, his eyes narrowing to slits as he considers my words. "I see." He reaches out to clap me on the shoulder, hand gripping in a friendly gesture. "You should be cautious in the time you spend with her. The brothers are starting to speak of you."

"In what manner?"

"Ryker says you look at her with longing."

"And?" I shrug, causing him to drop his hand from my shoulder.

"I've noticed it, too."

"All of us have looked at her with longing; she's an attractive woman. I don't understand the point you're trying to make."

"Don't let the sinner poison your mind, brother. We're concerned for you. There's a darkness inside her, and if you're not careful, she may bewitch you into sinning right along with her."

Too late to save me now, brother.

"I'm well aware of what she is, Killian. I have my method of relieving temptation when it's present." I lift my hand, showing him my leather glove as a reminder of my own manner of self-control.

"Right," he says. "But is a single burn upon your hand enough to remove the temptation of her from your mind?"

No.

"Yes. Is there a point to this conversation? I have other matters I need to tend to. I'd like to check in on Delle."

"I'm sure Theo has his newly appointed ward well cared for."

"I'm sure he does," I cock my head, "yet, somehow, I still find myself concerned for her well-being as a member of this community, and so I'd like to check in. Are we done?"

His stare lingers for a beat, his grin contorting into an accusatory grimace before he takes a step back. "Yes, of course. By all means, go and check in on Delle."

I side-step and move past him until I've reached Delle's door just a few steps away. He moves with me and pauses at my back.

"Just remember we're here for you, brother."

I turn my head over my shoulder and grant him a tight smile before he turns and walks back the way he came. Once he's passed a couple of doors, I lift my fist and knock softly, quietly, wondering if Delle is asleep and not wanting to disturb her if she is.

But quickly, the door swings open.

It isn't Delle standing behind it…it's Theo.

He holds a finger to his lips, indicating I should be quiet. "She's sleeping," he whispers, then waves, beckoning me to enter quietly.

I follow him into her spacious room and glance across at the regal bed. Sure enough, Delle is tucked in, sleeping soundly, peacefully. The room feels somber and tranquil—a welcome reprieve to the tension I feel every moment I'm with Mercy.

Theo moves to one of the two armchairs along the wall across from her bed. I move to sit beside him, in the chair angled toward his.

"How is she?" I whisper.

"She's fine. I don't think she's ill. I think it's the stress of the upcoming trial that makes her feel unwell."

I nod. Laying my arms on the armrests, my fingers curl around the edge.

"And Mercy?" he asks after a few silent beats. "Is she okay?"

"I don't know whether she would use the word, 'okay,' but she's settled for the night."

"Did you take her to the caves?"

"Yes."

I feel his eyes on me, heavy and warning. "Do you think that was a good idea?"

I turn my head to look at him squarely, casually lifting my ankle to cross over my knee. "Why wouldn't it be?"

The lies are coming again, and it twists my stomach.

"I'm just concerned about how it looks when you're alone with her."

"And aren't you concerned about how it looks when you're alone with *her*?" I incline my head to indicate Delle, sleeping in her bed.

Theo rakes a hand through his sandy blond hair. "Perhaps I should be." His gaze fixes on her sleeping form. "I find myself overwhelmed with worry for her well-being," he admits. "I know I should distance myself. She's in the trials now, and there's nothing to come from caring about her. She's just so small and frail…so young."

"Even if she weren't in the trials, there's nothing to come from it," I remind him. "Even if she weren't a servant, you know you wouldn't be allowed to choose the domestic assigned to you at your retirement."

I need the reminder myself, though admittedly, it shocks me with a sharp pang through my chest. The Shift happens every twenty-five years in Ember Glen. It happened a few years ago, when the previous members of the Control retired, and me and my brothers in God were selected to take their place.

Three of those retiring were elected to be the new Elders. The previous Elders and the other retired members of the Control were assigned domestics and sent through the caves to the Land of Kings.

There, they would live out the rest of their days in blissful retirement, happy with their domestic women and the children they bear.

No one returns to the village of Ember Glen after going to the Land of Kings. It's said the Impulse doesn't exist there—it's a holy land where no man is burdened by violent or sexual needs. And only those who have served Ember Glen as members of the Control become worthy enough to go there. Even so, they're not granted their choice of a domestic partner—that person is selected for them. One day, domestics will be chosen for me and Theo.

"I know," Theo whispers, and I hear pain in his words. I feel it, too. "The ache of compassion is a burden all men of God must carry."

Yes, he's right.

It's written in the Impulse Edict.

True men of God may feel compassion for the people they serve, but it doesn't mean that compassion has been earned by those who've sinned. It doesn't allow us to ignore the sins of our people. They must still be punished, and their pain is a burden we must carry.

Mercy must still be punished.

Regardless of my compassion for Mercy and Delle, regardless of my attraction to Mercy, my desire for her, my overwhelming need to sin with her again—*fuck*—I must recognize my compassion is a fault of my humanity and not reason granted by God.

Even as I think of this, every thought pounds with the ache of dissonance through my skull. When it comes to Mercy, all my thoughts feel painful, aching, throbbing with discordance against the harmony I held in my soul, harmony I'd earned through a lifetime of faith and acceptance of truth as it was written in the Edict.

Delle rolls in her bed, an innocent whimper slipping out in her slumber, and the sound of it returns a memory of a girl named Luna who was once my sister. We share the same mother, the same eyes and smile. She's five years younger than me, but we were always close.

I only see her in passing now. My place with the Control

doesn't allow me to recognize my family as mine. I'm allowed to speak with them if we cross paths in the village, but it's rare. My role as the authority of Ember Glen requires disconnection and objectivity—the subjectivity of one's feelings clouds judgment. I feel that cloudiness when I'm with Mercy, yet through the fog of her, I can see so clearly.

She's a contradiction of my faith.

Mercy's compassion for Delle mirrors the protectiveness I had for Luna when we were younger. I used to help care for her—not because I had to, as that was my mother's role, but because I wanted to. Luna was always bright, kind, and playful. She was always laughing and joyful. I don't ever see her that way now when we cross paths in the village. She has a permanent frown etched upon her face, always chasing after one of the three children she bore as a domestic. I think she's about to have another.

As I think of it, I realize how there's such a stark difference in the demeanor of the children of Ember Glen and the women that so many of the daughters grow to become. Their joy seems to have left them, but surely, that can't mean they're unhappy.

Maybe Luna would have been happier as a servant?

The image of it strikes me, a sixteen-year-old Luna bound and strung up for my brothers in God to defile in the first trial. My stomach lurches at the thought of it. I feel nausea tear through my gut and angry tension tug at my muscles. My fingers curl around the armrest, digging into the fabric.

What if Luna had done something stupid when she was sixteen?

What if Luna were in Delle's place right now?

How can I let this be done to her?

I have to let this be done to her…don't I?

"Perhaps we don't need to carry the burden of compassion in this case." The words escape me before I even realize I've opened my mouth.

Theo's eyes narrow on me. "What do you mean?"

"Mercy pled her case to take on Delle's burden."

"And she failed. Delle must complete the trial for herself."

"Yes, she must. There's no way around that. But does that mean that you and I can't find a way to…shift the burden if we can't remove it completely?"

Theo straightens in his seat, turning and leaning toward me on his arm. "I'm listening."

"Our brothers ache to punish Mercy, and for good reason. She's older and more experienced in service. She's the true rebel we worry could inspire others to rebel with her. She's already the focal point of these trials. No one really cares about making an example of Delle."

"You're suggesting that we capitalize on that."

I nod. "It wouldn't be difficult to ensure that our brothers' excitement for the punishment be directed at Mercy. Many of them already speak as if she's the only one on trial."

He inclines his head as he regards me with confusion. "Why would you want to do that for Delle? Why would you want to do that to Mercy?"

"Because Mercy is a temptation to me," I admit, though it doesn't sit well in my stomach. "Perhaps her temptation deserves to be punished. It's women like Mercy who inspire girls like Delle toward dissension."

Theo nods and slowly turns his head to look out in front of him, gazing toward where Delle sleeps in her bed. "You're right. We'll inspire our brothers to direct their punishment toward the one who deserves it most."

This is right.

This is necessary.

I feel the ache of shame brew within me, a sense of guilt that I'm somehow betraying Mercy in this. But I'm not beholden to her, and I owe her nothing.

She'll be dead before long.

chapter twenty-nine

Mercy

SERVICE OF THE *Flesh*.

The first of my three trials begins in thirty minutes.

I stand facing the full-length mirror in my bedroom, still fully clothed and wondering why I even bothered to dress today. These garments will be stripped from me soon. The crimson gown made of silk, which clings to my curves but covers me so modestly with its boat neck and long sleeves. The black bra and panties I wear beneath it, the garter belt holding up my black stockings, and even the boots on my feet will be stripped away.

My fingers play across the silk at my thighs, gripping it and lifting enough to show my boots beneath my dress. All the servants wear shoes like mine, and in a way, wearing them now makes me feel bound to them, serving as a reminder of the role I was selected to serve within this community.

Perhaps I should have shed them when I entered the Homestead and worn the difficultly tall shoes left for me in the wardrobe instead. Perhaps wearing the boots as the last symbol of my servitude should make me sad.

But it doesn't.

In some strange way, the connection to the servants makes me feel stronger. They were my sisters, and I loved them dearly—I still do. They're women I care for, even if I could never understand the joy they find in service, even if I could never reconcile my changing beliefs with their own.

Regardless of what's in our individual minds, we're the same inside, and my compassion for them knows no bounds.

I recall the looks on Ellary's and Cambria's faces when I tried to speak with them at Ivy Jane's memorial. They were heartbroken, devastated, and disappointed in me for sinning—because they believed that what I'd done was truly a sin. And though I'll never agree with them on that, I don't fault them for the beliefs that have been fed to them since birth. It's not their fault they believe what they believe. I don't judge them for it, and I don't love them any less.

Still, I feel lonelier than ever in these moments before my punishment is set to begin—the beginning of the end for me—and my boots make me feel just a little more connected to the sisterhood that once loved me as much as I love them.

I hear the door at my back click open, then close again gently.

It's Arlo.

I know without looking.

I feel the pulse of him as he crosses the room, slowly making his way toward me.

I drop my dress to cover my boots, then give myself one last glance in the mirror before lifting my eyes to meet his reflection. He stops behind me, his handsome face peeking over my shoulder in the reflection, regarding me with an expression I can't decipher.

We stand this way for what must be minutes, watching each other in the mirror, each of us trying to read the other for their aching thoughts in these moments before my defilement.

He's the first to speak. "It's a shame I'll have to remove the dress. You look lovely."

I glance down, then look up at his reflection. "I don't want your compliments, Arlo."

"I didn't mean it as a compliment. It's simply the truth."

"What do you want?"

"I want to help you."

"This time is meant to be mine. Can't you allow me some moments of peace before it begins?"

"That's why I'm here."

My brows furrow as my eyes narrow, and I spin to face him, meeting the perfect blue pools of his eyes with intensity. "You're presumptuous to think I can't find peace on my own. Do you think I can find a moment's peace with you? When I look at you, all I feel is fury."

It's true that I feel something intense when I look at him, though perhaps fury isn't the right word. If it isn't, then I don't know what other word to use in its place.

"I know I hurt you," he says, his gloved hand reaching up to tuck my shortened hair behind my ear.

The mere presence of his touch coaxes my head to tilt toward his hand, and he cups my cheek. I want to lift away, but I don't—I can't.

"I went too far with you, and I hurt you. But let me help you now."

"How could you possibly help me now? Do you understand what I'm about to go through? The pain, the shame, the horror I'm about to experience at the hand of your brothers in God?"

His jaw ticks. "You sinned, and it's your penance."

Fury is certainly the right word now. I lift my head from his palm, raise my dress at my thighs to keep from tripping, and move away from him. I walk across the room and stop at the end of the bed, reaching out to wrap my hand around one of its four posts.

I feel him at my back moments later, not touching me, but there all the same. He's so close I can feel the heat of him, and my fingers tighten their grip around the post.

"It's your penance, Mercy, but I still care about you...and I want to see you through this. Let me see you through this."

I turn my head over my shoulder to look at him, but I don't lift my eyes to meet his. I'm not even sure what to say to him right now, let alone what I would do if I let myself search for sincerity in his perfect blue eyes.

He steps closer, his heat rushing into my back. Delicately, his fingers play at the zipper of my dress where it touches the nape of my neck, resting over the seven scars marking me for the trials. I breathe slowly as he draws the zipper down. I see no sense in stopping him because I'll have to undress all the same.

But also...

My pulse quickens, my spine shudders, my breaths deepen at his touch.

The dress falls open as his fingers reach the top of my underwear. With my head still turned over my shoulder, I see him work to remove his gloves, and my lips part with anticipation of his next move.

I hate him and everything he stands for.

I hate that I can't force myself to loathe him.

I hate myself for feeling anything at all in his presence.

"I know you found some moments of peace with me in the cavern."

His bare palms flatten against my back, slipping up from the center beneath the split fabric, then grazing over my shoulders and pushing the sleeves down my arms. My shoulders shrug with tension at his touch—tension for the fear of it, tension for the desire of it.

His fingers trail down my arms as he pushes off the long sleeves, his touch trailing down my skin. Then his hands fall to my hips, nudging the tight gown over my curves and shoving it to the floor.

Lifting my hand to grip the bed post again, I step out of the ring of fabric dropped at my feet, and he kicks it aside before coming in closer, closing the distance between us. I startle at the way he invades my space so completely, so quickly, his warm hands slipping up my sides and stopping just beneath my breasts.

He pulls me back against him and sweeps his nose through my hair. I feel him breathe me in, and it's as though he inhales all my tension, taking it away from me and letting it seep inside him to unburden me.

I can't trust him.

This man has hurt me. He's used me. He's sinned and asked me to keep the secret for him. Arlo Rainn is not a good man—he's just not.

So why does my pain slip away whenever I fall into his arms?

"Warden Rainn," I whisper, keeping formality to try to distance myself from him again, "the trial hasn't begun yet."

He exhales in a rush as his hands slip around me, caressing my stomach, wrapping me into a close embrace. His head comes over my shoulder and his cheek nuzzles against mine. He hugs me close, and I don't want him to let go. I almost want to cry for the way he draws me in and takes away my loneliness.

I hate him for it.

I could almost love him for it.

"My brothers in God may use you today, but you are still mine."

His.

My hand leaves the bed post, intent on pulling his arms away. Instead, my arms cross over my belly and lay on top of his where they hold me, reveling in the comfort he offers. I lean back, letting him take the weight of me, allowing him to claim me for this moment.

"I don't want to share you," he says with a broken voice, planting a kiss on my cheek, then peppering a line along the side of my jaw.

Then don't.

Keep me.

Steal me away from Ember Glen…I'd rather face whatever is beyond the mountains.

I don't speak as he kisses a trail down the side of my neck, as he stops at my nape to nuzzle and lick and nip in a way that has me drawing in trembling breaths.

"I don't want you to go into this frightened, Mercy, not fearful and tense and dry. I want to give you something to hold on to through the next seven hours." My hands fall away as his slide across my stomach, running up my sides, palms reaching around to cover my breasts. I gasp as he gently squeezes. "No one has said you aren't allowed to enjoy this."

I shove his hands and try to step forward, but I only run into the edge of the mattress. "No. I'm not going to enjoy them."

He envelops me in his embrace, pulling me back again, hands roaming and groping me everywhere. I struggle against him for a moment, but I quickly fall victim to our confusing connection, to the combustible chemistry we share. I sink in his hold as one of his palms rubs flat down the center of my stomach, reaching low between my legs, over my underwear.

"I promised you," I pant, breathless, "I promised I would only come for you."

His fingers curl and he cups my sex to claim me. "And you will only come for me. Your greatest pleasure, Mercy, your peace today, will be found in the anticipation of it."

His fingers stroke gently over my underwear, drawing out a whimper of desire I hadn't expected him to be able to draw out of me. His other hand moves up my stomach as he speaks, traveling toward my breast.

"You won't come unless I tell you to. Even if you feel it building, even if your pussy aches for release, you will not let it overtake you without my permission."

How dare he demand such a thing?

I know it's wrong of him—he shouldn't be touching me at all right now—but the way he speaks, the way he wants me, the way he touches me lulls me into a submission that I struggle to fight.

I hate this.

His fingers dance across the mound of my breast and hook over the lacy black cup. He tugs it down, exposing my nipple to the cool air, and it hardens instantly. His hand continues moving, sliding over my chest, slipping up my throat, and cupping beneath my chin. Then his thumb reaches up to brush across my bottom lip.

"Open," he commands, and I obey.

He slips his thumb past my parted lips, gently pressing inside and running the pad of his thumb over my tongue. He gathers wetness there before bringing his hand down my chest and circles his wet thumb around my nipple. His cheek is pressed to mine—every part of him touching every part of me—as he speaks with command.

"Stay out of your mind and fixed on your senses. Find pleasure in the pain, sanity in the madness." He continues to circle my nipple, causing shocking jolts of pleasure as his other hand slips down into my panties, his fingers caressing my pussy. "Focus on feeling good without the release; remain in your heightened sense of anticipation, and when you're trapped in the purgatory of need, rely on me to release you."

I'm not sure I hear half of his words, or that I even understand the ones that I do, but his sultry voice is hypnotizing, intoxicating, lulling me into pleasure in the minutes before my trial is set to begin.

His thumb circles, his fingers brush and stroke, playing without purpose or intention, simply drawing me into lust. I moan, and my body rocks to seek more from his hand, which is buried in my underwear. At my movement, his hand stills.

"Don't seek," he says. "Take what's given to you and find peace in the pleasure of it. Don't chase release...it will only bring your pleasure to an end that much faster."

I want to protest his words and his actions in this vulnerable moment. What he's asking of me is deplorable. He wants me to find pleasure as his brothers use me but for me to stave off release until he grants it to me himself. He has no right to ask anything of me; he has no right to have his hands on me right now. His sins are so much worse than my own, yet I'm the one subjected to this disgusting punishment.

But even as my lips part to tell him this, I can't force out any sound other than a moan or a whimper, and I've never been so ashamed of myself.

He makes me feel shame, yet I let him.

I don't know how much time passes as we remain this way, my weight slumped against him as he strokes below and circles above. He works faster, drawing out my quickened breaths and desperate pleas, and then he slows again, stops altogether, then starts from the beginning.

It feels like forever and no time at all when he slowly pulls his hand from my panties and covers my breast with the lacy fabric of my bra.

He lets out a breath that's like fire against my scalp as it rustles my hair. "It's time," he says, and my heart drops like a lead ball, breaking past my ribs and falling heavily into my stomach.

I turn to face him and our eyes meet. I expect to see heat, but I don't expect to see regret. The recognition of it is jarring, and it nearly makes me want to cry. I press my eyes shut and focus my attention to the wetness he created between my legs, the throbbing of my swollen clit, and the need for touch that prickles beneath my skin.

Stay out of your mind and fixed on your senses.

It's as good advice as any going into such a horrible event. My mind has always been my own worst enemy, so maybe I'll make it through the next seven hours if I keep myself out of it.

Maybe Arlo knows what I need more than I do.

He bends to grab his leather gloves from the floor, but he doesn't put them on. When he rises, he sucks his fingers clean, the regret gone from his eyes and replaced with fiery desire.

"My focus will be intent on you tonight. I'll take care of every need you have before you even know you have it. You will survive this, starlight."

My heart grows wings at the nickname.

I know I can't trust him; I shouldn't. But somehow, I have faith he will take care of me; at least, in the ways I can't fathom needing caretaking in an event such as this trial.

It's the first of three, and though I know I'll survive this trial—even if it breaks me emotionally—I also know I'll be dead soon enough, and none of this will matter.

The way he sparks lust, the way he makes me hate him, the way he makes me feel so ashamed of myself, the way he claims me... none of it matters. I'll let him have this control over me because it makes no difference to my fate to deny him.

Because somehow, I can't bring myself to deny him.

chapter thirty

ARLO

I LEAD MERCY down the grand staircase in her undergarments, still wearing her black servants' boots. My heart thumps painfully against my ribcage as I spot my brothers standing around the tile starburst in the center of the foyer. All of them are there, waiting for Mercy, except for Theo and Owen. Killian, Ryker, Wesley, and Park turn their heads, watching Mercy as I lead her like a lamb to her slaughter.

Words I never expected to think about the Trials of Dissension blast into my mind—thoughts I'd never expected I could have for the punishment faced by a true sinner.

Depraved.

Abusive.

Abhorrent.

Something primal within me roars with the need to lift her over my shoulder and run from this place, far and fast. But there's nowhere to run. Even if there were, I know what's really happening within me.

It's the demon within her. The part of her that makes her sin has embedded in my heart, and it claws at my conscience. It tells me all the things I've always known to be good and godly and true are wrong.

It lies.

It can't be that everything I've ever known is wrong. It can't be that the doctrine, the Impulse, the Edict, the laws, and rules we uphold as members of the Control are wrong.

They're not.

They can't be.

Regardless of the connection I have to her, she's a sinner and she brought this upon herself. This is the punishment she's earned. It's her penance. It's her only chance at forgiveness and for her soul to be saved.

And it's my job to see her through it.

Our feet touch the foyer and time stands still. Mercy trembles at my side while my brothers spare a look to appraise her appearance. Wesley rubs his palms together with anticipation, and Ryker's grin is alarming.

Killian steps forward, crossing the sunburst, and stops in front of us. "Mercy Madness. We're finally here. I think this has been a long time coming. No sense in delaying the inevitable." He pauses, his eyes traveling down her form and back up again. He claps his hands together before spreading his arms wide. "Let's get this started, shall we? Wesley will lead prayer and the incitement of ceremony."

Killian steps back and I touch the small of Mercy's back. She jumps, startled by my touch, and her head snaps sideways to look at me. I want to give her something, anything—a look, a nod, a smile of encouragement.

Yet I give her nothing, and I don't know why.

Her throat bobs as she swallows, blinking, dragging her eyes away from me with the loneliest expression I've ever seen. I immediately feel sick about it, but I think the emotional distance between us is good for the moment…necessary.

She moves forward, carrying herself with grace to the center of the sun. She lifts her head to look up, noting that the chandelier has been removed, replaced by a suspension system that replicates the one I'd rigged in the caves. Candles have been placed around the room to create a flickering glow around us, and though the chandelier is gone, a single yellow spotlight has been fixed to the ceiling to shine down precisely on Mercy where she'll be suspended.

Every head in the room snaps to my left when we hear the click of a door from a bedroom that's just down the hall. Owen steps into the hallway, and just behind him are Delle and Theo. Delle is softly sobbing, tears streaming down her cheeks as she clutches her silk black robe. Her eyes scan the foyer as she approaches, and as she takes in the men all staring back at her, she draws her shoulders back and lifts her chin. It's a show of strength, though it's clear her strength is waning.

Depraved.

Abusive.

Abhorrent.

I have to press my eyes shut and suck in a deep breath to force the words away. We're only doing our duty to God. I have a purpose in this, and I must serve it. I must focus on Mercy and helping her pass this trial. The only thing I can do for her is to try to save her soul.

I've already worked this out with Theo. I've already made sure that Mercy will take the worst of this trial to spare Delle as much as possible, because I know that will weigh on Mercy's mind. Delle's pain must be spared to spare Mercy an emotional burden to her compassion.

Theo stops Delle by gripping her shoulders, and he turns her to face him. Silently his lips move, whispering something to her that we can't hear. Her eyes flutter shut and her lashes catch tears as she gives a single nod. When she opens her eyes again, she moves down the hall with grace, walking forward until she reaches the foyer. Taking in a shuddering breath, she removes her robe and drops it to the floor, revealing herself in her underwear and bra.

My eyes turn away from her, though I can't say the same for my brothers. I feel something strange roil in my gut at the sight of her lithe body. Her slenderness and slight curvature indicates her young age so clearly and looking at her as we're meant to now feels…wrong.

There's no reason that it should, yet it does.

I try to rectify this odd sense of shame that ripples inside me, but I can't seem to shake it. Not as Delle crosses the room in front of me and moves beside Mercy.

Sweet Mercy.

She reaches her hand out for Delle as she approaches, and quickly takes her palm, pulling her closer to her side. Mercy gently sweeps Delle's long hair behind her shoulder, and I feel regret—perhaps I should have cut Delle's hair to avoid my brothers twisting and jerking at the strands to control her. It's too late to think of it now.

Mercy leans and whispers in Delle's ear, words I can't hear, though I know they're filled with kindness and encouragement.

Mercy's compassion knows no bounds.

My head aches from the turmoil of contradictions—the compassionate sinner with starlight hair before me.

Delle nods at Mercy, and together, they lower to their knees.

Theo and I move to take our places, standing behind our two wards on the sunburst with a spotlight shining down on us. Killian turns on a camera which is placed on a table six feet in front of us. It clicks and rolls, and within moments, it will broadcast the scene live to the village of Ember Glen. Large screens line the village square from east to west, parallel to the front of the Homestead manor. For seven hours, the villagers and servants will be able to watch Mercy serve the first trial.

Only Mercy, not Delle because Theo and I worked together to direct our brothers' excitement toward Mercy. Delle will be closed off in the room from which she entered tonight, bound and suspended the same as Mercy, used the same as Mercy, but not watched the same as Mercy….and hopefully, not as brutalized. My brothers have far greater interest in the theatrics of it all, and greater still in punishing the true person of dissent—the real rebel, the girl with the fire that could burn everything we know to ashes if she's not stopped.

Sometimes I wonder if Mercy understands the true threat she

poses—I'm not even sure I have a full understanding of it. But we all know it's true that if she had the time to grow, to spread her influence with the servants of Ember Glen, she would. Her strength is only budding, and my brothers are eager to nip it.

Wesley moves with an air of ceremony, slowly working his way to stand in front of Mercy and Delle, facing the camera. His long dreadlocks are pulled together behind his back, wrapped with an elastic to keep them off his shoulders and out of the way for the night he intends to enjoy.

He rubs his palms slowly, solemnly in front of him, his head bowed slightly. A red light clicks on above the camera, indicating that we're now live-streaming in the village square, and Wesley lifts his head.

I feel no anxiety or fear pulsing from Mercy's back because all her attention is focused on Delle and providing her the comfort and strength she needs. I glance down to see Mercy squeeze Delle's hand tighter as she turns her head to look at her. I shuffle closer and strain my ears to hear as she leans in to tell her something.

"Have faith in yourself above all else," Mercy whispers to Delle. "Your strength is within you. These men don't control it, only you do. And I have faith that you'll find the best of your strength through these hours. You can endure this, and you will." They smile at each other, and an extra beat thuds in syncopation through the rhythm of my heart.

Then Wesley begins to speak.

"October sixth, twenty-one eighty-five. We gather days before the full moon to bear witness to this Service of the Flesh, the first of the three Trials of Dissension for sinners Mercy Madness and Delle Carter of Ember Glen. We welcome all who belong to the community of Ember Glen to bear witness to this trial, such that it brings awareness to the hardships that await servants who sin.

"It has been decided by the authority of Ember Glen that this trial shall be carried out by the seven members of the Control, who shall seek sexual service from the sinners over the course of seven hours. The sinners shall be bound and suspended for the entirety of the period, exclusive of two brief breaks to service their biological needs. Each break shall last no longer than ten minutes." He pauses. "Mercy Madness shall be the only sinner streamed for viewing in this intimate trial."

Mercy's head jerks up. "What?" she says with audible surprise.

"As the instigator of the events that prompted Delle to fall into sin and volunteer to participate in these trials, we, the Control and the Elders of Ember Glen, find this to be most appropriate given the circumstances."

Wesley side-steps, bringing Delle and Mercy into full view of the camera where they kneel in front of me. He turns sideways to speak to me and Theo.

"Arlo Rainn and Theo Hughes, as the selected wardens of these trial participants, please present them for this Service of the Flesh."

I step closer, close enough that I can see the way Mercy feels my presence at her back—it's evident in the way her shoulders stiffen the moment I move into her space.

"I present Mercy Madness for the first of these three Trials of Dissension. Mercy, do you enter this trial with the understanding of your sins and the means by which you are required to serve?"

She hesitates, but strongly replies, "Yes."

Theo speaks next. "I present Delle Carter for the first of these three Trials of Dissension. Delle, do you enter this trial with the understanding of your sins and the means by which you are required to serve?"

A small sob wracks her narrow shoulders, but she replies with a whimper, "Yes."

I take a step back as Mercy turns her head to the left, giving Delle a quick smile, but I see she uses it as a guise for looking back at me. Her eyes strain to look behind her, and I wish I could catch her gaze with mine.

Wesley moves in front of the girls again. "Let us share a prayer before we begin."

Clasping our hands in front of us, we all bow our heads, even Delle…but not Mercy.

Facing forward, she pulls her shoulders back as if to make it more obvious, clear that she refuses to pray. It should enrage me—and in many ways, it does—but it also impresses me. I'm not impressed by her defiance or her insolence; rather, I'm impressed by her commitment to rebellion. It's wrong and it's sinful, but regardless, it shows her strength.

I catch my brothers' stares as they notice from beneath their lashes, Killian turning his bowed head ever so slightly to look at Ryker beside him with a look of disgust on his face. He's disgusted by Mercy's show of rebellion, and that won't bode well for her in the upcoming hours.

My pulse is steady, but heavy, insistent through each beat that I have something to be concerned about with Killian.

I have nothing to be concerned about.

These are my brothers.

I swallow my conflicting feelings and close my eyes to shut them all out, to listen to Wesley's prayer and say a silent one of my own that God will find a way to remind me of what's right and true, that He'll guide me back to my purpose here in Ember Glen and take away this sinful longing I hold for Mercy.

"Our celestial creator and divine spirit, we come to You in this hour of trials and tribulations, seeking good favor in honor of our righteous choices," Wesley continues. "We bring these sinners before you, offering the sacrifice of their service in honor of the Impulse Edict, to the sanctity of Your divine word. We ask for Your righteous judgment of the souls of these sinners. Should they serve appropriately through these trials and prove themselves to be truly sacrificial servants, we ask for absolution of their wretched souls.

Please grant me and my brothers of the Control the strength and stamina to carry out this trial to the greatest extent of our endurance, such that we may present these sinners with a fair and exhaustive trial for their souls. *Malo mori quam foedari.*"

"*Malo mori quam foedari,*" we all repeat.

I open my eyes and lift my head at the same moment Killian steps forward to Mercy. "Say it," he demands, moving closer against her side.

She turns her head away in response, his belt buckle level with her eyes. "Say it, sinner," he demands. "*Malo mori quam foedari.*"

Bravely, she turns her head and lifts her chin high to meet his eyes. I don't have to see them clearly to know her stare has enough heat behind it to birth a thousand stars. She glares at him silently, refusing to speak a word.

This is perhaps the stupidest she's ever been. Either she doesn't understand or she doesn't care that my brothers loathe her and her rebellion. They're eager to show this woman just how wrong she is for standing against our values, against the authority they've been granted to uphold the sanctity of our community.

And she refuses now, in the moments before they prepare to take her and do vile things to her precious flesh.

I latch my fingers around the back of her neck. She cries out as I jerk her sideways, bending over her, coming in close and demanding with clear, concise insistence, "Say it, Mercy. Now is not the time to show your defiance."

I toss her forward before releasing her, and she drops to the floor, catching herself on her palms, which slap against the tile. She stays in place, chest rising and falling with her heavy, angry breaths.

Her silence continues, and my brothers close in, Killian dropping down to one knee at her side. He snatches her chin viciously in his hand, jerking her head up until she's forced to look at him. "I'll ask you one more time, sinner. Finish the prayer. *Malo mori quam foedari.*"

I know it's about to happen before it does—she's done it to me twice before. My heart kicks up in a flurry, punching adrenaline through my veins as I lunge for her, reaching out in hopes that I can cover her mouth before her furious boldness takes hold of her.

But I don't reach her in time.

She spits in Killian's face, and hell descends.

The circle closes around her as voices raise in a chorus of righteous indignation. Though I wish I could drag Mercy away and protect her, I know I can't.

Watching the rapidly shrinking circle, my concern shifts to Delle, the tiny thing who's just been knocked sideways by Ryker trying to slip around her to Mercy, blocking Theo along the way. I take my urge to protect and give it to Delle, because Mercy is beyond my help. I charge forward and pluck Delle from the floor, placing her on her feet just as Theo darts between Owen and Park to arrive at her side.

I lower my voice, though none of my brothers are listening anyway—they've busied themselves in taunting Mercy. "Take her, bind her, suspend her. Don't delay, it will draw questions." I look back at the group surrounding Mercy and nausea cuts through my stomach. "I'll encourage them to use Mercy as much as I can."

Mercy has served for four years.

She's older, stronger, braver.

And though Delle may have grown to become those things, right now, she's young and naïve, fragile, in need of care. Mercy is prepared to take this trial, and though I'm feeling oddly sick about what's happening to her right now, I know she will endure.

I'll make certain of it.

Theo nods and drags Delle away, back through the door from which they came, and closes it behind him.

I take a deep breath and turn to face the center of the foyer. My eyes behold a sight as reverent and terrifying as flickering firelight. In the center of the sun stands Mercy, naked, her shoes and undergarments already violently stripped from her body. Her fists are clenched at her sides and her head is bowed slightly as she fumes, dragging heavy breaths through her nose like a dragon preparing to breathe fire.

Sweet sin.

While my brothers look to me expectantly—ready for me to bind her and suspend her for them to use—I look directly at her.

"Mercy," I say sharply to gather her attention. I wait until she lifts her chin and meets my gaze, dark storms swirling through her gray-blue eyes. "Stay out of your mind…" I remind her of what I said earlier, to stay out of her mind and fixed on her senses.

It's a reminder that she can release her rage and try to find pleasure in this. But I can see she's already gone, lost to her anger.

And I don't know if I'll be able to bring her back.

chapter thirty-one
Mercy

STAY OUT OF *your mind…*

He dared to say it as if I could simply switch off this rage and allow this to happen to me. As if I could simply come out of fear and find some pleasure in this twisted rite. The men tower above me, surround me, cage me like an animal, and it's how I feel.

I'm ready to hiss and growl; ready to bare my teeth, show my claws, and scratch anyone who comes too close.

Malo mori quam foedari.

Death before dishonor. Though the men of Ember Glen speak it, it's not meant for them. It's meant for *us*—the servants. These vile creatures who call themselves men dishonor themselves and the humanity they claim to have more often than any woman in this village does. But we sacrificial servants are expected to seek death with pride, rather than sin in dishonor.

They live by the Impulse. As though women have none—as if servants have no purpose in this life but to meet their filthy needs. I desire, I rage, I feel intensely, just as men do. Yet I'm expected to repress it all for the sake of serving their uncontrollable needs.

It's disgraceful…*dishonorable.*

They should stand naked on this sun instead of me, be bound and hung, defiled and humiliated for enforcing the tenants of the vicious god they serve.

If they want to reduce the quality of their existence to being ruled by impulses, they can go right ahead. But I will not. I am more than an urge to act violently. I am more than a man ruled by his sexual needs in moments of weakness.

I am more than they want me to be.

And through my fuming rage, I know there is only one way to show it. Spitting fury, flinging words of hatred, screaming, and fighting the inevitable won't prove how much better I am. I must meet them with the dignity and grace of my entire being. I am not a raging impulse of emotion to be satiated by outbursts. I'm a woman— something stronger and far more spectacular than they'll ever be.

I breathe in deeply, and on the exhale, I force my shoulders to release their tension, my fingers to unclench from fists, my heart to calm from this passion. I search my mind for a breadcrumb of calmness I can follow along a path to serenity, and when I find it, I run toward it.

Stealing Arlo's gaze, I lower to my knees on the hard tile floor and cross my arms behind my back. "Start the damn clock."

Arlo's eyebrows flatten to a straight line and his eyes narrow to scrutinize me, his lips parting on a slow, steady exhale. Everyone's attention is pulled toward Arlo…watching and waiting. He's the one who must bind me and string me up for them. He's my warden, and his actions alone will determine when this nightmare officially begins.

Air catches in my lungs, threatening to reveal my sudden fear, but I shove it back down, refusing to show my weakness. Arlo steps slowly, his feet moving with a dull *thud* on the tile as he comes toward me. He stops in front of me, then holds his hand out at his side. "Bring me the rope," he says to everyone and no one.

Something sparks behind his eyes, something mad and powerful. I'm not quite certain if the look terrifies me or turns me on. It shouldn't turn me on, for heaven's sake. Not a single moment of this should, regardless of whether he's here. I'm enraged and horrified, and there's no room for lust. Except…the way he looks at me could easily set my insides on fire.

Someone places a length of rope in Arlo's hand, but I don't know who because I can't tear my eyes away from him. Winding the rope around his palm, his eyes skate over my naked form, drinking me in, taking his time. Then he moves so unexpectedly that it startles me, and my shoulders jump as he circles around me.

Inch by inch, he dresses me in coarse rope. Each twist, each tug, each drag of the rope across my skin cheats me into a shameful state of anticipation. It's as though he uses my anger as fuel for the fire he lights within me. I can hear his every breath as he works close to me, as he takes liberties to graze my skin with his fingers and draw sensations over my body.

I try to fight it when he jerks on a knot that tugs me backward, but his force is too strong. My lips part as I attempt to draw in a steeling breath, but it blows out shakily. I feel this way for *him*. Loathe as I am to admit it, I feel things for Arlo Rainn. I feel things that no one is allowed to feel. I feel things that are beyond the scope of reason. I feel things that could nearly restore my faith in a higher power—if only it weren't for the circumstances.

I want to fight the heaviness between my legs as my mind wanders, recalling his touch and the way he made me swell. I want to fight the pebbling of my nipples as ropes sweep across them before tugging tight around the mounds of my breasts to frame them. I want to fight the pull of tension through my core. But Arlo's voice whispers through my mind.

Moments later, it whispers against my ear. "Your strength is unmatchable. Don't let them take it from you." He speaks so softly that I have to strain to hear him—but at least I know none of the others will. He moves away from me and takes command, speaking loud enough that everyone can hear him. "Stand."

With Arlo's hand gripping my elbow, and my arms bound behind my back, I slowly climb to my feet. As soon as I'm steady, he lets go of me and begins looping the rope through one of the metal hoops dangling above me.

I tilt my head to look up at it, focusing on the rope as it moves through, trying to ignore the fact that I'm standing naked in the foyer of the Homestead with nearly every member of the Control surrounding me, staring at me, eagerly waiting for their turn to put me in my place.

My place is dancing on top of their fresh graves.

My jaw tenses as I lower my head to level, squeezing my eyes shut tightly, breathing through the heated resentment. In a heartbeat, the resentment disappears, giving way to a jolt of panic as the ropes around my body tighten, lifting me sideways from the ground. The knots that pull me into suspension are positioned along my side, just beneath my hip, and around my left ankle.

Hoisting me up, I hang sidelong to the ground. Arlo adjusts the rope so my body forms an angle, my head slightly higher than my hips. My left leg is straight, the knot around my ankle aiding in suspending my leg, and once it's secure, he reaches down, tapping my right knee, closest to the floor.

"Bend," he orders, and I do it, eager to lift my dangling leg as it hangs uncomfortably without support.

Bending my right knee and kicking my ankle back toward my bottom, he binds my leg to keep it that way, forever bent, kneecap pointing toward the floor in such a way that it keeps my thighs spread wide…

Accessible.

The familiar panic I had felt in the caves pricks in my mind, sending an electric current of frightened awareness rushing beneath my skin.

His hands leave me altogether, and I'm left to hang, settling in the ropes for a few moments. I listen to the sound of them creaking with the light sway of my body.

Then, a warm, heavy palm presses to my belly, an arm skimming along my side as it reaches around me from behind. I turn my head skyward to look behind me, and the air rushes from my lungs in relief. The hand belongs to Arlo. He's still right there at my back, running his palm down the center of my stomach.

Lower and lower he travels, and with each inch, my pounding heart beats a little faster. His fingers run down the tuft of hair before dipping between my legs.

"Let's see if you're ready for us, Mercy Madness."

My body twitches against my bindings as his fingers slip low, bending to press inside me and finding the wetness he dragged out of me in my bedroom. A low moan escapes me as he caresses, finding that wonderful spot inside and pressing against it with a perfectly pressured rhythm.

"Perfect," he mutters, catching my eyes and holding my stare.

How does he do this to me?

Damnit, how does he do this?!

Never once have I responded like this in service, not to anyone, not to a single other man.

Because none of them were him.

There is no one like him.

His lips curl in a smirk, drawing the lines of his dimples through his short beard. "This is how you serve, Mercy—with a warm, wet cunt that's prepared to take."

There's something odd about his words and the way he says them. His tone seems disingenuous. His words sound as though they're meant for his brothers, and not for me. He told me he didn't want to share me. He made me promise my pleasure was only for him. He had no right to say such things to me, but he did, and I feel they were real.

The way he speaks in front of the Control now, trying to come off as unaffected by my onrushing defilement, feels dissonant with how I know him. And I know him more intimately than anyone. He has to behave like them, speak like them, but the way his fingers move inside me whispers his truth.

He wants to help me through this.

He wants me to find pleasure if I can.

If it were only him using me, I could remain like this forever.

Then, someone else's hand touches my breast, and everything within me begs to shut down. My thighs clench, my inner walls squeeze around Arlo's fingers, but not with pleasure—with pressure to force him out. His fingers go still inside me, though he keeps them there all the same. Reluctantly, I turn my head to find my eyes level with Killian's belt buckle as he puts his hands on me.

"I'm going to enjoy painting you with cum," Killian says with a strangled voice. "I'll have you whispering the prayer you refused to speak between breaths as I choke you with my cock."

Panic pulses through my adrenaline-riddled veins, but then Arlo moves his hand again, dragging his fingers out and rubbing over my clit in perfect little circles.

I'm horrified by Killian's hand on my chest, but I can't ignore the perfect swirl of Arlo's fingers between my legs. A sickening swirl of disgust and lust storms through me, drawing me into a state of sexual awareness that begs for filth.

I hate it.

I'm sickened by it.

Yet pleasure builds in this detestable carnality.

Before long, Arlo has effortlessly stroked me toward an unwanted release.

Unwanted in every sense but physical—physically, it's needed.

He forces me up a cliff I don't want to climb because Killian's hands are on my breasts, kneading painfully, plucking harshly at my aching nipples. I can see the way his cock strains against his black slacks. When his hand falls to grip it, squeezing it through the fabric, the sparking madness within my mind combusts, burning in a blaze of misery.

I turn my head back to look at Arlo. "I don't want it," I whisper, though I'm breathless, panting, needy.

My thighs ache and twitch.

His pace and pressure remain steady, a blue flame in his eyes imploring me to finish. And just as I'm brought to the top of that peak, nearly ready to burst and tumble over the edge, he rips his hand away. He stops just before I detonate.

I cry out in frustration and confusion.

"Not yet," Arlo says, and I watch him back away.

He retreats as Ryker, Wesley, Park, and Owen close in around me.

He leaves me alone to the sound of belt buckles unlatching and zippers coming down. Five men with dark intent sketched across their faces encircle me, tower above me, strike me with fear, disgust, shame…all while the traitorous pulsing between my legs begs for a hand, a tongue, a cock—anything to put me out of my misery.

In front of me, I catch Arlo's movement beyond the outer rung of the sunburst on the tiled floor. Between Killian and Ryker's intimidating bodies, I watch as Arlo lowers to sit in a plush ivory armchair. I watch as he crosses his ankle over his knee, rests his elbows on the armrests, and steeples his fingers.

"Warden, shall we begin?" It's Killian's voice, but I don't look at him. I can't tear my gaze from Arlo and the way his eyes shift. It's like he's looking at me, but also looking past me…looking right through me.

Our connection is lost, and all that exists are the men who condemn me to be a creature used for their pleasure, all in the name of saving my soul.

In a moment of weakness—or perhaps, it's strength—I silently beg for mercy from an entity I don't believe in. I pray to a god who doesn't exist because no man will save me, I can't save myself…I'm alone in this. Even the man who promised to see me through this nightmare has stepped away, disconnected, and left me alone to endure this trial.

God help me.

Please, God help me through this.

With a brief nod, Arlo begins my ruin. "Let the trial begin."

Mercy and Arlo's story
continues in book two...

brynn's books

The Four Families Trilogy
Counts of Eight
Dance with Death
Pas de Trois

The Four Families Spin-Off
King of Masters

Ember Glen
Spark of Madness
Blaze of Misery
Embers of Mercy

Senseless
Unheard
Unseen

Lawless
(Coming Soon!)
The Darkness We Hide

Standalones
Jagged Line Paradise
Sugar Wood
The Alter

connect with brynn

Author Newsletter
brynnford.com/connect

Goodreads
goodreads.com/brynnfordauthor

BookBub
bookbub.com/profile/brynn-ford

Instagram
@brynnfordauthor
instagram.com/brynnfordauthor

TikTok
@brynnfordauthor
tiktok.com/@brynnfordauthor

Facebook Page
facebook.com/brynnfordauthor

Facebook Reader's Group
bit.ly/brynnsdarlings

acknowledgments

Mercy and Arlo's story has been in my mind for well over a year, and I can't believe this first part of their trilogy is complete! Stepping into a dystopian world to write their dark romance was no easy feat (world building in itself is a challenge), and I wouldn't have had the determination to go for it without all the people who hold me up while I'm writing like crazy.

I have to thank my husband and kids first, as I couldn't do this writing thing without their patience and support. Hubby, I appreciate all the time you give me to work on my art, knowing how important it is to me.

To Danielle, my incredible PA and amazing friend, thank you for doing the hard work of cheering me on when I'm struggling with writer life. I know you think you don't do much, but in reality you do *so, so much* for me. I couldn't do this without you!

To Danielle and Mary for your beta reads, and Maria for your notes early in the book, thank you so much for the time you spent and consideration you gave to my story. You've always been such an incredible support system for helping me to make my stories the best they can possibly be. Echo, Amanda, and Brandy, I appreciate you jumping in at the eleventh hour to do a read through and give me some last minute notes. I appreciate all of you more than I can express!

To my street team and ARC team, I absolutely adore you. Your support and love for my books humbles me. Thank you for sharing, reviewing, and helping other readers find my books!

Najla, Nada, and the team at Qamber Designs, thank you so much for making my book look beautiful! I adore your team and the work you do is always spectacular. I can always count on you to create gorgeous covers and stunning interior design for my stories.

To my incredible editor, Silvia, you are the best! My words are pretty okay when I send them your way, and you somehow always

manage to polish them to perfection. I feel so fortunate to have you as my editor!

I also want to thank Candi Kane PR, Xpresso Book Tours, and all the book bloggers who've read, reviewed, and shared my work. I appreciate you all so much!

My final thank you goes directly to you, reader. You picked up this book, you read the words I wrote, and for that alone, I am grateful. If you connected with the characters or the story and enjoyed this read, just know that you and I have met through these words, and I'm forever thankful you took the journey with me.

about the author

Brynn Ford is a USA Today Bestselling Author of dark romance for daring readers. She writes emotionally heavy love stories that will twist your soul and shatter your heart before pulling you back together with a hopeful happily-ever-after.

Brynn's books are dark, sometimes disturbing, and often overwhelming. But they're always brightened by an insistent, spicy romance that will live rent-free in your head long after you've turned the final page.

When Brynn isn't obsessively writing, you may find her binge-watching favorite shows while eating far too much junk food or fanatically reading, always seeking to lose herself in the emotional roller coaster of a damn good story. She's a firm believer that her characters continue to live outside the pages in the minds of her readers. Stories don't end just because there aren't any more pages to turn.

www.ingramcontent.com/pod-product-compliance
Lightning Source LLC
Chambersburg PA
CBHW060652190726
48289CB00002B/369